J. Arthur Thomson

Herbert Spencer

Outlook

J. Arthur Thomson

Herbert Spencer

1. Auflage | ISBN: 978-3-73263-012-7

Erscheinungsort: Frankfurt am Main, Deutschland

Erscheinungsjahr: 2018

Outlook Verlag GmbH, Frankfurt.

Reproduction of the original.

ENGLISH MEN OF SCIENCE

EDITED BY

J. REYNOLDS GREEN, D.Sc.

HERBERT SPENCER

HERBERT SPENCER

BY

J. ARTHUR THOMSON, M.A.

**REGIUS PROFESSOR OF NATURAL HISTORY IN
THE UNIVERSITY OF ABERDEEN
AUTHOR OF
THE STUDY OF ANIMAL LIFE; THE SCIENCE OF LIFE;
OUTLINES OF ZOOLOGY; PROGRESS OF SCIENCE;
ETC. ETC.**

PUBLISHED IN LONDON BY
J. M. DENT & CO. AND IN NEW
YORK BY E. P. DUTTON & CO.

1906

INTRODUCTION

This volume attempts to give a short account of Herbert Spencer's life, an appreciation of his characteristics, and a statement of some of the services he rendered to science. Prominence has been given to his *Autobiography*, to his *Principles of Biology*, and to his position as a cosmic evolutionist; but little has been said of his psychology and sociology, which require another volume, or of his ethics and politics, or of his agnosticism—the whetstone of so many critics. Our appreciation of Spencer's services is therefore partial, but it may not for that reason fail in its chief aim, that of illustrating the working of one of the most scientific minds that ever lived, "whose excess of science was almost unscientific."

The story of Spencer's life is neither eventful nor picturesque, but it commands the interest of all who admire faith, courage, and loyalty to an ideal. It is a story of plain living and high thinking, of one who, though vexed by an extremely nervous temperament, was as resolute as a Hebrew prophet in delivering his message. It is the story of a quiet servant of science, indifferent to conventional honours, careless about "getting on," disliking controversy, sensationalism, and noise, trusting to the power of truth alone, that it must prevail.

Another aspect of interest is that Spencer was an arch-heretic, one of the flowers of Nonconformity, against theology and against metaphysics, against monarchy and against molly-coddling legislation, against classical education and against socialism, against war and against Weismann. So that we can hardly picture the man who has not some crow to pick with Spencer.

It is not to be wondered at, then, that we find extraordinary difference of opinion as to the value of the great Dissenter's deliverances. In 1894, Prof. Henry Sidgwick spoke of Herbert Spencer as "our most eminent living philosopher," and in the same sentence described him as "an impressive survival of the drift of thought in the first half of the nineteenth century." Some have likened him to a second Aristotle, while others assure us that the author of the Synthetic Philosophy was not a philosopher at all. Similarly there are scientists who tell us that Spencer may have been a great philosopher, but that he was too much of an *a priori* thinker to be of great account in science. Many critics, indeed, devote so much time and ability to demonstrating Spencer's incompetence, in this or that field of thought, that the reader is left with the impression that it must be a tower of strength which requires so many assaults. And there are others, neither philosophers nor scientists, who are content to dismiss Spencer with saying that the least in the

Kingdom of Heaven is greater than he. Yet this much is conceded by most, that Herbert Spencer was an unusually keen intellectual combatant, who took the evolution-formula into his strong hands as a master-key, and tried (teaching others to try better) to open therewith all the locked doors of the universe—all the immediate, though none of the ultimate, riddles, physical and biological, psychological and ethical, social and religious. And this also is conceded, that his life was signalised by absolute consecration to the pursuit of truth, by magnanimous disinterestedness as to rewards, by a resolute struggle against almost overwhelming difficulties, and by an entire fearlessness in delivering the message which he believed the Unknown had given him for the good of the world. In an age of specialism he held up the banner of the Unity of Science, and he actually completed, so far as he could complete, the great task of his life—greater than most men have even dreamed of—that of applying the evolution-formula to everything knowable. He influenced thought so largely, he inspired so many disciples, he left so many enduring works—enduring as seed-plots, if not also as achievements— that his death, writ large, was immortality.

HERBERT SPENCER

CHAPTER I

HEREDITY

Ancestry—Grandparents—Uncles—Parents

Remarkable parents often have commonplace children, and a genius may be born to a very ordinary couple, yet the importance of pedigree is so patent that our first question in regard to a great man almost invariably concerns his ancestry. In Herbert Spencer's case the question is rewarded.

Ancestry.—From the information afforded by the *Autobiography* in regard to ancestry remoter than grandparents, we learn that, on both sides of the house, Spencer came of a stock characterised by the spirit of nonconformity, by a correlated respect for something higher than legislative enactments, and by a regard for remote issues rather than immediate results. In these respects Herbert Spencer was true to his stock—an uncompromising nonconformist, with a conscience loyal to "principles having superhuman origins above rules having human origins," and with an eye ever directed to remote issues. Truly it required more than "ingrained nonconformity," loyalty to principles, and far-sighted prudence to make a Herbert Spencer, and hundreds unknown to fame must have shared a similar heritage; but the resemblances between some of Spencer's characteristics and those of his stock are too close to be disregarded. Disown him as many nonconformists did, they could not disinherit him. Nonconformity was in his blood and bone of his bone.

Grandparents.—Spencer's maternal grandfather, John Holmes of Derby, was a business man and an active Wesleyan, with "a little more than the ordinary amount of faculty." The grandmother, née Jane Brettell, is described as "commonplace," but her portrait suggests a more charitable verdict. Spencer's paternal grandfather was a schoolmaster, a "mechanical teacher," somewhat oppressed by life, and "extremely tender-hearted." If, when a newspaper was being read aloud, there came an account of something cruel or very unjust, he would exclaim: "Stop, stop, I can't bear it!" Of this sensitive temperament his illustrious grandson had a large share. The most notable of the four grandparents was Catherine Spencer, née Taylor, "of good type both physically and morally." "Born in 1758 and marrying in 1786, when nearly 28, she had eight children, led a very active life, and lived till 1843: dying at the age of 84 in possession of all her faculties." A personal follower of John Wesley, intensely religious, indefatigably unselfish, combining unswerving integrity with uniform good temper and affection, "she had all the domestic virtues in large measures." Her grandson has said that "nothing was specially manifest in her, intellectually considered, unless, indeed, what would be called sound common sense." Grandparents taken together count on an *average* for about a quarter of the individual inheritance, but we would note that in Herbert Spencer's case, Catherine Spencer should be regarded as a peculiarly dominant hereditary factor.

Uncles.—Two of her children died in infancy, the only surviving daughter (*b.* 1788) was an invalid; then came Herbert Spencer's father, William George (*b.* 1790), and there were four other sons. Henry Spencer, a year and a half younger than Herbert Spencer's father, was "a favourable sample of the type," independent with "a strong dash of chivalry," an energetic, though in the end unsuccessful man of business, an ardent radical and with "a marked sense of humour." The next son, John, had strong individuality; he was a notably self-assertive, obstinate solicitor, successful only in out-living all his brothers. Thomas, the next brother, began active life as a school-teacher near Derby, was a student of St John's, Cambridge, achieved honours (ninth wrangler), and became a clergyman of the Church of England at Hinton. He was "a reformer," "anticipating great movements," a "radical," a "Free-Trader," a "teetotaler," "an intensified Englishman." The youngest son, William, "distinguished less by extent of intellectual acquisitions than by general soundness of sense, joined with a dash of originality," carried on his father's school, and was one of Herbert Spencer's teachers. He was a Whig and a nonconformist, but more moderate than his brothers in either direction.

These facts in regard to Herbert Spencer's uncles corroborate the general thesis that heredity counts for much. The four uncles had individuality, rising sometimes to the verge of eccentricity; in their various paths of life they were independent, critical, self-assertive, and with a characteristic absence of reticence.

Parents.—George Spencer, Herbert's father (*b.* 1790) was "the flower of the flock." "To faculties which he had in common with the rest (except the humour of Henry and the linguistic faculty of Thomas), he added faculties they gave little sign of. One was inventive ability, and another was artistic perception, joined with skill of hand." He began very early to teach in his father's school, and was for most of his life a teacher. As such, he was noted for his reliance on non-coercive discipline, and at the same time for his firmness; he continually sought to stimulate individuality rather than to inform. His *Inventional Geometry* and *Lucid Shorthand* had some vogue for a time.

He was an unconventional person, as shown in little things—by his repugnance to taking off his hat, to donning signs of mourning, or to addressing people as "Esq." or "Rev^{d}.," and in big things by his pronounced "Whigism." With "a repugnance to all living authority" he combined so much sympathy and suavity that he was generally beloved. He found Quakerism "congruous with his nature in respect of its complete individualism and absence of ecclesiastical government." He had unusual keenness of the senses, delicacy of manipulation, and noteworthy artistic skill. A somewhat fastidious and finicking habit of trying to make things better was expressed in his annotations on dictionaries and the like, but he had also a larger "passion for reforming the world." As his son notes, the one great drawback was lack of considerateness and good temper in his relations with his wife. For this, however, a nervous disorder was in part to blame. He lived to be over seventy.

Herbert Spencer's mother, née Harriet Holmes (1794-1867), introduced a new strain into the heritage. "So far from showing any ingrained nonconformity, she rather displayed an ingrained conformity." A Wesleyan by tradition rather than by conviction, she was constitutionally averse to change or adventure, non-assertive, self-sacrificing, patient, and gentle. "Briefly characterised, she was of ordinary intelligence and of high moral nature—a moral nature of which the deficiency was the reverse of that commonly to be observed: she was not sufficiently self-asserting: altruism was too little qualified by egoism."

Spencer did not think that he took after his mother except in some physical features. He had something of his father's nervous weakness, but he had not his large chest and well developed heart and lungs. Believing that "the mind is as deep as the viscera," he does not scruple to state that his "visceral constitution was maternal rather than paternal."

"Whatever specialities of character and faculty in me are due to inheritance, are inherited from my father. Between my mother's mind and my own I see scarcely any resemblances, emotional or intellectual. She was very patient; I am very impatient. She was tolerant of pain, bodily or mental; I am intolerant of it. She was little given to finding fault with others; I am greatly given to it. She was submissive; I am the reverse of submissive. So, too, in respect of intellectual faculties, I can perceive no trait common to us, unless it be a certain greater calmness of judgment than was shown by my father; for my father's vivid representative faculty was apt to play him false. Not only, however, in the moral characters just named am I like my father, but such intellectual characters as are peculiar are derived from him" (*Autobiography* ii., p. 430).

CHAPTER II

NURTURE

Boyhood—School—At Hinton—At Home

Herbert Spencer was born at Derby on the 27th of April 1820. His father and mother had married early in the preceding year, at the age of about 29 and 25 respectively. Except a little sister, a year his junior, who lived for two years, he was practically the only child, for of the five infants who followed none lived more than a few days. As Spencer pathetically remarks: "It was one of my misfortunes to have no brothers, and a still greater misfortune to have no sisters." But is it not recompense enough of any marriage to produce a genius?

In reference to his father's breakdown soon after marriage, Spencer writes: "I doubt not that had he retained good health, my early education would have been much better than it was; for not only did his state of body and mind prevent him from paying as much attention to my intellectual culture as he doubtless wished, but irritability and depression checked that geniality of behaviour which fosters the affections and brings out in children the higher traits of nature. There are many whose lives would have been happier had their parents been more careful about themselves, and less anxious to provide for others."

Boyhood.—The father's ill-health had this compensation, that Herbert Spencer spent much of his childhood (æt. 4-7) in the country—at New Radford, near Nottingham. In his later years he had still vivid recollections of rambling among the gorse-bushes which towered above his head, of exploring the narrow tracks which led to unexpected places, and of picking the blue- bells "from among the prickly branches, which were here and there flecked with fragments of wool left by passing sheep." He was allowed freedom from ordinary "lessons," and enjoyed a long latent receptive period.

In 1827 the family returned to Derby, but for some time the boy's life was comparatively unrestrained. There was some gardening to do—an educational discipline far too little appreciated—and there was "almost nominal" school-drill; but there was plenty of time for exploring the neighbourhood, for fishing and bird-nesting, for watching the bees and the gnat-larvæ, for gathering mushrooms and blackberries. "Beyond the pleasurable exercise and the gratification of my love of adventure, there was gained during these excursions much miscellaneous knowledge of things, and the perceptions were beneficially disciplined." "Most children are instinctively naturalists, and were they encouraged would readily pass from careless observations to careful and deliberate ones. My father was wise in such matters, and I was not simply allowed but encouraged to enter on natural history."

He had the run of a farm at Ingleby during holidays; he enjoyed fishing in the Trent, in which he was within an ace of being drowned when about ten years old; he was a keen collector of insects, watching their metamorphoses, and often drawing and describing his captures; and he was also encouraged to make models. In short, he had in a simple way not a few of the disciplines which modern pædagogics—helped greatly by Spencer himself—has recognised to be salutary.

In his boyhood Spencer was extremely prone to castle-building or day-dreaming—"a habit which continued throughout youth and into mature life; finally passing, I suppose, into the dwelling on schemes more or less practicable." For his tendency to absorption, without which there has seldom been greatness of achievement, he was often reproached by his father in the words: "As usual, Herbert, thinking only of one thing at a time."

He did not read tolerably until he was over seven years old, and *Sandford and Merton* was the first book that prompted him to read of his own accord. He rapidly advanced to *The Castle of Otranto* and similar romances, all the more delectable that they were forbidden fruits. While John Stuart Mill was working at the Greek classics, Herbert Spencer was reading novels in bed. But the appetite for reading was soon cloyed, and he became incapable of enjoying anything but novels and travels for more than an hour or two at a time.

School.—As to more definite intellectual culture, the first school period (before ten years) seems to have counted for little, and is interesting only because it revealed the boy's general aversion to rote-learning and dogmatic statements. Shielded from direct punishment, he lived in an atmosphere of reproof, and this "naturally led to a state of chronic antagonism." But when he was ten (1830) he became one of his Uncle William's pupils, and this led to some progress. There was drawing, map-making, experimenting, Greek Testament without grammar, but comparatively little lesson-learning. "As a consequence, I was not in continual disgrace." The boy was quick in all matters appealing to reason, and "had a somewhat remarkable perception of locality and the relations of position generally, which in later life disappeared."

Apart from school he had the advantage of hearing discussions between his father and his friends on all sorts of topics, of preparing for the scientific demonstrations which his father occasionally gave, of sampling scientific periodicals which came to the Derby Philosophical Society of which his father was honorary secretary, and of reading such works as Rollin's *Ancient History* and Gibbon's *Decline and Fall of the Roman Empire.* He was continually prompted to "intellectual self-help," and was continually stimulated by the question, "Can you tell me the cause of this?"

"Always the tendency in himself, and the tendency strengthened in me, was to regard everything as naturally caused; and I doubt not that while the notion of causation was thus rendered much more definite in me than in most of my age, there was established a habit of seeking for causes, as well as a tacit belief in the universality of causation." "A tacit belief in the universality of causation" seems a big item to be put to the credit of a boy of thirteen, but we have the echo of it in Clerk Maxwell's continual boyish question, "What is the go of this?" That the question of cause was acute in both cases implies that both had hereditarily fine brains, but it also suggests that the question is normal in those who are naturally educated. The sensitive, irritable, invalid father was no ideal parent, but he did not snub his son's inquisitiveness, nor coerce his independence, nor appeal to authority as such as a reason for accepting any belief.

Spencer has given in his *Autobiography* a picture of himself as a boy of thirteen. His constitution was distinguished "rather by good balance than by great vital activity"; there was "a large margin of latent power"; he was more fleet than any of his school-fellows. He was decidedly peaceful, but when enraged no considerations of pain or danger or anything else restrained him. He was affectionate and tender-hearted, but his most marked moral trait was disregard of authority. His memory was rather below par than above; he was "averse to lesson-learning and the acquisition of knowledge after the ordinary routine methods," but he picked up general information with facility; he could not bear prolonged reading or the receptive attitude. From about ten years of age to thirteen he habitually went on Sunday morning with his father to the Friends' Meeting House, and in the evening with his mother to the Methodist Chapel. "I do not know that any marked effect on me followed; further, perhaps, than that the alternation tended to enlarge my views by presenting me with differences of opinion and usage." While John Mill kept his son away from conventional religious influences, Spencer's father excluded none; and the result seems to have been much the same in the two cases. In this and other connections, Prof. W. H. Hudson points out the contrast between the methods of the two fathers of the two remarkable sons—John Stuart Mill was constrained along carefully chosen paths, Herbert Spencer enjoyed more elbow-room and free-play, what German biologists call "Abänderungsspielraum."

At thirteen, Herbert Spencer had little Latin and less Greek; he was wholly uninstructed in "English"; he had no knowledge of mathematics, English history, ancient literature, or biography. "Concerning things around, however, and their properties, I knew a good deal more than is known by most boys." Through physics and chemistry in certain lines, through entomology and general natural history, through miscellaneous reading in physiology and geography, he had in many ways an intellectual grip of his environment; but on the lines of the "humanities" he was wofully uneducated.

On the other hand, his education had been stimulating and emancipating, and even as a boy of thirteen his intelligence was alert and independent. Much in the open air, he had kept an open mind. He had learned to use his brains and to enjoy nature. After that, everything is possible.

At Hinton.—When Herbert Spencer was thirteen (in the summer of 1833) his parents took him to his Uncle Thomas, at Hinton Charterhouse, near Bath. The journey was a revelation to the boy, and his early days at Hinton were full of delight, especially in regard to the new butterflies. But when he discovered that he had come to stay and to be schooled, he had a feverish *Heimweh*, and soon followed his parents homewards. "That a boy of thirteen should, without any food but bread and water and two or three glasses of beer, and without sleep for two nights, walk 48 miles one day, 47 the next, and some 20 the third, is surprising enough." It was a rather absurd boyish escapade, mainly due to lack of parental frankness, but not without the compliment implied in all nostalgia, and it gives us an inkling of Spencer's obstinacy and doggedness.

A fortnight after the escapade, the runaway returned peacefully to Hinton—content with his dramatic assertion of himself. For about three years he remained under his uncle's tutorship, and this was a formative period. Hinton stands high in a hilly country, between Bath and Frome, with picturesque places all round. His uncle was "a man of energetic, strongly-marked character," "intellectually above the average," with a good deal of originality of thought. Like his kindly wife, he belonged to the evangelical school.

"The daily routine was not a trying one. In the morning Euclid and Latin, in the afternoon commonly gardening, or sometimes a walk; and in the evening, after a little more study, usually of algebra I think, came reading, with occasionally chess. I became at that time very fond of chess, and acquired some skill." The aversion to linguistic studies continued, but there was an enthusiasm for mathematics and physics. To a modern educationist the regime at Hinton cannot but seem narrow; there was no history, no letters, no concrete science, and no play. There was certainly no over-pressure, but there was some brain-stretching and some salutary moral discipline. Stimulating, doubtless, was the table-talk and Mr Spencer's arguments with his nephew, whom he found "very deficient in the principle of *Fear*." We must not forget the visits to London (including the then private Zoological Gardens), or the first appearances in print—two letters in the newly started *Bath Magazine* on curiously shaped floating crystals of common salt, and on the New Poor Law! In June 1836, Herbert Spencer returned to Derby, benefited by the rural life and bracing climate of Hinton, "strong, in good health, and of good stature."

Looking backward after many years, Herbert Spencer felt that he was treated as a youth "with much more consideration and generosity than might have been expected. There was shown great patience in prosecuting what seemed by no means a hopeful undertaking." It is interesting, of course, to speculate what might have been the result if the boy's education had been less of a family affair; and it would be unfair to conclude that the success which attended the easy-going, personal, familiar instruction of this boy of uncommon brains would also attend a similar treatment of those of humbler parts. But would it not be well to make the experiment oftener, since the material abounds, and since the results of the conventional discipline of public schools and the like are not dazzlingly successful?

Spencer felt strongly, as he indulged in retrospect, that his well-meaning educators "had to deal with intractable material—an individuality too stiff to be easily moulded." That we may, in time, come to have not an occasional stiff haulm with a big ear, but a whole crop of them, must be the prayer of all who believe in education and race-progress.

Another of Spencer's retrospective convictions is one that makes all human nature kin—that he was not so black as he was painted. His father and his uncle had been eminently "good" boys, and they gauged boy-nature by their own standard. Had he gone to a public school, Spencer thinks that his "*extrinsically-*wrong actions would have been many, but the *intrinsically* wrong actions would have been few." This distinction will doubtless appeal to the wise.

At Home.—For a year and a half after leaving Hinton, Herbert Spencer remained at home, enjoying another period of freedom. He made in a day, without previous experience, a survey of his father's small property at Kirk Ireton—two fields and three cottages with their gardens; he made designs for a country house; he hit upon a remarkable property of the circle; and he fished. Meanwhile, however, his father who "held, and rightly held, that there are few functions higher than that of the educator," induced him to engage in school-work, and this experiment lasted for three months. It appears to have been directly a success, Spencer's lessons were at once "effective and pleasure-giving," and "complete harmony continued throughout the entire period"; it was not less important eventually, for we cannot doubt that part of the effectiveness of Herbert Spencer's book on *Education* is traceable to the fact that he had, for a term at least, personal experience of teaching.

Even at this early age (17 years) Spencer had ideals of "intellectual culture, moral discipline, and physical training." But as he disliked mechanical routine, had a great intolerance of monotony, and had ideas of his own, it seems likely enough that if he had embraced the profession of teacher, he would sooner or later have "thrown it up in disgust." The experiment was not to be tried further, however, for in November 1837, his uncle William wrote from London that he had obtained for his nephew a post under Mr Charles Fox as a railway engineer. "The profession of a civil engineer had already been named as one appropriate for me; and this opening at once led to the adoption of it."

We may sum up the first two periods of Spencer's life. The period of childhood was marked by a more than usual freedom from the conventional responsibilities of juvenile tasks, by the large proportion of open-air life, and by much more intercourse with adults than with other children. The table talk between his father and uncles had an important moulding influence, all the more that there was "a comparatively small interest in gossip." "Their conversation ever tended towards the impersonal.... There was no considerable leaning towards literature.... It was rather the scientific interpretations and moral aspects of things which occupied their thoughts." The period of boyhood and of more definite education was marked by freedom and variety, by a relative absence of linguistic discipline, by a preponderance of scientific training, by much family influence, and by an unusual amount of independent thinking.

CHAPTER III

PERIOD OF PRACTICAL WORK

Engineering—Many Inventions—Glimpse of Evolution-Idea—A Resting Period—Beginning to Write—Experimenting with Life

Herbert Spencer's life after boyhood may be conveniently divided into four periods:—

1. For about ten years he was engaged in varied practical work—surveying, plan-making, engineering, secretarial business, and superintendence (1837-1846).

2. After an unattached couple of years, during which he continued his self-education, experimented, invented, and meditated, there began a period of miscellaneous literary work, of journalism, and essay-writing, during which he wrote his *Principles of Psychology* and felt his way to his System (1848- 1860).

3. At the age of forty, he settled down to something like unity of occupation—developing and writing *The Synthetic Philosophy* (1860-1882).

4. Finally, during a prolonged period of pronounced invalidism, he withdrew almost completely from social life, husbanding his meagre supply of mental energy for the completion of his System, the revision of his works, and his *Autobiography* (1882-1903).

Engineering.—For about ten years (1837-46) Herbert Spencer had a varied experience of practical life. He began as assistant, at £80 a year, to Mr Charles Fox, who had been one of Mr George Spencer's pupils,—a man of mechanical genius, who was at that time resident engineer of the London division of the "London and Birmingham" railway, and afterwards became well known as the designer and constructor of the Exhibition-Building of 1851. Spencer had surveying and measuring, drawing and calculating to do, and he threw off the slackness which marked his school-days. During the first six months in London he never went to any place of amusement and never read a novel, but gave his leisure to mathematical questions and to suggesting little inventions or improved methods.

A transference for the summer months to Wembly, near Harrow, gave him even more time for study, and we read of an appliance by which he proposed to facilitate some kinds of sewing. He seems to have pleased his employer well, for in September 1838 he was advanced to a post of draughtsman in connection with the "Gloucester and Birmingham" railway, at a salary of £120 yearly. Thus the next two years were spent at Worcester, where he had his first experience of working alongside of other young men, to whom he appeared rather an "oddity," though not one to be "quizzed." His "mental excursiveness" grew stronger and stronger, and had occasionally useful results, leading, for instance, to an article in *The Civil Engineer and Architect's Journal* (May 1839) on a new plan of projecting the spiral courses in skew bridges, to a re-invention of Nicholson's Cyclograph, and to an improvement in the apparatus for giving and receiving the mail-bags carried by trains.

Many Inventions.—In 1840, Spencer became engineering secretary to his chief, Captain Moorson, and went to live in the little village of Powick, about three miles out of Worcester. He enjoyed his work, and had the new experience of establishing relations with a number of children, with whom he soon became a favourite. Long afterwards, in his declining years he found much gratification in making friends with children, and referred to it quaintly as "a vicarious phase of the philoprogenitive instinct." It was at Powick that Spencer first began to have a conscience about his very defective spelling (his *morals* had always been *sans reproche*) and to take an interest in style. It was at Powick, too, in a physical and social environment that suited him, that Spencer invented his "Velocimeter," a little instrument for showing by inspection the velocity of an engine, and two or three other devices. He had inherited his father's constructive imagination, and his father's discipline had increased it. The father wrote on July 3rd, 1840, "I am glad you find your inventive powers are beginning to develop themselves. Indulge a grateful feeling for it. Recollect, also, the never-ceasing pains taken with you on that point in early life." And the son remarks gratefully that this conveys a lesson to educators; the inherited endowment is much, but the fostering of it is also much. "Culture of the humdrum sort, given by those who ordinarily pass for teachers, would have left the faculty undeveloped." On the whole, however, Spencer attached most importance to the hereditary endowment, for he goes on to say that Edison, "probably the most remarkable inventor who ever lived," was a self-trained man, and that Sir Benjamin Baker, "the designer and constructor of the Forth Bridge, the grandest and most original bridge in the world, received no regular engineering education." It was at Powick, too, that place of many inventions, that Herbert Spencer (aetat. 20) made the intimate acquaintance of an "intelligent, unconventional, amiable, and in various ways attractive" young lady, who "tended to diminish his *brusquerie*." Luckily or unluckily, the young lady was engaged; and Spencer remarks, "It was pretty clear that had it not been for the pre-engagement our intimacy would have grown into something serious. This would have been a misfortune, for she had little or nothing and my prospects were none of the brightest." Here the ancestral prudence crops out.

Glimpses of Evolution-Idea.—The year 1840-41 was "a nomadic period," of bridge-building at Bromsgroove and Defford, of "castle-building," too, for he dreamt of making a fortune by successful inventions, of testing engines, and other routine duties,—a life involving considerable wear and tear which began to tell on Spencer's eyes. During this period he renewed his youth by collecting fossils, and "making a collection is," as he afterwards said, "the proper commencement of any natural history study; since, in the first place, it conduces to a concrete knowledge which gives definiteness to the general ideas subsequently reached, and, further, it creates an indirect stimulus by giving gratification to that love of acquisition which exists in all." It was then that the purchase of Lyell's *Principles of Geology* led him, curiously enough, to adopt the supposition that organic forms have arisen, not by special creation, but by progressive modifications, physically caused and inherited. In spite of Lyell's chapter refuting Lamarck's views concerning the origin of species, it was with Lamarck that Spencer, at the age of twenty, sided. The idea of natural genesis was in harmony with the general idea of the order of Nature towards which Spencer had been growing. "My belief in it never afterwards wavered, much as I was, in after years, ridiculed for entertaining it."

"The incident illustrates the general truth that the acceptance of this or that particular belief, is in part a question of the type of mind. There are some minds to which the marvellous and the unaccountable strongly appeal, and which even resent any attempt to bring the genesis of them within comprehension. There are other minds which, partly by nature and partly by culture, have been led to dislike a quiescent acceptance of the unintelligible; and which push their explorations until causation has been carried to its confines. To this last order of minds mine, from the beginning, belonged."

Spencer's engagement with Capt. Moorson came to a natural termination, and an offer of a permanent post on the Birmingham and Gloucester railway was declined, one motive being a desire to prepare for the future by a course of mathematical study, another being to work at an idea his father had arrived at of an electro-magnetic engine. Thus his twenty-first birthday was spent at home in Derby, after an absence of three and a half years,—which had been on the whole "satisfactory, in so far as personal improvement and professional success were concerned."

A Resting Period.—But when he got home he found his study of a work on the Differential Calculus a weariness to the flesh. "To apply day after day merely with the general idea of acquiring information, or of increasing ability," was not in him, though he could work hard when the end in view was definite or large enough. Moreover an article in the *Philosophical Magazine* led to an immediate abandonment of the idea of an electro-magnetic engine. "Thus, within a month of my return to Derby, it became manifest that, in pursuit of a will-o'-the-wisp, I had left behind a place of vantage from which there might probably have been ascents to higher places."

As a consolation for what was at the time a disappointment, Herbert Spencer made a herbarium, which still retained in 1894 a specimen of Enchanter's Nightshade gathered in the grove skirting the river near Darley. In company with Edward Lott, with whom he formed a life-long friendship, he often spent the early summer morning, in rowing up the Derwent, which in those days was rural and not unpicturesque above Derby. As they rowed they sang popular songs, making the woods echo with their voices, and now and then arresting their "secular matins" for the purpose of gathering a plant. It is refreshing to read of Spencer having in his head a considerable stock of sentimental ballads.

It was during this fallow year that at the age of one-and-twenty he went with his father on a walking tour in the Isle of Wight, and first saw the sea. "The emotion produced in me was, I think, a mixture of joy and awe,—the awe resulting from the manifestation of size and power, and the joy, I suppose, from the sense of freedom given by limitless expanse." His father and he were good companions.

We read of various activities during this period,—of investigations, with inadequate mathematics, concerning the strength of girders, of experiments in electrotyping and the like, of botanical excursions, of some enthusiastic exercise in part-singing, drawing and modelling. In the early summer of 1842 Spencer paid a visit to his old haunts at Hinton. "The journey left its mark because, in the course of it, I found that practice in modelling had increased my perception of beauty in form. A good-looking girl, who was one of our fellow-passengers for a short interval, had remarkably fine eyes: and I had much quiet satisfaction in observing their forms." Our hero had not much sense of humour.

Beginning to write.—Of greater importance is the fact that Spencer began in 1842 to write letters to *The Nonconformist* on social problems, in which prominence was given to such conceptions as the universality of law and causation, progressive adaptation in organisms and in Man, and the tendency to equilibrium through self-adjustment. "Every day in every life there is a budding out of incidents severally capable of leading to large results; but the immense majority of them end as buds, only now and then does one grow into a branch, and very rarely does such a branch outgrow and overshadow all others." The visit to Hinton led to political conversations with Thomas Spencer, to a letter of introduction to the editor of *The Nonconformist*, to the letters on "The Proper Sphere of Government," to the *Social Statics* and eventually to the *Synthetic Philosophy*!

Spencer's next activity was an inquiry into his father's system of short-hand, which he found to be better than Pitman's. He passed to speculations on the methods to be followed in forming a universal language, and to shrewd criticisms of the decimal system of enumeration. In the autumn of 1842 he interested himself enthusiastically in "The Complete Suffrage Movement." For a youth of twenty-two he took a big plunge into politics. "It produced in me a high tide of mental energy"; the signature on a draft democratic bill "has a sweep and vigour exceeding that of any other signature I ever made, either before or since."

In the spring of 1843 Herbert Spencer went to London and tried very unsuccessfully to get editors to accept his wares. He made a pamphlet of his *Nonconformist* letters, but perhaps a hundred copies were sold! "The printer's bill was £10 2s. 6d., and the publisher's payment to me on the first year's sales was fourteen shillings and threepence!"

Experimenting with Life.—Spencer's half year in London came to little. As he says, he was too much "in the mood of Mr Micawber,—waiting for something to turn up, and waiting in vain." So he raised the siege and retreated to Derby. There he read Mill's *System of Logic*, Carlyle's *Sartor Resartus* and some of Emerson's essays. He tried his hand at improving watches, printing-presses, type-making, and what not; he speculated on the rôle of carbon in the earth's history, and on phrenology; and in 1844 he migrated to Birmingham to be sub-editor of a short-lived paper called *The Pilot*.

It was then that he made a superficial acquaintance with Kant's *Critique of Pure Reason*, only to give it "summary dismissal." He was deterred from pursuing the acquaintance by the "utter incredibility" of the proposition that time and space are "nothing but" subjective forms, and by "want of confidence in the reasonings of any one who could accept a proposition so incredible."

After about a month of sub-editing, he reverted to his former profession of railway engineer, having been commissioned to help with mapping out a projected branch line between Stourbridge and Wolverhampton. The country was dreary enough, but Spencer had abundant open-air work, and it was during this short period that he made a lasting friendship with Mr W. F. Loch which was important in his life.

Then followed an interval, partly in London and partly in the fields of Warwickshire, occupied in various ways connected with railway development, which was then becoming a mania. He seems to have done his work effectively, but it led to no important personal results, and the failure of his chief employer's schemes in 1846 ended Spencer's connection with railway projects and engineering. In afterwards discussing the question whether he should have made a good engineer or not, Spencer notes with his characteristic self-impartiality that he had adequate inventiveness but insufficient patience, enough of intelligence but too little tact. He had an "aversion to mere mechanical humdrum work," "inadequate regard for precedent," no interest in financial details, and a "lack of tact in dealing with men, especially superiors." The frank analysis is interesting, especially in indicating how Spencer was weak where Darwin was strong, in "la patience suivie," in dogged persistence at detailed work. It may seem strange to say this when we think of his indomitable perseverance with his life-work, but this was quite consistent with a "constitutional idleness," with a shirking from everything tedious except his own thinking. As Thomas Hardy says of one of his characters, "he was a thinker by instinct, but he was only a worker by effort." He never learned or tried to learn what it was to put his nose to the grindstone: he would not learn "lessons," he recoiled from languages, he baulked at the differential calculus, he trifled with Kant and Comte, he was always "an impatient reader." He elected to think for himself, and had the defect of this rare quality.

CHAPTER IV

PREPARATION FOR LIFE-WORK

More Inventions—Sub-editing—Avowal of Evolutionism—Friendships—
Books and Essays—Crystallisation of his Thought—Settling to Life-work

Thrown out of regular employment once more, Spencer was left free for a time to follow his own bent. He lived a "miscellaneous and rather futile kind of life," reading a little and thinking much over a proposed book on Social Statics, holidaying a good deal and trying in vain to make money by inventions.

More Inventions.—In 1845 he had a scheme of quasi-aerial locomotion: not a flying machine but "something uniting terrestrial traction with aerial suspension"; but even on paper it broke down. In 1846 he patented an effective "binding pin" for fastening loose sheets, which might have been a financial success if it had been properly pushed. About the same time he was speculating on a method of multiplying decorative patterns,—a sort of "mental kaleidoscope," and on a systematic nomenclature for colours, analogous to that on which the points of the compass are named. More ambitious was a new planing engine and an improvement in type-making, but neither got much beyond the paper stage. In fact Spencer discovered, as so many have done, that it is one thing to invent and another thing to make inventions boil the pot. For a year and a half, he lamented, time and energy and money had been simply thrown away. The proceeds of the binding pin just about served to pay for his share in the cost of the planing machine patent.

Seven years spent in experimenting towards a livelihood had not brought Spencer much success. In point of fact he was "stranded," and there was talk of emigration to New Zealand, or of "reverting to the ancestral profession" of teaching, but the year of suspense ended with his appointment (1848) as sub-editor in *The Economist* office, at a salary of one hundred guineas a year. "Thus an end was at last put to the seemingly futile part of my life which filled the space between twenty-one and twenty-eight—futile in respect of material progress, but in other respects perhaps not futile."

He had enjoyed a varied intercourse with men and things during these seven lean years of railway-making, sub-editing, experimenting, inventing; he had had experience of field work and office work, of doing what he was told and of exercising authority; he had had time for drawing, modelling, music, and some natural history; he had come to know something of life's ups and downs. "In short, there had been gained a more than usually heterogeneous, though superficial, acquaintance with the world, animate and inanimate. And along with the gaining of it had gone a running commentary of speculative thought about the various matters presented." *Vivendo discimus.*

Sub-editing.—Spencer's duties as sub-editor of *The Economist* were not onerous; he had abundant leisure for reading and reflection, for music and that pleasant conversation which is one of the ends of life. He had great Sunday evening talks with his broad-minded philanthropic uncle Thomas who had come to live in London, and he began to know interesting people, notably, perhaps, Mr G. H. Lewes. His reading was mainly in connection with the journal he had charge of, and Coleridge's *Idea of Life*, with its doctrine of individuation, was the only serious work which seems to have left any impression during that early period. He tried Ruskin but recoiled disappointed from his "multitudinous absurdities." He also tried vegetarianism but found that it lowered his bodily and mental vigour.

He worked hard at his first book, sitting late over it with an assiduity to which he looked back with astonishment in after years. The subject of the book was "A system of Social and Political Morality" and he had great searchings for a suitable title, his own preference for "Demostatics" yielding finally in favour of "Social Statics." This phrase had been used by Comte as the heading of one of the divisions of his Sociology, but Spencer was quite unaware of this, and at that time "knew nothing more of Auguste Comte, than that he was a French philosopher." There were also great difficulties in securing publication, although to get the work printed and circulated without loss was as much as he hoped for. "At that time I was, and have since remained, one of those classed by Dr Johnson as fools—one whose motive in writing books was not, and never has been, that of making money."

What Spencer calls "an idle year" (1850-1) followed the publication of *Social Statics*, but it was then that he attended a course of lectures by Prof. Owen on Comparative Osteology, and doubtless got a firmer hold of those principles of organic architecture which make even dry bones live. It was then, too, that he had walks with George Henry Lewes, which were profitable on both sides. Lewes received an impulse which awakened interest in scientific inquiries, and Spencer became interested in philosophy at large. He read Lewes's *Biographical History of Philosophy*, and there was one memorable ramble during which a volume by Milne-Edwards in Lewes's bag was the means of vivifying for Spencer the idea of "the physiological division of labour." "Though the conception was not new to me, as is shown towards the end of *Social Statics*, yet the mode of formulating it was; and the phrase thereafter played a part in the course of my thought." About the same time, in preparing a review of Carpenter's *Physiology*, he came across von Baer's formula expressing the course of development through which every living creature passes—"the change from homogeneity to heterogeneity"; and from this very important consequences ensued.

Through Lewes he got to know Carlyle, but the acquaintance was never deepened. While he admired Carlyle's vigour and originality, he was repelled by his passionate incoherence of thought, his prejudices, his dogmatism, his "insensate dislike of science." "Carlyle's nature was one which lacked co-ordination, alike intellectually and morally. Under both aspects, he was, in a great measure, chaotic." To Carlyle, on the other hand, Spencer appeared "an unmeasurable ass."

Avowal of Evolutionism.—In 1852 Spencer definitely began his work as a pioneer of Evolution Doctrine by publishing the famous *Leader* article on "The Development Hypothesis," in which he avowed his belief that the whole world of life is the result of an age-long process of natural transmutation. In the same year he wrote for *The Westminster Review* another important essay, "A Theory of Population deduced from the General Law of Animal Fertility," in which he sought to show that the degree of fertility is inversely proportionate to the grade of development, or conversely that the attainment of higher degrees of evolution must be accompanied by lower rates of multiplication. Towards the close of the article he came within an ace of recognising that the struggle for existence was a factor in organic evolution. It is profoundly instructive to find that at a time when pressure of population was practically interesting men's minds, not Spencer only, but Darwin and Wallace, were being independently led from this social problem to a biological theory of organic evolution. There could be no better illustration, as Prof. Geddes has pointed out, of the Comtian thesis that science is a "social phenomenon."

Friendships.—About this time a strong friendship arose between Spencer and Miss Evans (George Eliot). To him she was "the most admirable woman, mentally," he ever met, and he speaks enthusiastically of her large intelligence working easily, her remarkable philosophical powers, her habitual calm, her deep and broad sympathies. It is interesting to learn that he strongly advised her to write novels, and that she tried in vain to induce him to read Comte. As they were often together and the best of friends, the gossips had it that he was in love with her and that they were about to be married. "But neither of these reports was true."

Another friendship, formed about the same time, was an important factor in Spencer's life; he got to know Huxley and thus came into close touch with a scientific worker of the first rank, useful alike in suggestion and in criticism. He found another friend in Tyndall, whom he greatly admired for his combination of the poetic with the scientific mood, for "his passion for Nature quite Wordsworthian in its intensity," and for his interest in "the relations between science at large and the great questions which lie beyond science."

In 1853, by the death of his uncle Thomas, who had persistently overworked himself, Spencer received a bequest of £500. On the strength of this and the extended literary connections which the good offices of Mr Lewes and Mr (afterwards Prof.) David Masson had secured for him, he resigned his sub-editorship of *The Economist* in order to obtain leisure for larger works. He always believed in burning his ships before a struggle.

Looking back on the "*Economist*" period, Spencer felt that his later career had been "mainly determined by the conceptions which were then initiated and the friendships which were formed."

Books and Essays.—Spencer's life of greater freedom began with a holiday in Switzerland (1853), which "fully equalled his anticipations in respect of its grandeur, but did not do so in respect of its beauty." The tour was greatly enjoyed, for Spencer was a lover of mountains, but some excesses in walking seem to have overtaxed his heart, and immediately after his return "there commenced cardiac disturbances which never afterwards entirely ceased; and which doubtless prepared the way for the more serious derangements of health subsequently established."

For a time he settled down to essay-writing; *e.g.*, on "Method in Education," in which he sought to justify his own experience of his father's non-coercive liberating methods by affiliating these with the Method of Nature; on "Manners and Fashions," in which he protested against unthinking subservience to social conventions, some of which are mere survivals of more primitive times without present-day justification; on "The Genesis of Science," in which he showed how the sciences have grown out of common knowledge; and on "Railway Morals and Railway Policy," in which he made some salutary disclosures with characteristic fearlessness.

Spencer's second book, "The Principles of Psychology," began to be written in 1854 in a summer-house at Tréport, and it was in the same year that the author made his first acquaintance with Paris. Preoccupied with his task, he wandered from Jersey to Brighton, from London to Derby, often writing about five hours a day, and thinking with but little intermission. The result was that he finished the book in about a year and almost finished his own career. The nervous breakdown that followed cost him a year and a half for recuperation, and his pursuit of truth was ever afterwards involved with a pursuit of health.

In search of health Spencer reverted to the best of his ability to a simple life, but he found it difficult not to think. Thought rode behind him when he tried horseback exercise, and novels brought only sleeplessness. He tried yachting and he tried fishing, shower-baths and sea-bathing, playing with children and sleeping in a haunted room, but the cure was slow; music was almost the only thing he could enjoy with impunity. It was when fishing one morning in Loch Doon that he vented his first oath, at the age of thirty-six, because his line was tangled, and became, he tells us, more fully aware of the irritability produced by his nervous disorder!

As entire idleness seemed futile, and as two and a half years had elapsed since he had made any money, Spencer returned to London (1857)—to a home with children—and began in a leisurely way to write more essays. He composed the article on "Progress: its Law and Cause" at the pathetically slow rate of about half a page per day, and the effort proved beneficial. A significant essay entitled, "Transcendental Physiology," dates from the same year, and during an angling holiday in Scotland he wrote another on the "Origin and Function of Music." Starting from the fact that feeling tends to discharge itself in muscular contractions, including those of the vocal organs, he sought to show that music is a development of the natural language of the emotions.

Crystallisation of his Thought.—Spencer settled down in London in a home "with a lively circle," and pursued his calling as a thinker with quiet resolution. He had Sunday afternoon walks and talks with Huxley, and he occasionally dined out to meet interesting people such as Buckle and Grote; but the tenor of his life was uninterrupted by much incident. In this year he published a volume of essays new and old, *Essays: Scientific, Political, and Speculative*; and this was probably in part responsible for a great unification in Spencer's thought. It was in the beginning of 1858 that he made the first sketch of his System, and on the 9th of January he wrote to his father as follows: "Within the last ten days my ideas on various matters have suddenly crystallised into a complete whole. Many things which were before lying separate have fallen into their places as harmonious parts of a system that admits of logical development from the simplest general principles."

In this *annus mirabilis* (1858) when Darwin and Wallace read their papers at the Linnæan Society expounding the idea of Natural Selection, Spencer was also thinking keenly along evolutionary lines. He ventured on a defence of the Nebular Hypothesis and a criticism of Owen's Vertebral Theory of the Skull; and he was working at the question of the form and symmetry of animals, which he interpreted as "determined by the relations of the parts to incident forces." Vigorous as he was in his intelligence, he was still unable to work for more than about three hours a day, and his pecuniary prospects were dismal.

In view of his determination to go on working out his System, it was a fortunate chance that led him in an emergency to discover that he could greatly increase his productivity by dictating instead of writing.

Spencer made various efforts (1859-60) to secure some Government appointment which would afford him a steady income and yet leave him free for his life-work, but as nothing came of these, he went on quietly with his essay-writing, with many pleasant holidays interspersed, and produced his "Illogical Geology," "The Social Organism," "Prison Ethics," "The Physiology of Laughter," and so on.

Settling to his life-work.—Baffled in other plans, he at length organised a scheme of publishing his projected series of volumes by subscription. His influential friends headed the list and four hundred names were soon secured in Britain; the disinterested energy of an American admirer, Prof. E. S. Youmans, raised the total to six hundred. And thus Spencer, at the age of forty, handicapped by lack of means and health, calmly sat down to a task which was calculated to occupy him for twenty years…. "To think that an amount of mental exertion great enough to tax the energies of one in full health and vigour, and at his ease in respect of means, should be undertaken by one who, having only precarious resources, had become so far a nervous invalid that he could not with any certainty count upon his powers from one twenty-four hours to another! However, as the result proved, the apparently unreasonable hope was entertained, if not wisely, still fortunately. For though the whole of the project has not been executed, yet the larger part of it has." In one form of faith Spencer was in no wise lacking.

CHAPTER V

THINKING OUT THE SYNTHETIC PHILOSOPHY

Thinking by Stratagem—The System Grows—Difficulties—Italy—Habits of Work—Sociology—Ill-health—Citizenship—Visit to America—Closing Years

Having theoretically secured the requisite number of subscribers to the projected series of volumes, Spencer tried to settle down to "something like unity of occupation." In the Spring of 1860 he began the *First Principles*— only to break down before he had finished the first chapter; and the same depressing experience was continually repeated. Fortunately for Spencer's peace of mind, his uncle William left him some money; one may well say fortunately, since the number of defaulters in the subscription list was so large that in the absence of other resources even the first volume could not have been published.

Thinking by Stratagem.—Spencer's devices for keeping off the cerebral congestion which work induced were many and various—some almost laughable, if the whole business had not been so tragic. He would ramble into the country, find a sheltered nook or sunny bank, do a little work, and move on like a "Scholar Gipsy"; he would take his amanuensis on the Regent's Park water, row vigorously for five minutes, dictate for fifteen, and so on *da capo*; he frequented an open racquet-court at Pentonville, and sandwiched games and *First Principles*; even in the Highlands he would dictate while he rowed. It was altogether like thinking by stratagem, and the tension of working against time became so irksome, that he issued a notice to the subscribers that successive numbers would come out when they were ready. Nevertheless, he completed the *First Principles* in June 1862.

The System Grows.—Having safely set forth his doctrine, Spencer turned with zest to relaxation, acting as cicerone to his friends at the International Exhibition, climbing in Wales, fishing in Scotland, revisiting Paris, and so forth. The years passed in alternate work and play, and the next great event was the publication of the first volume of the *Principles of Biology* in 1864. In spite of inadequate preparation Spencer produced by the strength of his intelligence a biological classic. At the time, of course, little notice was taken of it; thus in "The Athenæum" of 5th November 1864, a paragraph concerning the book commenced thus: "This is but one of two volumes, and the two but a part of a larger work: we cannot therefore but announce it." "In

1864," Spencer says, "not one educated person in ten or more knew the meaning of the word Biology; and among those who knew it, whether critics or general readers, few cared to know anything about the subject" (*Autobiography*, ii. p. 105).

It was in the same year (1864) that Spencer formulated his views on the classification of the sciences and his reasons for dissenting from the philosophy of Comte.

Of considerable interest was the formation of a decemvirate of Spencer's friends, which was first called "The Blastodermic" and afterwards the "X" club. It consisted of Huxley, Tyndall, Hooker, Lubbock, Frankland, Busk, Hirst, Spottiswoode, and Spencer, with one vacancy which was never filled up. The members dined together occasionally and talked at large. "Among its members were three who became Presidents of the Royal Society, and five who became Presidents of the British Association. Of the others one was for a time President of the College of Surgeons; another President of the Chemical Society; and a third of the Mathematical Society...." "Of the nine I was the only one who was fellow of no society, and had presided over nothing." The club lasted for at least twenty-three years (1887), and had considerable influence both on its members and externally.

In 1865 Spencer took considerable interest in a new weekly journal, called "The Reader," in which many prominent workers were implicated, but the enterprise ended in disappointment, unless, indeed, it was a step towards the establishment of *Nature*. In this and the following year he busied himself with an investigation regarding circulation in plants,—the only concrete piece of biological work he ever indulged in. But the great event of 1866 was the completion of *The Principles of Biology*.

Difficulties.—In the beginning of 1866 Spencer found that many of the subscribers to his serial publications had withdrawn, and that not a few were much in arrears, and he sorrowfully decided that he must abandon his undertaking. It was at this juncture that he discovered what stuff his friends were made of. Mr John Stuart Mill wrote proposing to help to indemnify Spencer for losses incurred, and offering to guarantee the publisher against any loss on the next treatise. He called this "a simple proposal of co-operation for an important public purpose, for which you give your labour and have given your health." As Spencer felt himself obliged to decline this generous proposal, the next move among his friends was to arrange to take a large number of copies (250) for distribution. To this, with mingled feelings of satisfaction and dissatisfaction, Spencer agreed. Meanwhile, however, his American admirers, organised by Professor Youmans, invested in Spencer's name a sum of 7000 dollars as a fund to ensure the continued publication of his works. This, in combination with an improvement in Spencer's financial position, consequent on his father's death (1866), made publication once more secure without the aid of the subsidising scheme proposed by his English friends.

In September 1866 Herbert Spencer settled himself in London, *en pension* at 37 Queen's Gardens, Lancaster Gate, which remained his home for over a score of years. Henceforth he was less of a nomad, and he secured himself against all interruptions by taking a secret study a few doors off.

There are two records for the beginning of 1867 which are interesting in their contrast. The first is that Spencer declined without hesitation certain overtures by his friends that he should stand for the professorship of Moral Philosophy at University College, London, and for a similar post in Edinburgh; the second is that he invented a most elaborate invalid-bed, which, like most of his inventions, fell flat.

The invalid-bed had been suggested by his mother's prolonged feebleness, but it was not long to be used. Spencer was left in 1867 with no nearer relatives than cousins. In reference to his mother, we quote with all reverence one of the few strong personal touches in the *Autobiography*.

"Thus ended a life of monotonous routine, very little relieved by positive pleasures. I look back upon it regretfully: thinking how small were the sacrifices which I made for her in comparison with the great sacrifices which, as a mother, she made for me in my early days. In human life, as we at present know it, one of the saddest traits is the dull sense of filial obligations which exists at the time when it is possible to discharge them with something like fulness, in contrast with the keen sense of them which arises when such discharge is no longer possible."

In the spring of 1867 Spencer finished publishing the second volume of the *Biology*, and immediately set to work to recast *First Principles*. And as if that was not enough, he began in the same year, with the help of his secretary, Mr David Duncan, his collection of sociological data, which was intended to afford the foundation for a treatise on the *Principles of Sociology*. In spite of occasional holidays at Yarrow, at Glenelg, and in other delightful places, the usual nemesis of industry was not avoided. Spencer's nerve-centres, which could never endure prolonged attention, showed the usual symptoms of over-fatigue; and though he tried morphia and skating, hydropathy and rackets, he had to give up work early in 1868. He betook himself to Italy for rest, attracted partly by the fact that Vesuvius was in eruption! About this time he was elected a member of the Athenæum Club, the sedative amenities of which proved a useful prophylactic in after years.

Italy.—Of Spencer's Tour in Italy the *Autobiography* gives us some interesting reminiscences. He arrived in Naples in a state of extreme exhaustion, wearied with the voyage, wearied with a menu in which tunny was the *pièce de résistance*, and finding comfort only in the shelter of his Inverness cape. And yet, the day after his arrival, the author of *Social Statics* might have been seen giving swift chase to an audacious thief who had taken advantage of the philosopher's preoccupation to abstract his opera-glass. "Most likely had the young fellow had a knife about him I should have suffered, perhaps fatally, for my imprudence." A few days later, the same characteristic rashness impelled him to ascend the burning mountain without a guide and at great risk. "How to account for the judicial blindness I displayed, I do not know; unless by regarding it as an extreme instance of the tendency which I perceive in myself to be enslaved by a plan once formed—a tendency to become for a time possessed by one thought to the exclusion of others."

Nothing that Spencer saw in Italy impressed him so much as "the dead town" of Pompeii. The man who "took but little interest in what are called histories" was stirred by this concrete historical fossil. "It aroused sentiments such as no written record had ever done." He enjoyed Rome, but rather for its harmonious colouring than for its historical associations, of which he had no vivid perception. He was more irritated than pleased by the old masters. He got most pleasure from the scenery, but Italy is "a land of beautiful distances and ugly foregrounds." Companionless and impatient, his chief thought was how to get home most comfortably, and so he returned no better than he went.

Habits of Work.—About this time the tide had turned as regarded the sale of his works, and he wrote gratefully "the remainder of my life-voyage was through smooth waters." As the *Autobiography* shows, it was a quiet and uneventful voyage. Periods of work alternated with holidays, many parts of the country were visited, and angling became more and more his best recreation. "Nothing else served so well to rest my brain and fit it for resumption of work." Another resource was billiards, which he greatly enjoyed. He never could remember whist or similar games.

On fine mornings he used to spend two or three hours on the Serpentine, alternating rowing and dictating. After his morning's work and after lunch he used to walk through Kensington Gardens, Hyde Park, and the Green Park, without more than a quarter of a mile upon pavement, to the Athenæum Club, where he skimmed through periodicals and books, and played his game. Thereafter he sauntered back to dinner at seven, "which was followed by such miscellaneous ways of passing the time without excitement as were available. Thus passed my ordinary days." By this time he had given up novel-reading, only treating himself to one about once a year, and then in a dozen or more instalments. He did not care to multiply social relations, he "avoided acquaintanceships and cultivated only friendships." "There is in me very little of the *besoin de parler*; and hence I do not care to talk with those in whom I feel no interest." And thus, though far from being a recluse, he lived his life of thought quietly.

In 1871 Spencer was nominated for the office of Lord Rector at the University of St Andrews, but he declined the honour for the sake of his work. He also declined the honorary degree of Doctor of Laws from the same University, and subsequently, similar honours, chiefly on the ground "that the advance of thought will be most furthered, when the only honours to be acquired by authors are those spontaneously yielded to them by a public which is left to estimate their merits as well as it can."

The first (synthetic) volume of the new edition of the *Psychology* begun in 1867 was finished in 1870, the second (analytic) volume begun in 1870 was completed in the end of 1872. Having become much interested in the well-known "International Scientific Series," Spencer contributed to it in 1873 the volume known as *The Study of Sociology*, which has done much in Britain and America to secure the position of Sociology as a workable science. It was unusually successful for a book of its kind, and brought Spencer about £1500.

Sociology.—From 1867 onwards Spencer had been collecting Sociological Data to serve as a basis for generalised interpretation. With the help of Mr David Duncan, Mr James Collier, and Dr Scheppig, this big piece of work made steady progress, and its publication began to be discussed in 1871. It was hoped that the plan of "exhibiting sociological phenomena in such wise that comparisons of them in their co-existences and sequences, as occurring among various peoples in different stages, were made easy, would immensely facilitate the discovery of sociological truths." The first part of this *Descriptive Sociology* was published in 1873, but the demand for it was very slight; not quite 200 copies were asked for in eight months. "I had," Spencer says, "greatly over-estimated the amount of desire which existed in the public mind for social facts of an instructive kind. They greatly preferred those of an uninstructive kind." In this and similar connections, the reader of the *Autobiography* cannot but be impressed by two facts,—on the one hand, the chivalrous eagerness on the part of American friends to be allowed to lessen Spencer's pecuniary burden, and, on the other hand, the almost ultra-sensitive resoluteness which Spencer exhibited in declining these offers.

In 1874, with the materials and memoranda of a quarter of a century around him, the thinker, who was blamed for not being inductive, set himself to write the *Principles of Sociology*, "feeling much as might a general of division who had become commander-in-chief; or rather, as one who had to undertake this highest function in addition to the lower functions of all his subordinates of the first, second, and third grades. Only by deliberate method persistently followed was it possible to avoid confusion."

The period of work on the *Sociology* was broken by some delightful holidays in the Highlands and elsewhere, by the British Association meeting at Belfast (1874) when Tyndall gave his famous Presidential Address, and by the usual ill-health. The first volume was completed in 1877. Apart from the nemesis of nerves, Spencer's life at this time seems to have been a happy one; he was fairly free from pecuniary cares; he was no longer tied to a serial issue of his publications; he could afford pleasant holidays, and he had a small circle of loyal friends. The philosopher began a series of annual picnics, which he seems to have engineered with great skill; in various ways he acted up to what he says was his habitual maxim, "Be a boy as long as you can." In 1877 he had the excitement of a shipwreck near Loch Carron, and the encouragement of having his *Descriptive Sociology* translated into Russian.

Ill-Health.—In spite of all his care, the year 1878 opened with a serious illness, and this prompted him to begin dictating *The Data of Ethics* lest an aggravation of his ill-health should hinder him from raising this coping-stone of his system. Just before Christmas of this year, he went with Prof. Youmans to the Riviera, and for a couple of months was more than usually successful in combining work and play. He finished *The Data of Ethics* in June 1879, and *Ceremonial Institutions* later in the year. As a reward of industry, and as a safeguard against too much of it, a holiday up the Nile in pleasant company was then arranged, and Spencer entered upon it in great spirits. But an ill- considered meal at Alexandria brought on dyspepsia and morbid fancies, and he was forced to return at the first cataract. He had seen many of the sights and was inevitably impressed, but he seems to have been glad to get out of the "melancholy country"—"the land of decay and death—dead men, dead races, dead creeds," as it appeared to his jaundiced eyes.

On his return journey he spent three days in Venice, but though he derived much pleasure from the general effects, he was repelled by the obtrusiveness and superficiality of the decorations. He regarded St Mark's as "a fine sample of barbaric architecture"; "it has the trait distinctive of semi-civilised art— excess of decoration"; "it is archæologically, but not æsthetically precious."

The entry in his journal for Feb. 12th, 1880 reads: "Home at 7-10; heartily glad—more pleasure than in anything that occurred during my tour."

Although he did not greatly enjoy his tour in Egypt, and brought back his packet of work unopened, the break seems to have been "decidedly beneficial." "It has apparently worked some kind of constitutional change;

for, marvellous to relate, I am now able to drink beer with impunity and, I think, with benefit—a thing I have not been able to do for these fifteen years or more." He thought that it had also perhaps furthered his work to have had contact with people in a lower stage of civilisation.

In 1881 Spencer published the eighth part of his *Descriptive Sociology* and put a full stop to the undertaking which left him with a deficit of between three and four thousand pounds, and which had half-killed two secretaries.

Spencer's next task was the completion of *Political Institutions*, another instalment of the *Sociology*, which he had begun in 1879, and he was at this time also occupied in considering and answering the more formidable of the criticisms which his system had aroused, and in revising new editions of the *First Principles* and *The Study of Sociology*. It is interesting to note that the last work was carefully revised sentence by sentence five times.

Citizenship.—In 1881 Spencer felt in a new way the universal call "*Il faut être citoyen*"; he was drawn into practical action, and although this led to the greatest disaster of his life, the cause was worthy of the sacrifice. It was the cause of peace. While writing *Political Institutions* he had become more firmly convinced than ever that "the possibility of a higher civilization depends wholly on the cessation of militancy and the growth of industrialism." Conversations with Mr Frederic Harrison and others led to meetings of those who were sympathetic with what might be called a non- aggression policy, and Spencer was so keenly interested that in spite of forebodings he undertook some organising work, and even went the length of moving a resolution and making a speech at a public meeting. There was no direct political result of the "Anti-Aggression League," but there was most mischievous result to Spencer. "There was produced a mischief which, in a gradually increasing degree, undermined life and arrested work." He had now begun to descend the inclined plane which brought him down in the course of subsequent years to "the condition of a confirmed invalid, leading little more than a vegetative life." What Spencer did in connection with the Anti- Aggression movement was probably only the last straw, but he could not look back on his intrinsically right action without regret. "Right though I thought it, my course brought severe penalties and no compensations whatever. I am not thinking only of the weeks, months, years, of wretched nights and vacant days; though these made existence a long-drawn weariness. I refer chiefly to the gradual arrest and final cessation of my work; and the consciousness that there was slipping by that closing part of life during which it should have been completed." He was too honest to profess a pleasure he did not feel in a *mens sibi conscia recti*. "It is best," he said, "to recognise the facts as they are, and not try to prop up rectitude by fictions."

Visit to America.—In 1882 in the hope of recovering tone, not, as some of the papers said, of recouping his finances, Spencer went on a visit to America, along with Mr Lott his friend of forty years. He was, of course, pressed to lecture, and was offered terms up to 250 dollars per night, but he would have none of it. Lecturing was not his metier, and his health was broken. "As matters stand," he wrote, "the giving a lecture or reading a paper, would be nothing more than making myself a show; and I absolutely decline to make myself a show." The only public appearance he made was at a dinner in his honour at New York, where, with his fatigued brain, he spoke straight to the Americans on the sin of over-devotion to work. With his friend Lott as a buffer, he succeeded in avoiding all interviewers until he had got on board the *Germanic* on his return voyage, when he was taken unawares at the last moment.

Spencer saw some of the finest sights in America and Canada; he met congenial spirits, and everything possible was done to make his visit a tonic; but he came back in a worse state than he went, "having made another step downwards towards invalid life."

Closing Years.—From 1882 till 1889, when the *Autobiography* ends, Spencer's life was one of invalidism with occasional gleams of health. There was nothing organically wrong with him, but he had no reserve of nervous energy, and he was not able to work for more than brief intervals at a time. Yet he produced during these years *The Man Versus the State*, a volume on *Ecclesiastical Institutions*, and *The Factors of Organic Evolution*. He also dictated the *Autobiography* at the average rate of about fifteen lines per day!

As years went on Spencer became more and more of a recluse, more and more a man of nerves, the grasshopper became a burden, and as he watched himself with scientific minuteness, hypochondria naturally grew upon him. He continued, however, to use for work the minute fractions of a day when he felt relatively vigorous, and thus he at length actually finished his *Synthetic Philosophy* in 1896.

He gives an account of his daily routine when he had attained the age of seventy-three. In the mornings he did a little work, dictating for ten minutes at a time, and repeating the process from two to five times. During the rest of the day he killed time, walking a few hundred yards, driving for an hour or so in a carriage with india-rubber tyres, or "sitting very much in the open air, hearing and observing the birds, watching the drifting clouds, listening to the sighings of the wind through the trees." He could not read or bear being read to, he could not play games or listen to music, he used ear-stoppers to shut out conversation whenever he got tired of it, and without respect of persons, and he took opium to secure a few hours sleep at nights. He might have been more comfortable, physically, if he had abandoned all attempt at work, but the architectonic instinct tyrannised over him. He really lived for the sake of the little oases of work-time which broke the monotony of his daily journey.

It should be remembered, that invalid as he was, Spencer aggravated matters by his scientific hypochondria, and perhaps also by his soporifics. His disturbances of health involved little positive suffering, and, till he was considerably over sixty, he had few deprivations. Even in old age he had no invalid appearance. "Neither in the lines of the face nor in its colour, is there any such sign of constitutional derangement as would be expected. Contrariwise, I am usually supposed to be about ten years younger than I am" (1893).

> "Spencer's closing years," Prof. Hudson writes, "were clouded with much sadness and disappointment." His days were vacant and his nights a weariness; he had outlived most of his friends and was lonely; and "the completion of his *Synthetic Philosophy* in 1896 did not bring him the keen satisfaction he fairly might have expected." He saw his political advice disregarded, and on all sides an exuberant growth of the socialistic organisations which he had spent himself in criticising. "He saw, too, with profound sorrow, unmistakable signs everywhere of reaction in religion, politics, society. The recrudescence of militarism, the development of a sordidly materialistic spirit throughout the modern nations and their abandonment of the principles of sanity and political righteousness—all these things cast a very black shadow over his declining path. I do not wonder that, as he looked back over his magnificent life-work, his mind should have been darkened by the doubt as to whether some of the truths, to which he attached the greatest value, might not after all have been set forth in vain" ("Fortnightly Review," 1904, p. 17).

Spencer's life closed in his eighty-third year, on December 8th, 1903.

CHAPTER VI

CHARACTERISTICS:—PHYSICAL AND INTELLECTUAL

The Autobiography—Physical Characteristics—Intellectual Characteristics—Limitations—Development of Spencer's Mind—Methods of Work—Genius?

Spencer was much given to summing up what he called the "traits" of the men he met, and he extended the process to himself in his *Autobiography*, which is an elaborate piece of self-portraiture.

The Autobiography.—Some one has called autobiography the least credible form of fiction, but that is not the impression which Spencer's gives. His self-analysis is candid and continuous; he is always revealing his feet of clay, and that with a self-complacency which is unintelligible to those who do not understand the impersonal scientific mood which had become habitual to Spencer. He almost achieved the impossible, of looking at himself from the outside.

Huxley wrote an autobiography in a score of pages, and he never wrote anything better; Spencer occupied over a thousand pages with his account of himself, and he never wrote anything worse. Dictated in outline in 1875, it was elaborated piecemeal, in small daily instalments, after the most serious of the many breakdowns in health had precluded more difficult work. Naturally enough, therefore, the *Autobiography* is often prolix and lacking in proportion, often slack in style and, it must be confessed, tedious. Little details in a picture may be essential to the effective impression, but Spencer often wearies us with trifling incidents whose narration has no excuse except as happening in a great life. Yet, if we lay the volumes aside, bored by their monumental egotism, we return to them with sympathy, and are won again by their unaffected frankness and candid sincerity.

With the *Autobiography* before us, but exercising the right of private judgment, we propose in this and the next chapter to sum up Spencer's characteristics—physical, intellectual, and emotional, and to refer to his methods of work and conduct of life.

Physical Characteristics.—Spencer at his best was an impressive figure, "tall, erect, a little gaunt, with a magnificent broad brow and high domed head." "His face," Prof. W. H. Hudson writes, "was a strikingly expressive one, with its strong frontal ridge, deep-set eyes, prominent nose, and firmly-cut mouth and jaw—the face of a man marked out for intellectual leadership."[1] It was not wrinkled with thought, as one might have expected, but was smooth as a child's or as a bishop's, the explanation being, as Spencer said, that he never worried over things, but allowed his brain to do its own thinking without pressure. He looked anything but an invalid, for his cheeks were ruddy even in later years. He had a fine voice and "a rather rare laugh of deep-chested musical qualities."

[1] Herbert Spencer: A Character Study, "Fortnightly Review,"1904.

He lamented that he had not inherited his father's finely developed chest organs, and that in consequence his cerebral circulation was under par. More positively, he seems to have inherited a readily fatigued nervous system, which limited his powers of protracted attention and made him not infrequently irritable and difficult to get on with. As we have seen he suffered periodically from over-taxing his brain, which induced terrible insomnia. Like Carlyle, he suffered from dyspepsia.

Intellectual Characteristics.—1. Among his intellectual characteristics, Spencer gave the foremost place to his "unusual capacity for the intuition of cause." The capacity was inherited and it was carefully nurtured. His restlessness to discover causes—"natural causes"—was illustrated when, as a boy of thirteen, he called in question the dictum of Dr Arnott respecting inertia, and it was characteristic of his whole intellectual life. He cultivated this inquisitiveness for causes till the mood became habitual, and resulted in what we may almost call an interpretative instinct. That this never led him astray, not even his most enthusiastic disciples would venture to maintain.

While the scientific method is always fundamentally the same, there is happily some legitimate elasticity in the order of procedure. Some minds start with a clue perceived by a flash of insight and then proceed to test and verify; others collect their data laboriously and never get a glimpse of their conclusion until the induction is complete. Some seem to have a selective instinct for getting hold of the most significant facts, or for making the crucial experiment; others have to plod on patiently from fact to fact and must make many "fools' experiments." Some find a nugget while their neighbours get their gold in dust particles after washing much ore.

Now Spencer had that passion for facts which is fundamental to all solid scientific work, but he had the greater gift of getting rapidly beneath facts to the question of their significance. He had not the love of details which is essential to the descriptive naturalist for instance, which sometimes becomes intellectual avarice for copper coinage, but he was instinctively an ætiologist, an interpreter.

In his account of the working of his mind, he says:—

> "There was commonly shown a faculty of seizing cardinal truths rather than of accumulating detailed information. The implications of phenomena were then, as always, more interesting to me than the phenomena themselves. What did they prove? was the question instinctively put. The consciousness of causation, to which there was a natural proclivity, and which had been fostered by my father, continually prompted analyses, which of course led me below the surface and made fundamental principles objects of greater attention than the various concrete illustrations of them. So that while my acquaintance with things might have been called superficial, if measured by the *number* of facts known, it might have been called the reverse of superficial, if measured by the *quality* of the facts. And there was possibly a relation between these traits. A friend who possessed extensive botanical knowledge, once remarked to me that, had I known as much about the details of plant-structure as botanists do, I never should have reached those generalisations concerning plant-morphology which I had reached." (*Autobiography* I.)

2. Another inherited capacity was "the synthetic tendency," the power of generalising or of working out unifying formulæ. His first book *Social Statics* set out with a general principle; his first essay was entitled, "A theory of population, *deduced from the general law* of animal fertility"; his life-work was the *Synthetic Philosophy*. One of George Eliot's witticisms made game of Spencer's aptitude for generalisation. He had been explaining his disbelief in the critical powers of salmon, and his aim in making flies "the best average representation of an insect buzzing on the surface of the water." "Yes," she said, "you have such a passion for generalising, you even fish with a generalisation." And this exactly describes what he spent much of his life in doing.

Mr Francis Galton has graphically stated his impression, that Spencer's composite mental photographs, in forming a generalisation, or in using a general formula-term, were many times multiple of those of ordinary mortals. A composite mental photograph from a small number of intellectual negatives yields a blurred outline—a woolly idea, with ragged edges and loose ends—but a composite mental photograph from a very large number of impressions, yielded, in Spencer's case, a generalisation which was crisp and well-defined. Some one has said that Ruskin had the most analytic mind in modern Christendom: that Spencer had one of the most synthetic minds can hardly be questioned.

3. It was one of the open secrets of Spencer's power that his analytic tendency was almost equal to his synthetic tendency. "Both subjectively and objectively, the desire to build up was accompanied by an almost equal desire to delve down to the deepest accessible truth, which should serve as an unshakable foundation." "It appears that in the treatment of every topic, however seemingly remote from philosophy, I found occasion for falling back on some ultimate principle in the natural order."

The first volume of the Psychology is synthetic, the second volume is analytic, "taking to pieces our intellectual fabric and the products of its actions, until the ultimate components are reached"; and we find the same two methods pursued in his other books.

> "While, on the one hand, they betray a great liking for drawing deductions and building them up into a coherent whole; on the other hand, they betray a great liking for examining the premises on which a set of deductions is raised, for the purpose of seeing what assumptions are involved in them, and what are the deeper truths into which such assumptions are resolvable. There is shown an evident dissatisfaction with proximate principles, and a restlessness until ultimate principles have been reached; at the same time there is shown a desire to see how the most complex phenomena are to be interpreted as workings of these ultimate principles. It is, I think, to the balance of these two tendencies that the character of the work done is mainly ascribable."

But while Spencer had beyond doubt analytic powers of a very high order, it is to be feared that there is some justice in the criticism that he sometimes confused abstraction with analysis, and reached an apparently simple result by abstracting away some essential components.

4. "One further cardinal trait, which is in a sense a result of the preceding traits, has to be named—the ability to discern inconspicuous analogies." It was in part this ability that gave Spencer his power of handling so many different orders of facts. "The habit of ignoring the variable outer components and relations, and looking for the invariable inner components and relations, facilitates the perception of likeness between things which externally are quite unlike—perhaps so utterly unlike that, by an unanalytical intelligence, they cannot be conceived to have any resemblance whatever." It is this kind of insight which enables the morphologist to unify a whole series of organic types by detecting the similarities of architecture underlying the exceedingly diverse external expression. It was this kind of insight which led Spencer to his analogy between a social organism and an individual organism, and to many others which have been found fruitful. But it is to be feared that some

of his analogies, notably that between inanimate mechanisms and living creatures led him far astray.

5. Another power strongly developed was constructive imagination. The boy who was so fond of building castles in the air, who grudged the sleep which put an end to his fanciful adventures, grew up a man whose mind was his kingdom. All sorts of things and thoughts pulled the trigger of his imagination, with which he was often so preoccupied that he would pass those living in the same house with him and look them in the face without knowing that he had seen them.

> Spencer found in the delight of constructive imagination part of the explanation of his versatility. The products of his mental action ranged "from a doctrine of State functions to a levelling-staff; from the genesis of religious ideas to a watch escapement; from the circulation in plants to an invalid bed; from the law of organic symmetry to planing machinery; from principles of ethics to a velocimeter; from a metaphysical doctrine to a binding-pin; from a classification of the sciences to an improved fishing-rod joint; from the general Law of Evolution to a better mode of dressing artificial flies." "But for every interest in either the theoretical or the practical, a requisite condition has been—the opportunity offered for something new. And here may be perceived the trait which unites the extremely unlike products of mental action exemplified above. They have one and all afforded scope for constructive imagination."

Clearness in exposition was another of Spencer's gifts, and he connected this with the fact that his grandfather and father had been teachers. But lucidity of exposition usually accompanies clear thinking, and increases if there is opportunity for practice. His fearlessness and his self-confidence, he also connected with the fact that in school the master must be the absolute authority, but it seems much more plausible to regard this characteristic independence of judgment as an outcrop of the Nonconformist mood of his ancestors.

Limitations.—Spencer was too scrupulous a self-analyst not to be aware of many of his own limitations, and he has exposed the defects of his qualities with the utmost frankness. Thus his disregard of authority, which helped him to independent positions in science and philosophy, seemed to become a habit of mind which prompted him to react from current beliefs and opinions without always doing them justice. His anti-classical bias led him "to underestimate the past as compared with the present". "Lack of reverence for what others have said and done has tended to make me neglect the evidence of early achievements."

One concrete instance may be selected,—his failure to appreciate Plato's dialogues, which the wise are at one in regarding as masterpieces of philosophical discussion, and as affording invaluable discipline for the most modern of thinkers. Spencer approached them with a strong bias, with a predisposition to depreciate, and what was the result? "Time after time I have attempted to read, now this dialogue and now that, and have put it down in a state of impatience with the indefiniteness of the thinking and the mistaking of words for things: being repelled also by the rambling form of the argument. Once when I was talking on the matter to a classical scholar, he said—'Yes, but as works of art they are well worth reading.' So, when I again took up the dialogues, I contemplated them as works of art, and put them aside in greater exasperation than before. To call that a 'dialogue' which is an interchange of speeches between the thinker and his dummy, who says just what it is convenient to have said, is absurd. There is more dramatic propriety in the conversations of our third-rate novelists; and such a production as that of Diderot, *Rameau's nephew*, has more strokes of dramatic truth than all the Platonic dialogues put together, if the rest are like those I have looked into. Still, quotations from time to time met with, lead me to think that there are in Plato detached thoughts from which I might benefit had I the patience to seek them out. The like is probably true of other ancient writings." (!)

Disregard of authority is a great gift, if it go hand in hand with a careful examination of the reasons which lead to a conclusion becoming authoritative, but Spencer does not seem to have felt this responsibility. He began every subject by cleaning the slate. Thus one of the most conspicuous, and in some ways least agreeable characteristics of his intellectual work was his indifference as to what previous investigators had said. This was in part an expression of his own strength and independence, but it also savoured of arrogance. The virtue of it was that he approached a subject with the vigour of a fresh mind, but its vice was repeatedly disclosed in his failure to realise all the difficulties and subtleties of a problem—a failure which sometimes involved nothing short of amateurishness. A skilful naturalist has said that in tackling an unsolved problem there are only two commendable methods,— one to read everything bearing on the question, the other to read nothing. It was the second method that Spencer habitually practised. He gathered facts, but took little stock in opinions or previous deliverances.

Thus in beginning to plan out his *Social Statics* he "paid little attention to what had been written either upon ethics or politics. The books I did read were those which promised to furnish illustrative material." He wrote his

First Principles with a minimal knowledge of the philosophical classics, and his *Psychology* as if he had been living before the invention of printing. Some one thought certain parts of his *Education* savoured of Rousseau, but he had not heard of *Emile* when he wrote. He was greatly indebted to von Baer for a formula, but there is no evidence that he ever read any part of the great embryologist's works. The suggestion that he was indebted to Comte for some sociological ideas might have been dismissed at once on *a priori* grounds as absurd. And in point of fact when Spencer wrote his *Social Statics* he knew no more of Comte than that he was a French philosophical writer, and it was not till 1853 that he began to nibble at Comte's works, to which Lewes and George Eliot had repeatedly directed his attention. He adopted two of Comte's words— "altruism" and "sociology"—but beyond that his indebtedness was little. We may take his own word for it: "The only indebtedness I recognise is the indebtedness of antagonism. My pronounced opposition to his views led me to develop some of my own views." That they both tried to organise a system of so-called philosophy out of the sciences indicates a community of aim, but there the resemblance ceases.

Spencer's intellectual development seems to have been peculiarly detached and independent. He was of course influenced by his father and by two of his uncles during his formative period, and he was also doubtless influenced by George Henry Lewes and George Eliot, Huxley and Hooker in later years—as who could help being—but in the main he was a strong, self-sufficient, self-made Ishmaelite. Similarly as regards authors, he was influenced by Lamarck's transformist theory, by Laplace's nebular hypothesis, by Malthus's theory of population, by Milne-Edwards' idea of the physiological division of labour, by von Baer's formula, by Hamilton and Mansel, by Grove's correlation of the physical forces, by Darwin's *Origin of Species*, and so on, but his own thought was always far more to him than anything he ever read.

Just as independence may become a vice, so with criticism, and Spencer had certainly the defect of this quality. Like his grandfather and his father before him, he was perpetually criticising, and he developed a hypersensitiveness to mistakes and shortcomings. For while sound criticism is an intellectual saving grace, it defeats its own end when the critic is constantly looking for reasons for disagreement, rather than for supplementary construction. Comte was assuredly right in saying that one only destroys when one replaces. Morever, Spencer's dominant tendency greatly interfered with his power of admiration. He was so keenly alive to "the many mistakes in *chiaroscuro* which characterise various paintings of the old masters" that he found little pleasure in them. When looking at Greek sculpture he constantly discovered unnatural drapery. When he went to the opera with George Eliot he remarked "how much analysis of the effects produced deducts from enjoyment of the effects."

He could not even look at a beautiful woman without his "phrenological diagnosis" discovering something which took the edge off his admiration. "It seems probable," he quaintly remarks, "that this abnormal tendency to criticise has been a chief factor in the continuance of my celibate life."

Development of Spencer's Mind.—Spencer has himself given us an account of his mental development.

As a boy his mind was always set upon discovering natural causes, and under his father's influence there grew up in him "a tacit belief that whatever occurred had its assignable cause of a comprehensible kind." Insensibly he relinquished the current creed of supernaturalism and its associated story of creation.

The doctrine of the universality of natural causation has for its inevitable corollary the doctrine that the Universe and all things in it have reached their present forms through successive stages physically necessitated. But no such corollary suggested itself definitely until Spencer was twenty when he read Lyell's *Principles of Geology*, and was led by Lyell's arguments against Lamarck to a partial acceptance of Lamarck's evolutionist point of view.

Two years afterwards, in *The proper Sphere of Government*, "there was shown an unhesitating belief that the phenomena of both individual life and social life conform to law"; and eight years later in *Social Statics*, the social organism was discussed in the same sort of way as the individual organism; a physiological view of social actions was taken, and the same mode of progress was shown to be common to all changing phenomena.

In 1852 the essay on the "Development Hypothesis" was an open avowal of evolutionism; and other essays on population and over-legislation "assumed that social arrangements and institutions are products of natural causes, and that they have a normal order of growth."

An acquaintance with von Baer's description of individual development gave definiteness to Spencer's conception of progress, and the idea of change from homogeneity to heterogeneity became his formula of evolution, applicable to style, to manners and fashions, to science itself, and to the growing mind of the child, as was shown in a succession of essays on these themes.

The next great step was in the *Principles of Psychology* which sought to trace out the genesis of mind in all its forms, sub-human and human, as produced by the organised and inherited effects of mental actions.

Increase of faculty by exercise, hereditary entailment of gains, and consequent progressive adaptation, were prominent ideas in this treatise. "Progressive adaptation became increasing adjustment of inner subjective relations to outer objective relations—increasing correspondence between the two."

So far, then, Spencer had recognised throughout a vast field of phenomena the increase of heterogeneity, of speciality, of integration—as traits of progress of all kinds; and thus arose the question: Why is this increasing heterogeneity universal? "A transition from the inductive stage to the deductive stage was shown in the answer—the transformation results from the unceasing multiplication of effects. When, shortly after, there came the perception that the condition of homogeneity is an unstable condition, yet another step towards the completely deductive stage was made." "The theorem passed into the region of physical science."

"The advance towards a complete conception of evolution was itself a process of evolution. At first there was simply an unshaped belief in the development of living things; including, in a vague way, social development. The extension of von Baer's formula expressing the development of each organism, first to one and then to another group of phenomena, until all were taken in as parts of a whole, exemplified the process of integration. With advancing integration there went that advancing heterogeneity implied by inclusion of the several classes of inorganic phenomena and the several classes of super-organic phenomena in the same category with organic phenomena. And then the indefinite idea of progress passed into the definite idea of evolution, when there was recognised the essential nature of the change, as a physically determined transformation conforming to ultimate laws of force."

It is difficult to state with any certainty what led Spencer in 1857 to a coherent body of beliefs—to the first sketch of his system. In the main the unification was probably a natural maturation and integration of his thoughts, but it was perhaps helped by the immediate task of revising and publishing a collection of essays, and also by the fact that "the time was one at which certain all-embracing scientific truths of a simple order were being revealed." Notably the doctrine of the conservation and transformability of energy was beginning to possess scientific minds, and the doctrine of evolution was beginning to make its grip felt.

Furthermore, in trying to understand Spencer, we must recognise that he was the flower of a nonconformist dissenting stock, that his mind matured in contact with engines and other mechanisms, and that he was almost forced to exclude new influences after he settled down with his system at the age of forty.

Methods of Work.—While there was nothing remarkable in Spencer's methods of work, it may be of interest to indicate certain general features which the *Autobiography* discloses.

In the first place, after a few disastrous experiments, he abandoned any attempt at what is usually called working hard. Like many an artist who will only paint when he feels in the mood and in good form, Spencer would never write or dictate under pressure, or when he felt that his brain was not working smoothly. When he was writing the *Principles of Psychology* (1854-5), he began between nine and ten and continued till one; he then paused for a few minutes to take some slight refreshment, usually a little fruit, and resumed till three, altogether about five hours at a stretch. He then went for a walk, returned in time for dinner between five and six, and did considerable proof- correcting thereafter. But, as we have seen, the result of this strenuousness— which would be quite normal to many students—was his first serious breakdown, involving a loss of eighteen months. Thereafter, it was his custom to work for short spells at a time, to sandwich work and exercise, and to take a holiday whenever he began to feel tired.

His output of work was so large even for a long life that one naturally thinks of him as a hard worker. But the reverse would be nearer the truth. Partly as a self-justification of his "constitutional idleness," and partly as a precaution against his hereditary tendency to nervous breakdown, he was a strong advocate of the proposition that "Life is not for work, but work is for life." "The progress of mankind is, under one aspect, a means of liberating more and more life from mere toil and leaving more and more life available for relaxation—for pleasurable culture, for æsthetic gratification, for travels, for games." Industry is not a virtue in itself; over-work is blameworthy.

In the second place, Spencer made it a rule never to force his thinking. If a problem was not clear to him, he let it simmer. "On one occasion George Eliot expressed her surprise that the author of *Social Statics* had no lines on his forehead, to which he answered, 'I suppose it is because I am never puzzled.' This called forth the exclamation: 'O! that's the most arrogant thing I ever heard uttered.' To which I rejoined: 'Not at all, when you know what I mean.' And I then proceeded to explain that my mode of thinking did not involve that concentrated effort which is commonly accompanied by wrinkling of the brows" (*Autobiography*, i. p. 399).

Spencer did not set himself a problem and try to puzzle out an answer. "The conclusions at which I have from time to time arrived, have not been arrived at as solutions of questions raised; but have been arrived at unawares—each as the ultimate outcome of a body of thoughts which slowly grew from a germ."

He had "an instinctive interest in those facts which have general meanings"; he let these accumulate and simmer, thinking them over and over again at intervals. "When accumulation of instances had given body to a generalisation, reflexion would reduce the vague conception at first framed to a more definite conception; and perhaps difficulties or anomalies at first passed over for a while, but eventually forcing themselves on attention, might cause a needful qualification and a truer shaping of the thought. Eventually the growing generalisation, thus far inductive, might take deductive form: being all at once recognised as a necessary consequence of some physical principle—some established law. And thus, little by little, in unobtrusive ways, without conscious intention or appreciable effort, there would grow up a coherent and organised theory" (*Autobiography*, i. 400, 401). In short, Spencer gave his thinking machine time to do its work, or in other words he let his thoughts grow. He distrusted strain and all forcing. Like a good golfer, he would not "press." "The determined effort causes perversion of thought."

A third feature in his work has been already alluded to—his practical indifference to the literature of the subject at which he was working. For this characteristic there were doubtless several reasons, though none of them justified it. He was not fond of hard reading, and conserved his energy for his own production; he had abundant thought-material of his own, and no lack of confidence in its value. Furthermore, he explains, "It has always been out of the question for me to go on reading a book the fundamental principles of which I entirely dissent from. Tacitly giving an author credit for consistency, I, without thinking much about the matter, take it for granted that if the fundamental principles are wrong, the rest cannot be right, and thereupon cease reading—being, I suspect, rather glad of an excuse for doing so" (i. p. 253). "All through my life," he says, "Locke's 'Essay' had been before me on my father's shelves, but I had never taken it down; or at any rate I have no recollection of having read a page of it." More than once he tackled Kant's *Critique of Pure Reason*, but was baulked at the start by the doctrine that time and space are merely subjective forms. Nor did Mill's *Logic* interest him.

At the same time it is not to be supposed that Spencer wove his system out of himself as a spider its web. He had a wonderful aptitude for collecting data by a strange sort of skimming reading.

"Though by some I am characterised as an *a priori* thinker, it will be manifest to any one who does not set out with an *a priori* conception of me, that my beliefs, when not suggested *a posteriori*, are habitually verified *a posteriori*. My first book, *Social Statics*, shows this in common with my later books. I have sometimes been half-amused, half- irritated, by one who speaks of me as typically deductive, and whose own conclusions, nevertheless, are not supported by facts anything like so numerous as those brought in support of mine. But we meet with men who are such fanatical adherents of the inductive method, that immediately an induction, otherwise well established, is shown to admit of deductive establishment, they lose faith in it" (*Autobiography*, i. pp. 304-5).

No one who studies Spencer's works can fail to be impressed with the logical orderliness and lucidity of his method. Thus, in beginning *The Principles of Biology*, for instance, we are first asked to consider what truths the biologist takes for granted; *e.g.*, the conservation of energy and the indestructibility of matter; then we are asked to notice the inductions in regard to the phenomena of life which biologists agree in accepting as well-established; and only then do we pass to Spencer's particular interpretation of the facts in the light of his evolutionist ideas. The same logical method is illustrated in his treatment of psychology, sociology and ethics.

Like most men who get through much work, Spencer was very methodical and orderly. In reference to his *Sociology*, he tells us how he classified and reclassified his materials in fasciculi, placing them in a semi-circle on the floor round his chair, inserting new "covers" where there seemed need for them, and gradually filling these. As the plan became clear, the materials for a chapter were raised to his large desk, and then began a grouping into sections, and a grouping within each section.

He did not begin to compose until he had thought out his subject to the best of his ability. He then wrote or dictated a little at a time, criticising every sentence with especial reference to clearness and force. Except for his first book, which he revised, copied out, and revised afresh, the original copy was always sent to press "sprinkled with erasures and interlineations." He was more interested in vigour and lucidity of style than in its beauty, and it was characteristic of him to try to correlate effectiveness of style with the doctrine of the conservation of energy. The main thesis in the essay on "The Philosophy of Style" may be briefly stated. The reader has only a limited amount of nervous energy, and it is important that this should not be dissipated before he comes to the ideas of which the style is the vehicle. "In proportion as there is less energy absorbed in interpreting the symbols, there is more left for representing the idea, and, consequently, greater vividness of the idea." "Every resistance met with in the progress from the antecedent idea to the consequent idea, entails a deduction from the force with which the consequent idea arises in consciousness."

It is common to speak of Spencer's works as "hard reading," but those who say so must have a strange scale of hardness. He may be difficult to agree with, but he is rarely difficult to understand; he deals with difficult themes, but he is singularly clear in his expression of his convictions. When he discusses less abstract questions, as in his *Study of Sociology* or *Education,* his style has almost every good quality except beauty. And when he occasionally "lets himself go" a little, as in the famous passage in the *First Principles* at the end of the discussion of the Unknowable, there is a ring of nobility in his sentences.

Sometimes he sums up with epigrammatic terseness, and we submit a few of his utterances which we have noted down as illustrating various qualities:—

"Life is not for learning nor is life for working, but learning and working are for life."

"It is best to recognise the facts as they are, and not try to prop up rectitude by fictions."

"Beliefs, like creatures, must have fit environments before they can live and grow."

"Mind is not as deep as the brain only, but is, in a sense, as deep as the viscera."

"Melody is an idealised form of the natural cadences of emotion."

"Logic is a science of objective phenomena."

"In proportion as intellect is active, emotion is rendered inactive."

"Inherited constitution must ever be the chief factor in determining character."

"Each nature is a bundle of potentialities of which only some are allowed by the conditions to become actualities."

"Considering that the ordinary citizen has no excess of individuality to boast of, it seems strange that he should be so anxious to hide what little he has."

"Englishmen are averse to conclusions of wide generality."

"The ultimate result of shielding men from the effects of folly is to fill the world with fools."

"A nation which fosters its good-for-nothings will end by becoming a good-for-nothing nation."

"I don't mean to get on. I don't think getting on is worth the bother."

Genius.—It doubtless requires genius to define genius, and until that is done, the question of awarding or refusing this supreme title to our hero need not be very seriously discussed. All will agree that genius is more than unusually great talent; that it is neither "une patience suivie" nor "an infinite capacity for taking pains"; that it is not to be judged by its effectiveness; and that it may never receive the unwithering laurels of immortality. Spencer poured contempt on Carlyle's assertion that genius "means transcendent capacity of taking trouble first of all"; the truth being, he said, that genius may be rightly defined quite oppositely, as an ability to do with little trouble that which cannot be done by the ordinary man with any amount of trouble.

Another of Spencer's remarks about genius is worth citing. Speaking of Huxley's wonderful versatility as a thinker, he said that it lent "some colour to the dictum—quite untenable, however—that genius is a unit, and, where it exists, can manifest itself equally in all directions." As it seems to us, there is much truth in the dictum which Spencer dismissed as "quite untenable." The genius is a new variation of high potential and is as such a unity, capable of expressing itself in many diverse ways, and always with originality. The expression of genius may be intellectual, emotional, or practical, according to the mood which is constitutionally dominant and according to the opportunities afforded by education and circumstances; but there seems much to be said, both on general grounds and from a study of historical examples, for the view that genius means something distinctive in the whole mental pattern or personality, and is potentially at least many-sided.

Biologically regarded, a genius is a transilient variation on the up-grade of psychical evolution, of such magnitude that it stands apart as a new mental pattern, as a peculiar combination of moods at a high potential, as a secret amalgam. Whether it be intellectual, emotional, or practical, it sees or feels or does things in a new way. It makes what it touches new; it affords a new outlook. "God said: Let Newton be! and there was light"—that is genius.

In this sense we venture to think that Spencer was not far from the kingdom of genius. He saw all things in the light of the evolution-idea; he had a fresh vision of the unity of nature and the unity of science, and the light that was in him was so clear that it radiated into other minds. Had his emotional nature been stronger, had he been more than luminiferous, he might have set the world aflame.

CHAPTER VII

CHARACTERISTICS: EMOTIONAL AND ETHICAL

Emotional—The Genius Loci—Poetry—Science and Poetry—Art—Humour—Callousness—Nature—Human Relations—Fundamental Motives

Emotional.—Spencer found great delight in scenery and sunsets; he enjoyed music within certain limits; he was very fond of children, but he was essentially a man of thought, not of feeling or of action. The scientific mood dominated him, the artistic and practical moods were in abeyance. Although he delighted in imaginative construction, he does not seem to have had much imaginative life. Although he pondered over the great mysteries of the universe, there was no mystical element in his composition. Of course no Englishman wears his heart on his sleeve, but Spencer was more than usually callous, and our sketch would be far from true if it ignored his emotional limitations.

The Genius Loci.—To begin with, let us refer to his indifference to places which are rich in human associations. On his many holidays he visited not a few of these, and yet he seems to have been rarely touched or impressed by their significance. He frankly confessed that he took but little interest in what are called histories, but was interested only in sociology, and therefore his appreciation of the genius loci was always limited. He could not people the palaces, the cathedrals, the castles, the ancient cities that he visited. "When I go to see a ruined abbey or the remains of a castle, I do not care to learn when it was built, who lived or died there, or what catastrophes it witnessed. I never yet went to a battle-field, although often near to one—not having the slightest curiosity to see a place where many men were killed and a victory achieved." He had few historical associations even in Rome, and when at Florence he did not go three miles to Fiesole. The forms and colours of time-worn walls and arches excited pleasant sentiments, he said, but that seems to have been all. It was a sort of conchological interest that he had.

One is unfortunately familiar with the cosmic preoccupation which the dominant scientific mood is apt to engender, as also with historical erudition which loses the wood in the trees or leaves Nature out altogether. These are the defects of our limited mental capacities and our ill-organised education; but that a man of Spencer's powers could be so complacent with his limitations is extraordinary. And that he could write, "It is always the poetry rather than the history of a place that appeals to me," is more extraordinary still; as if the history were not half the poetry.

Poetry.—Spencer's attitude to poetry was characteristic; he took it all too intellectually and was usually bored. He did not find enough thought in it, and it may be doubted if he ever surrendered himself to the artistic mood. At one time he regarded Shelley as "by far the finest poet of his era," and of "Prometheus Unbound" he said, "It is the only poem over which I have ever become enthusiastic." It satisfied one of his organic needs—variety; "I say organic, because I perceive that it runs throughout my constitution, beginning with likings for food." Another requirement of poetry for Spencer was intensity. "The matter embodied is idealised emotion, the vehicle is the idealised language of emotion." For this reason he was in but small measure attracted to Wordsworth. "Admitting, though I do, that throughout his works there are sprinkled many poems of great beauty, my feeling is that most of his writing is not wine but beer" (i. p. 263). Similarly, he found the "Iliad" "tedious" and Dante "too continuously rich"… "a gorgeous dress ill made up."

"About others' requirements I cannot of course speak; but my own requirement is—little poetry and of the best. Even the true poets are far too productive." More will agree with him when he says: "The poetry commonly produced does not bubble up as a spring, but is simply pumped up; and pumped-up poetry is not worth reading. No one should write verse if he can help it. Let him suppress it if possible; but if it bursts forth in spite of him, it may be of value."

In reference to the supposed antagonism between Science and Poetry, Spencer refers to the story that Keats once proposed after dinner, some such sentiment as "Confusion to Newton," for having by his analysis destroyed the wonder of the rainbow. "In so doing," Spencer says, "Keats did but give more than usually definite expression to the current belief that science and poetry are antagonistic. Doubtless it is true that while consciousness is occupied in the scientific interpretation of a thing, which is now and again "a thing of beauty," it is not occupied in the æsthetic appreciation of it. But it is no less true that the same consciousness may at another time be so wholly possessed by the æsthetic appreciation as to exclude all thought of the scientific interpretation. The inability of a man of science to take the poetic view simply shows his mental limitation; as the mental limitation of a poet is shown by his inability to take the scientific view. The broader mind can take both. Those who allege this antagonism forget that Goethe, predominantly a poet, was also a scientific inquirer" (*Autobiography*, i. p. 419). This is sound sense, and is the excuse for Spencer's own limitations in regard to poetry; he usually found it too difficult to lay aside the intellectual preoccupation that gave part of the point to Huxley's jest in the course of a talk on tragedy: "Oh! you know, Spencer's idea of a tragedy is a deduction killed by a fact."

The same sort of desperately serious intellectual attitude is seen in Spencer's remarks on the Opera. His "intolerance of gross breaches of probability" spoilt his enjoyment of the music. "That serving-men and waiting-maids should be made poetical and prompted to speak in *recitative,* because their masters and mistresses happened to be in love, was too conspicuous an absurdity; and the consciousness of this absurdity went far towards destroying what pleasure I might otherwise have derived from the work. It is with music as with painting—a great divergence from the naturalness in any part so distracts my attention from the meaning or intention of the whole, as almost to cancel gratification."

In connection with Spencer's relative lack of interest in poetry and the drama, or in the works of men like Carlyle and Ruskin, we have simply to deplore the fact and remember that his mind was preoccupied with big problems and was dominated by the scientific mood. From his boyhood he was "thinking about only one thing at a time," and he had to husband his energies. This is well illustrated by his note on Carlyle's *Cromwell*: "If, after a thorough examination of the subject, Carlyle tells us that Cromwell was a sincere man, I reply that I am heartily glad to hear it, and that I am content to take his word for it; not thinking it worth while to investigate all the evidence which has led him to that conclusion." This might seem to betray a somewhat Philistinish contempt for historical study and complacence therewith, but the real state of the case is revealed in the sentence that follows the above: "I find so many things to think about in this world of ours, that I cannot afford to spend a week in estimating the character of a man who lived two centuries ago." What he somewhat strangely calls "interests of an entirely unlike kind" were at that time strongly attracting him to Humboldt's *Kosmos.* His outlook was characteristically cosmic, not human.

Art.—One of Spencer's heresies concerned the old masters of painting, whose works he regarded as highly over-rated. On the one hand, he detected insincerity in the conventional veneration in which the works of Raphael and Michael Angelo, to name no smaller names, are held. Subject is not dissociated from execution, and "the judicial faculty has been mesmerised by the confused halo of piety which surrounds them." There is an æsthetic orthodoxy from which few are bold enough to dissent. On the other hand, Spencer detected in the works themselves "fundamental vices," "the grossest absurdities," "gratuitous contradictions of Nature," impossible light and shade, and no end of technical defects in what he was pleased to call "physioscopy."

Art-criticism is probably now more emancipated from authority than it was when Spencer promulgated his heresies and Ruskin wrote his *Modern Painters*, and doubtless many experts will admit that some of the philosopher's strictures are justified. More will probably maintain that in his intellectual criticism Spencer was blind to artistic genius. In his criticism, for instance, of Guido's "Phœbus and Aurora," to which he allowed beauty in composition and grace in drawing, he applied commonplace physical criteria to show that "absurdity was piled upon absurdity." "The entire group—the chariot and horses, the hours and their draperies, and even Phœbus himself— are represented as illuminated from without: are made visible by some unknown source of light—some other sun! Stranger still is the next thing to be noted. The only source of light indicated in the composition—the torch carried by the flying boy—radiates no light whatever. Not even the face of its bearer immediately behind it is illumined by it! Nay, this is not all. The crowning absurdity is that the non-luminous flames of this torch are themselves illuminated from elsewhere!" And so on.

All this is dismally intellectual, and reminds us of the medical man's discovery that Botticelli's "Venus," in the Uffizi at Florence, is suffering from consumption, and should not be riding across the sea in an open shell, clad so scantily.

Humour.—Prof. Hudson speaks of Spencer's capital sense of humour, but it is difficult for a reader of the *Autobiography* to believe this. The ponderous way in which he analyses his own little jokes, for instance, is too quaint to be consistent with much sense of humour. Thus he tells us that it was only the sudden access of moderately good health that enabled him to remark to G. H. Lewes, on a little tour they had, that the Isle of Wight produced very large chops for so small an island. The fact is that he always took himself and other people very seriously in little things as well as great. With what physiological seriousness does he discuss the experience he had coming down Ben Nevis after some wine on the top of whisky: "I found myself possessed of a quite unusual amount of agility; being able to leap from rock to rock with rapidity, ease, and safety; so that I quite astonished myself. There was evidently an exaltation of the perceptive and motor powers."… "Long-continued exertion having caused unusually great action of the lungs, the exaltation produced by stimulation of the brain was not cancelled by the diminished oxygenation of the blood. The oxygenation had been so much in excess, that deduction from it did not appreciably diminish the vital activities."

Callousness.—In his extreme sang-froid, Spencer sometimes did violence to the unity of the human spirit. We venture to give one example. In referring to a ramble in France (*Autobiography*, ii. p. 236), he wrote as follows: "We passed a wayside shrine, at the foot of which were numerous offerings, each formed of two bits of lath nailed one across the other. The sight suggested to me the behaviour of an intelligent and amiable retriever, a great pet at Ardtornish. On coming up to salute one after a few hours' or a day's absence, wagging her tail and drawing back her lips so as to simulate a grinning smile, she would seek around to find a stick, or a bit of paper, or a dead leaf, and bring it in her mouth; so expressing her desire to propitiate. The dead leaf or bit of paper was symbolic, in much the same way as was the valueless cross. Probably, in respect of sincerity of feeling, the advantage was on the side of the retriever." The animal psychology here expressed seems pretty bad, and the human psychology much worse.

Turning, however, to pleasanter subjects and correcting any unduly harsh judgment, we would remind the reader that Spencer was genuinely fond of music and of scenery, two loves which cover a multitude of sins.

> "The often-quoted remark of Kant that two things excited his awe—the starry heavens and the conscience of man—is not one which I should make of myself. In me the sentiment has been more especially produced by three things—the sea, a great mountain, and fine music in a cathedral. Of these the first has, from familiarity I suppose, lost much of the effect it originally had, but not the others."

Nature.—One of the lasting pleasures of Spencer's life was a simple delight in the beauty of Nature, especially in varied scenery. Thus he writes (in 1844) to his friend Lott, regarding a journey into South Wales: "I wish you had been with me. Your poetical feelings would have had great gratification. A day's journey through a constantly changing scene of cloud-capped hills with here and there a sparkling and romantic river winding perhaps round the base of some ruined castle is a treat not often equalled. I enjoyed it much. When I reached the seaside, however, and found myself once again within sound of the breakers, I almost danced with pleasure. To me there is no place so delightful as the beach. It is the place where, more than anywhere else, philosophy and poetry meet—where in fact you are presented by Nature with a never-ending feast of knowledge and beauty. There is no place where I can so palpably realise Emerson's remark that 'Nature is the circumstance which dwarfs every other circumstance.'"

> One evening in August 1861 Spencer stood looking over the Sound of Mull from Ardtornish house. "The gorgeous colours of clouds and sky, splendid enough even by themselves to be long remembered, were

reflected from the surface of the sound, at the same time that both of its sides, along with the mountains of Mull, were lighted up by the setting sun; and, while I was leaning out of the window gazing at this scene, music from the piano behind me served as a commentary. The exaltation of feeling produced was unparalleled in my experience; and never since has pleasurable emotion risen in me to the same intensity" (*Autobiography*, ii. p. 69).

Spencer's feeling for Nature was for the most part limited to scenic effects. Occasionally, when he was at leisure, he felt some "admiration of the beauties and graces" of flowers, but this was so unusual that it surprised him, "for, certainly," he says, "intellectual analysis is at variance with æsthetic appreciation." This does not of course mean that there is any opposition between scientific interpretation and artistic enjoyment; it simply means that the scientific mood is quite different from the artistic mood, and that for most people only one can be dominant at a time. There are many naturalists of undoubted analytic skill who have a "love exceeding a simple love of the things that glide in grasses and rubble of woody wreck"; the modern botanist may still see the Dryad in the tree; and if the scientific mood is not allowed by over-specialisation to over-ride all others, increase in knowledge may mean not increase of sorrow, but a deepening of the joy of life.

Human Relations.—That Spencer lacked emotional warmth and expansiveness not only in regard to nature and art, literature and history, but in his human relations, will be admitted by all, but when a great man has an obvious limitation there is often a tendency to make too much of it. We think that Mr Gribble has done this in his interesting comparison of Spencer and Carlyle,[2] whom he contrasts as philosopher and sage. We condense his comparison. Both were big men, both were egotists, both were dyspeptics. Neither suffered fools gladly, and each tended to be an outspoken judge of all the earth. But while Carlyle loved and hated intensely, Spencer judged callously. Carlyle was more like a human being, Spencer "made his heart wait on his judgment—indefinitely." "What is almost uncanny about Herbert Spencer is his triumphant superiority to natural instincts." "It is difficult for the average man to believe that Spencer was a human being of like passions with himself." In reference to love he said, "Physical beauty is a *sine qua non* with me"; "in every walk of life," Mr Gribble says, "it seems, some *sine qua non* stood like an angel with a flaming sword between Herbert Spencer and his emotions." "In the main, he suggests abstract intellect performing in a morality play, exhibiting no emotion but intellectual pride." But this tends to suggest that Spencer was a sort of synthetic ogre, which he certainly was not.

[2] Francis Gribble: "Fortnightly Review," 1904, p. 984.

Emotion is distinctively impulsive, and it was Spencer's nature and deliberate purpose not to yield to the strain of impulse. Yet we must not misunderstand his reserve and restraint for cold-bloodedness. Some have referred to the cold impersonal way in which he refers to his father in the *Autobiography*, but when we consider facts not words we find that the relations of sympathy, companionship, and mutual understanding between father and son were very perfect. The human male is slow to learn that it is not only necessary to love, but to say that one loves.

In his human relations, Spencer was loyal, if somewhat too candid, as a friend; he was by no means non-social, but enjoyed conversation with those who interested him, and was himself a good talker and raconteur; he was fond of, and was a favourite with children, which is saying a great deal. One of his friends has called him a thoroughly "clubbable" man, which is probably going too far, but it was only in later years that he became an almost monastic recluse and used ear-stoppers. Many who met him for a short time thought him cold and difficult of access, with reserved chilly talk "like a book," rather restrained, scrupulous and severe; but those who knew him well speak of his large, simple, and eminently sympathetic nature. George Eliot said, "He is a good, delightful creature, and I always feel better for being with him." Prof. Hudson writes: "The better one knew him the more one grew to understand and admire his quiet strength, steadiness of ethical purpose, and unflinching courage, the purity of his motives, his rigid adherence to righteousness and truth, and his exquisite sense of justice in all things." He was often terribly provoked by unjust criticisms and stupid or wilful misunderstandings of his positions, but "in controversy he was scrupulously fair, aiming at truth, and not at the barren victories of dialectics."[3]

> *[3]* Gribble, *op. cit.*

Besides his love of truth and justice, besides his courage and self-sacrificing altruism, Spencer reveals a strength of purpose which has rarely been surpassed. In fact it is difficult to over-estimate the resolution with which he effected his life-work. Apart from the inherent difficulty of his task, apart from the long delay of public appreciation, and apart from ill-health, the pecuniary obstacles were very serious. Had it not been for the £80 which came to him in 1850 under the Railway Winding-up Act, he would have been unable to publish *Social Statics*; a bequest from his uncle Thomas made the publication of the *Principles of Psychology* possible; he would have been forced to desist before the completion of *First Principles* had it not been for a bequest from his uncle William; at a later stage an American testimonial and his father's death just saved the situation. Well might he say:—

"It was almost a miracle that I did not sink before success was reached."

When we read the detailed story of his preparation, his endeavour, his struggle, his achievement, we cannot but feel that his resolute strenuousness was not far from heroism.

As a nervous subject, Spencer was naturally at times irritable, as others can be without his excuse, and even petulant, severe in his utterances, and a little intolerant. But normally he was habitually just and tried to understand people, if not as persons, at least as phenomena. What he said of Carlyle was much more just than what Carlyle said of him, though it may have been what we call less "human." In his own way Spencer felt that "tout comprendre, c'est tout pardonner," but it has been truly said that "the natural man would rather be passionately denounced than treated as a phenomenon to be co- ordinated."[4] But this was just Spencer's way, and he applied it equally to himself.

> In speaking of his seven years' experience as a committee-man in connection with the Athenæum, he notes certain traits of nature which were manifest to himself at least. "The most conspicuous is want of tact. This is an inherited deficiency. The Spencers of the preceding generation were all characterised by lack of reticence.... I tended habitually to undisguised utterance of ideas and feelings; the result being that while I often excited opposition from not remembering what others were likely to feel, I, at the same time, disclosed my own intentions in cases where concealment of them was needful as a means to success" (*Autobiography*, ii. p. 280).

[4] Gribble, *op. cit.*

It must be admitted that there was little out of the common in Herbert Spencer's daily walk and conversation; in fact, there was a fair share of commonplaceness. Spencer himself was rather amused at those who came expecting extraordinary intellectual manifestations or traits of character greatly transcending ordinary ones. There was the pretty poetess and heiress, whom two of his friends (Chapman and Miss Evans) selected as a suitable wife for the philosopher, and who seems to have been as little favourably impressed with him as he was with her. "Probably she came with high anticipations and was disappointed." There was the Frenchman who found Spencer playing billiards at the Athenæum Club, and "lifted up his hands with an exclamation to the effect that had he not seen it he could not have believed it." And there was the American millionaire, Mr Andrew Carnegie, who was so greatly astonished to hear Spencer say at the dinner-table on the *Servia*, "Waiter, I did not ask for Cheshire; I asked for Cheddar." To think that a philosopher should be so fastidious about his cheese!

Spencer seems never to have fallen in love, and his early utterances on marriage savour somewhat of the non-mammalian type of bachelor. "If as somebody said (Socrates, was it not?)—marrying is a thing which whether you do it or do it not you will repent, it is pretty clear that you may as well decide by a toss up. It's a choice of evils, and the two sides are pretty nearly balanced." He was too wise to marry out of a sense of duty, and too preoccupied to marry by inclination. "As for marrying under existing circumstances, that is out of the question; and as for twisting circumstances into better shape, I think it is too much trouble."… "On the whole I am quite decided not to be a drudge; and as I see no probability of being able to marry without being a drudge, why, I have pretty well given up the idea." As a matter of fact, however, he was not altogether so callous as his words suggest. Indeed when balancing the alternatives of emigrating to New Zealand or staying in England, he gave 110 marks to the latter and 301 to the former, allowing no less than 100 for the marriage which emigration would render feasible!

In short Spencer could not marry when he would, and would not when he could. He had a great admiration for women, especially beautiful women; he had a natural fondness for children and got on well with them; but in his struggling years he could not have supported a wife and family, and besides he was very hard to please. On the one hand there was the economic difficulty, for he felt assured that his friend was right in saying "Had you married there would have been no system of philosophy." It does not seem to have occurred to him that there might have been a better one! On the other hand, there was his eternally critical attitude. "Physical beauty is a *sine quâ non* with me; as was once unhappily proved where the intellectual traits and the emotional traits were of the highest." From the point of view of the race it seems a pity that his *sine quâ non* was so stringent; an emotional graft on the Spencerian stock might have given us for instance a new religious genius. But Spencer's own conclusion was:—

> "I am not by nature adapted to a relation in which perpetual compromise and great forbearance are needful. That extreme critical tendency which I have above described, joined with a lack of reticence no less pronounced, would, I fear, have caused perpetual domestic differences. After all my celibate life has probably been the best for me, as well as the best for some unknown other."

A critical yet appreciative estimate of Spencer has been given by Prof. A. S. Pringle-Pattison, which we venture to quote to correct our own partiality.

"Paradoxical as the statement may seem in view of Spencer's achievement, the mind here pourtrayed, save for the command of scientific facts and the wonderful faculty of generalisation, is commonplace in the range of its ideas; neither intellectually nor morally is the nature sensitive to the finest issues. Almost uneducated except for a fair acquaintance with mathematics and the scientific knowledge which his own tastes led him to acquire, with the prejudices and limitations of middle-class English Nonconformity, but untouched by its religion, Spencer appears in the early part of his life as a somewhat ordinary young man. His ideals and habits did not differ perceptibly from those of hundreds of intelligent and straight-living Englishmen of his class. And to the end, in spite of his cosmic outlook, there remains this strong admixture of the British Philistine, giving a touch almost of banality to some of his sayings and doings. But, just because the picture is so faithfully drawn, giving us the man in his habit as he lived, with all his limitations and prejudices (and his own consciousness of these limitations, expressed sometimes with a passing regret, but oftener with a childish pride), with all his irritating pedantries and the shallowness of his emotional nature, we can balance against these defects his high integrity and unflinching moral courage, his boundless faith in knowledge and his power of conceiving a great ideal and carrying it through countless difficulties to ultimate realisation, and a certain boyish simplicity of character as well as other gentler human traits, such as his fondness for children, his dependence upon the society of his kind, and his capacity to form and maintain some life-long friendships. A kindly feeling for the narrator grows as we proceed; and most unprejudiced readers will close the book with a genuine respect and esteem for the philosopher in his human aspect."

Fundamental Motives.—There seems something approaching self-vivisection in Spencer's analysis of the motives prompting his career, and the reader who is not moved by it must be callous indeed. We shall not do more than refer to the general results arrived at.

> "So deep down is the gratification which results from the consciousness of efficiency, and the further consciousness of the applause which recognised efficiency brings, that it is impossible for any one to exclude it. Certainly, in my own case, the desire for such recognition has not been absent. Yet, so far as I can remember, ambition was not the primary motive of my first efforts, nor has it been the primary motive of my larger and later efforts."… "Still, as I have said, the desire for achievement and the honour which achievement brings, have doubtless been large factors."… "Though from the outset I have had in view the effects to be wrought on men's beliefs and courses of action—especially in respect of social affairs and governmental functions; yet the sentiment

of ambition has all along been operative."

The other prompters were the pleasure of intellectual hunting and "the architectonic instinct." On the one hand, "It has been with me a source of continual pleasure, distinct from other pleasures, to evolve new thoughts, and to be in some sort a spectator of the way in which, under persistent contemplation, they gradually unfolded into completeness." On the other hand, "during thirty years it has been a source of frequent elation to see each division, and each part of a division, working out into congruity with the rest —to see each component fitting into its place, and helping to make a harmonious whole." "Once having become possessed by the conception of Evolution in its comprehensive form, the desire to elaborate and set it forth was so strong that to have passed life in doing something else would, I think, have been almost intolerable." Like an architect he was restless till his edifice was completed, and on working towards this there was æsthetic as well as intellectual gratification. "There appears to be in me a dash of the artist, which has all along made the achievement of beauty a stimulus; not, of course, beauty as commonly conceived, but such beauty as may exist in a philosophical structure."

Spencer had a high sense of his responsibility to deliver the truth that was in him, and he had a strong faith in human progress. It is in the light of these two sentiments, perhaps, that we best understand the heroism of his strenuous life. "Not only is it rational to infer that changes like those which have been going on during civilisation will continue to go on, but it is irrational to do otherwise. Not he who believes that adaptation will increase is absurd, but he who doubts that it will increase is absurd. Lack of faith in such further evolution of humanity as shall harmonise with its conditions adds but another to the countless illustrations of inadequate consciousness of causation. One who, leaving behind both primitive dogmas and primitive ways of looking at them, has, while accepting scientific conclusions, acquired those habits of thought which science generates, will regard the conclusion above drawn as inevitable" (*Data of Ethics*, chap. x.).

"Whoever hesitates to utter that which he thinks the highest truth, lest it should be too much in advance of the time, may reassure himself by looking at his acts from an impersonal point of view. Let him duly realise the fact that opinion is the agency through which character adapts external arrangements to itself—that his opinion rightly forms part of this agency—is a unit of forces, constituting, with other such units, the general power which works out social changes; and he will perceive that he may properly give full utterance to his innermost conviction, leaving it to produce what effect it may. It is not for nothing that he has in him these sympathies with some principles and repugnance to others. He with all his capacities, and aspirations, and beliefs, is not an accident, but a product of his time. He must remember that while he is a descendant of the past, he is a parent of the future; and that his thoughts are as children born to him, which he may not carelessly let die. He, like every other man, may properly consider himself as one of the myriad agencies through whom works the Unknown Cause; and when the Unknown produces in him a certain belief, he is thereby authorised to profess and act out that belief" (*First Principles*, p. 123).

CHAPTER VIII

SPENCER AS BIOLOGIST—THE DATA OF BIOLOGY

The Principles of Biology—Organic Matter—Metabolism—Definition of Life—The Dynamic Element in Life—Life and Mechanism

The Principles of Biology.—If there is any book that will save a naturalist from being easy-going it is Spencer's *Principles of Biology*. It is a biological classic, which, in its range and intensity, finds no parallel except in Haeckel's greatest and least known work, the *Generelle Morphologie*, which was published in 1866 about the same time as the *Principles*. As one of our foremost biologists, Prof. Lloyd Morgan has said[5]: "What strikes one most forcibly is the extraordinary range and grasp of its author, the piercing keenness of his eye for essentials, his fertility in invention, and the bold sweep of his logical method. In these days of increasingly straitened specialism, it is well that we should feel the influence of a thinker whose powers of generalisation have seldom been equalled and perhaps never surpassed."

[5] Mr Herbert Spencer's Biology, "Natural Science," xiii. (1898) pp. 377-383.

Much that is in *The Principles of Biology* has now become common biological property; much has been absorbed or independently reached by others; consciously or unconsciously we are now, as it were, standing on Spencer's shoulders, but this should not blind us to the magnitude of Spencer's achievement. The book was more than a careful balance-sheet of the facts of life at a time when that was much needed; it meant orientation and systematisation; it was the introduction of order, clearness, and breadth of view. It gave biology a fresh start by displaying the facts of life and the inductions from these for the first time clearly in the light of evolution. For if the evolution idea is an adequate modal formula of the great process of Becoming, then we need to think of growth, development, differentiation, integration, reproduction, heredity, death—all the big facts—in the light of this. And this is what the *Principles of Biology* helps us to do. It is of course saturated with the theory of the transmissibility of acquired characters—an idea integral to much of Spencer's thinking—which had hardly begun to be questioned when the work was published, which is now, however, a very moot point indeed. For this and other reasons, we doubt whether Spencer was wise in making a re-edition of what might well have remained as a historical document, especially as the re-edition is not so satisfactory for 1898 as the original was for 1864.

The chief purpose of *The Principles of Biology* was to interpret the general facts of organic life as results of evolution. Manifestly, as a preliminary step, "it was needful to specify and illustrate these general facts; and needful also to set forth those physical and chemical properties of organic matter which are implied in the interpretation." "What are the antecedent truths taken for granted in Biology, and what are the biological truths, which, apart from theory, may be regarded as established by observation?" Thus Part I. deals with organic matter and its activity or metabolism, the action and reaction between organisms and their environment, the correspondence between organisms and their circumstances, and similar general data. Part II. states the big inductions regarding growth, development, adaptation, heredity, variation, and so on. Part III. deals with the arguments suggestive of organic evolution and with the factors in the process. Part IV. is a detailed interpretation of the evolution of organic structure, and Part V. an analogous interpretation of the evolution of functions. Part VI. deals with the laws of multiplication.

Before illustrating Spencer's workmanship in dealing with these great themes, we cannot but ask what preparation he had for a task so ambitious. He had an inborn interest in Natural History; he had dabbled in Entomology and done a little microscopic work; he had attended lectures by Owen and had enjoyed many a talk with Huxley; he had been influenced by Lamarck, Milne-Edwards, and von Baer; he had read hither and thither in medical and biological literature; but it is manifest that his own admission was true that he was "inadequately equipped for the task." That he succeeded in producing a biological classic is a signal proof of his intellectual strength. He was kept right by his power of laying hold of cardinal facts and by his grip of the Evolution-clue. Not to be forgotten, moreover, was the generous help rendered by Professor Huxley and Sir Joseph Hooker, who checked his proofs. Spencer made but one biological investigation (1865-6), and that of little moment—on the circulation in plants—but his contact with the facts of organic life was by no means superficial. His intelligence was such that he got further into them than most concrete workers have ever done. And in some measure it was an advantage to him in his task that he was no specialist, that he did not know too much. It enabled him to approach the facts with a fresh mind, and to see more clearly the general facts of Biology which lie behind the details of Botany and Natural History. He was in no danger of not seeing the wood for the trees.

Organic Matter.—"In the substances of which organisms are composed, the conditions necessary to that redistribution of Matter and Motion which constitutes Evolution, are fulfilled in a far higher degree than at first appears."

Thus the most complex compounds into which Carbon, Hydrogen, Oxygen, and Nitrogen enter, together with small proportions of two other elements (Sulphur and Phosphorus) which very readily oxidise, "have an instability so great that decomposition ensues under ordinary atmospheric conditions"; the component elements have an unusual tendency to unite in different modes of aggregation though in the same proportions, thus forming analogous substances with different properties; the colloid character of the most complex compounds that are instrumental to vital actions gives them great molecular mobility—a plastic quality fitting them for organisation; "while the relatively great inertia of the large and complex organic molecules renders them comparatively incapable of being set in motion by the ethereal undulations, and so reduced to less coherent forms of aggregation, this same inertia facilitates changes of arrangement among their constituent molecules or atoms, since, in proportion as an incident force impresses but little motion on a mass, it is the better able to impress motion on the parts of the mass in relation to one another"; "lastly, the great difference in diffusibility between colloids and crystalloids makes possible in the tissues of organisms a specially rapid redistribution of matter and motion; both because colloids, being easily permeable by crystalloids, can be chemically acted on throughout their whole masses, instead of only on their surfaces; and because the products of decomposition, being also crystalloids, can escape as fast as they are produced, leaving room for further transformations." In short, organic matter is chemically and physically well-suited to be the physical basis of life.

The colloid character of organic matter facilitates modification by arrested momentum or by continuous strain. There is often strong capillary affinity and rapid osmosis. Heat is an important agent of redistribution in the animal organism, and light is an all-important agent of molecular changes in organic substances. But the extreme modifiability of organic matter by chemical agencies is the chief cause of that active molecular rearrangement which organisms, and especially animal organisms, display. In short, the substances of which organisms are built up are specially sensitive to the varied environing influences; "in consequence of its extreme instability organic matter undergoes extensive molecular rearrangements on very slight changes of conditions."

The correlative general fact is that during these extensive molecular rearrangements, there are evolved large amounts of energy, in the form of motion, heat, and even light and electricity. On the one hand the components of organic matter are regarded as falling from positions of unstable equilibrium to positions of stable equilibrium; on the other hand, "they give out in their falls certain momenta—momenta that may be manifested as heat, light, electricity, nerve-force, or mechanical motion, according as the conditions determine." It follows from the law of the Conservation of Energy that "whatever amount of power an organism expends in any shape, is the correlate and equivalent of a power which was taken into it from without."

Metabolism.—"The materials forming the tissues of plants as well as the materials contained in them, are progressively elaborated from the inorganic substances; and the resulting compounds, eaten, and some of them assimilated by animals, pass through successive changes which are, on the average, of an opposite character: the two sets being constructive and destructive. To express changes of both these natures the term 'metabolism' is used; and such of the metabolic changes as result in building up from simple to compound are distinguished as 'anabolic,' while those which result in the falling down from compound to simple are distinguished as 'katabolic.'"

"Regarded as a whole, metabolism includes, in the first place, those anabolic or building-up processes specially characterising plants, during which the impacts of ethereal undulations are stored up in compound molecules of unstable kinds; and it includes, in the second place, those katabolic or tumbling-down changes specially characterising animals, during which this accumulated molecular motion (contained in the food directly or indirectly supplied by plants) is in large measure changed into those molar motions constituting animal activities. There are multitudinous metabolic changes of minor kinds which are ancillary to these—many katabolic changes in plants and many anabolic changes in animals—but these are the essential ones."

Definition of Life.—Spencer's first definition of life (*Theory of Population*, 1852) was simply "the co-ordination of actions." But he soon saw that this was too wide. "It may be said of the Solar System, with its regularly-recurring movements and its self-balancing perturbations, that it, also, exhibits co-ordination of actions." "A true idea of Life must be an idea of some kind of change or changes." Therefore he carefully considered assimilation on the one hand, as an example of bodily life, and reasoning on the other hand, as an example of that life known as intelligence, and inquired into the common features of these two processes of change. Thus there emerged the formula that life is *the definite combination of heterogeneous changes, both simultaneous and successive.* But this formula also fails, as he said, by omitting the most distinctive peculiarity. It is universally recognised that living creatures continually exhibit *effective* response to external stimuli. To be able to do this is the very essence of life, distinguishing its responses from non-vital responses. Thus a clause must be added to the proximate conception, and the formula reads: "Life is the definite combination of heterogeneous changes, both simultaneous and successive, *in correspondence with external co-existences and sequences*." There are internal relations, namely, "definite combinations of heterogeneous changes, both simultaneous and successive," and there are external relations, "external co-existences and sequences," and life is the connexion of correspondence between them. Thus under its most abstract form, Spencer's conception of Life is:—"*The continuous adjustment of internal relations to external relations*."

In an appendix to the revised edition of the *Principles of Biology*, Spencer admits that he had not sufficiently emphasised the fact of *co-ordination*. "The idea of co-ordination is so cardinal a one that it should be expressed not by implication but overtly." The formula defining the phenomenon of life thus reads: "*The definite combination of heterogeneous changes, both simultaneous and successive, co-ordinated into correspondence with external co-existences and sequences*." It may be needful to remark that this was not intended to define Life in its essence, but Life as manifested to us. "The ultimate mystery is as great as ever: seeing that there remains unsolved the question: What *determines* the co-ordination of actions?"

If life be correspondence between internal and external relations, then "allowing a margin for perturbations, the life will continue only while the correspondence continues; the completeness of the life will be proportionate to the completeness of the correspondence; and the life will be perfect only when the correspondence is perfect." As organisms become more differentiated they enter into more complex relations with their environment, and as the environment becomes more complex organisms become more differentiated. The internal and external relations increase in number and intricacy *pari passu*, and the correspondences between them become more complex, numerous, and persistent. "The highest life is that which, like our own, shows great complexity in the correspondences, great rapidity in the succession of them, and great length in the series of them." "The highest Life is reached when there is some inner relation of actions fitted to meet every outer relation of actions by which the organism can be affected." "This continuous correspondence between inner and outer relations which constitutes Life, and the perfection of which is the perfection of Life, answers completely to that state of organic moving equilibrium which arises in the course of Evolution and tends ever to become more complete."

The Dynamic Element in Life.—But Spencer was not satisfied with his formula of Life. He recognised that there were vital phenomena which were not covered by it. The growth of a gall on a plant, due to irritant substances produced by an insect, shows no internal relations adjusted to external relations; the heart of a frog will live and beat for a long time after excision; the segmentation of an egg shows no correspondence with co-existences and sequences in its environment; when rudimentary organs are partly formed and then absorbed, no adjustment can be alleged between the inner relations which these present and any outer relations: the outer relations they refer to ceased millions of years ago; no correspondence, or part of a correspondence, by which inner actions are made to balance outer actions, can be seen in the dairymaid's laugh or the workman's whistle; the struggles of a boy in an epileptic fit show no correspondence with the co-existences and sequences around him, but they betray vitality as much as do the changing movements of a hawk pursuing a pigeon; "both exhibit that principle of activity which constitutes the essential element in our conception of life."

> "When it is said that Life is the definite combination of heterogeneous changes, both simultaneous and successive, in correspondence with external co-existences and sequences, there arises the question— Changes of what?… Still more clearly do we see this insufficiency when we take the more abstract definition—"the continuous adjustment of internal relations to external relations." Relations between what things? is the question to be asked. A relation of which the terms are unspecified does not connote a thought but merely the blank form of a thought. Its value is comparable to that of a cheque on which no amount is written."

This self-criticism led Spencer to the conclusion that "that which gives substance to our idea of Life is a certain unspecified principle of activity. The dynamic element in life is its essential element."

But how are we to conceive of this dynamic element? "Is this principle of activity inherent in organic matter, or is it something superadded?" Spencer at once rejected the second alternative, because the hypothesis of an independent vital principle has a bad pedigree, carrying us back to the ghost-theory of the savage, and because it is an unrepresentable 'pseud-idea,' which cannot even be imagined.

But the alternative of regarding Life as inherent in the substances of the organisms displaying it is also full of difficulties. "The processes which go on in living things are incomprehensible as results of any physical actions known to us." "We are obliged to confess that Life in its essence cannot be conceived in physico-chemical terms. The required principle of activity, which we found cannot be represented as an independent vital principle, we now find cannot be represented as a principle inherent in living matter. If, by assuming its inherence, we think the facts are accounted for, we do but cheat ourselves with pseud-ideas."

"What then are we to say—what are we to think? Simply that in this direction, as in all other directions, our explanations finally bring us face to face with the inexplicable. The Ultimate Reality behind this manifestation, as behind all other manifestations, transcends conception."

"Life as a principle of activity is unknown and unknowable—while its phenomena are accessible in thought the implied noumenon is inaccessible—only the manifestations come within the range of our intelligence, while that which is manifested lies beyond it."

But "our surface knowledge continues to be a knowledge valid of its kind, after recognising the truth that it is only surface knowledge."

The chapter on "The Dynamic Element in Life," which concludes the section of the book called *The Data of Biology*, was interpolated in the revised edition (1898). It indicates, as it seems to us, that Spencer's point of view had changed considerably since he stereotyped his *First Principles*. We must pause to consider what this change was.

In his *First Principles* Spencer wrote: "The task before us is that of exhibiting the phenomena of Evolution in synthetic order. Setting out from an established ultimate principle [the Persistence of Force] it has to be shown that the course of transformation among all kinds of existences cannot but be that which we have seen it to be." [This refers to the formula: Evolution is an integration of matter and concomitant dissipation of motion during which the matter passes from an indefinite, incoherent homogeneity to a definite, coherent heterogeneity; and during which the retained motion undergoes a parallel transformation.] "It has to be shown that the redistribution of matter and motion must everywhere take place in those ways and produce those traits, which celestial bodies, organisms, societies alike display. And it has to be shown that this universality of process results from the same necessity which determines each simplest movement around us, down to the accelerated fall of a stone or the recurrent beat of a harp string. In other words, the phenomena of Evolution have to be deduced from the Persistence of Force. As before said, 'to this an ultimate analysis brings us down; and on this a rational synthesis must build up.'" And again he wrote: "The interpretation of all phenomena in terms of Matter, Motion, and Force, is nothing more than the reduction of our complex symbols of thought to the simplest symbols."

These were brave words, and if we understand them aright it is, to say the least, surprising to be told when we come to the life of organisms that "the processes which go on in living things are incomprehensible as results of any physical actions known to us."

On the first page of the *Principles of Biology* we read: "The properties of substances, though destroyed to sense by combination, are not destroyed in reality. It follows from the persistence of force, that the properties of a compound are *resultants* of the properties of its components—*resultants* in which the properties of the components are severally in full action, though mutually obscured." But on p. 122 it is written: "We find it impossible to conceive Life as emerging from the co-operation of the components."

In the frankest possible way Spencer admitted that his definition of Life did not cover the facts, that it did not recognise the essential or dynamic element, that "Life in its essence cannot be conceived in physico-chemical terms." But if so, it can only be by great faith or great credulity that we can believe that an Evolution-formula in terms of "Matter, Motion, and Force" is adequate to describe its genesis.

At an earlier part of the *Data of Biology* Spencer assumed the origin of active protoplasm from a combination of inert proteids during the time of the earth's slow cooling, and did not suggest that there was any particular difficulty in the assumption; yet in the end we are told that it is "impossible even to imagine those processes going on in organic matter out of which emerges the dynamic element in Life."

"One can picture," Prof. C. Lloyd Morgan writes,[6] "how certain folk will gloat and 'chortle in their joy' over this confession, for such it will almost inevitably be regarded. But it is not likely that Mr Spencer is here, in so vital a matter, false to the evolution he has done so much to elucidate. The two seemingly contradictory statements are not really contradictory; they are made in different connections; the one in reference to phenomenal causation, the other to noumenal causation—to an underlying 'principle of activity.' The simple statement of fact is that the phenomena of life are data *sui generis*, and must as such be accepted by science. Just as when oxygen and hydrogen combine to form water, new data for science emerge; so, when protoplasm was evolved, new data emerged which it is the business of science to study. In both cases we believe that the results are due to the operation of natural laws, that is to say, can, with adequate knowledge, be described in terms of antecedence and sequence. But in both cases the results, which we endeavour thus to formulate, are the outcome of principles of activity, the mode of operation of which is inexplicable. We formulate the laws of evolution in terms of antecedence and sequence; we also refer these laws to an underlying cause, the noumenal mode of action of which is inexplicable. This, if I interpret him rightly, is Mr Spencer's meaning."

[6] "Natural Science," xiii., December 1898, p. 380.

Our own impression is that Spencer was guilty of "wobbling" between two modes of interpretation, between scientific description and philosophical explanation, a confusion incident on the fact that his *Principles of Biology* was also part of his *Synthetic Philosophy*. Biology as such has of course nothing to do with "the Ultimate Reality behind manifestations" or with the "implied noumenon." And when Spencer says "it is impossible even to imagine those processes going on in organic matter out of which emerges the dynamic element in Life," or when he illustrates his difficulty by pointing out how impossible it is to give a physico-chemical interpretation of the way a plant cell makes its wall, or a coccolith its imbricated covering, or a sponge its spicules, or a hen eats broken egg-shells, we do not believe he was thinking of anything but "phenomenal causation." When he says "The processes which go on in living things are incomprehensible as results of any physical actions known to us," we see no reason to take the edge off this truth by saying that Spencer simply meant that the Ultimate Reality is inaccessible.

In any case, whether Spencer meant that we cannot give any scientific analysis in physico-chemical terms of the unified behaviour of even the simplest organism, or whether he simply meant that the *raison d'être*, the ultimate reality of life, was an inaccessible noumenon, he confesses that we have "only a surface knowledge"; "only the manifestations come within the range of our intelligence while that which is manifested lies beyond it"; "the order existing among the actions which living things exhibit remains the same whether we know or do not know the nature of that from which the actions originate." This seems to us to sound a more modest note than is heard in the sentence: "The interpretation of all phenomena in terms of Matter, Motion and Force, is nothing more than the reduction of our complex symbols of thought to the simplest symbols."

Life and Mechanism.—But are not all biologists confronted with the difficulty that gave Herbert Spencer pause? Physiological analysis has done much in revealing chains of sequence within the organism, but no vital phenomenon has as yet been redescribed in terms of chemistry and physics. Again and again some success in discovering physico-chemical chains of sequence has awakened the expectation that the dawn of a mechanical theory of life was drawing nigh, but the dawn seems further off than ever. The residual phenomena left uninterpreted by mechanical categories loom out more persistently than they did a century ago. As Bunge once said "the more thoroughly and conscientiously we endeavour to study biological problems, the more are we convinced that even those processes which we have already regarded as explicable by chemical and physical laws, are in reality infinitely more complex, and at present defy any attempt at a mechanical explanation." As Dr J. S. Haldane puts it: "If we look at the phenomena which are capable of being stated, or explained in physico-chemical terms, we see at once that there is nothing in them characteristic of life…. The action of each bodily mechanism, the composition and structure of each organ, are all mutually determined and connected with one another in such a way as at once to distinguish a living organism from anything else. As this mutual determination is the characteristic mark of what is living, it cannot be ignored in the framing of fundamental working hypotheses."

The fact is that we have to regard the living organism as a new synthesis which we cannot at present analyse, and life as an activity which cannot at present be redescribed in terms of the present physical conceptions of matter and energy. And even if a living organism were artificially made, the problem would not be altered; though our conception of what we at present call inanimate might be.

Prof. Karl Pearson states the position from another point of view.

For the biologist as a scientific inquirer "the problem of whether life is or is not a mechanism is not a question of whether the same things, 'matter' and 'force,' are or are not at the back of organic and inorganic phenomena—of what is at the back of either class of sense-impressions we know absolutely nothing—but of whether the conceptual shorthand of the physicist, his ideal world of ether, atom, and molecule, will or will not also suffice to describe the biologist's perceptions." That it does not at present seems the conviction of the majority of physiologists; if it ever should it would be "purely an economy of thought; it would provide the great advantages which flow from the use of one instead of two conceptual shorthands, but it would not 'explain' life any more than the law of gravitation explains the elliptic path of a planet."

"Atom" and "molecule" and the rest are scientific concepts, not phenomenal existences, therefore even if the physicist's formulæ should fit vital phenomena—which they seem very far from doing—there would be no explanation forthcoming, for "mechanism does not explain anything."

Thus, like Spencer, we find the secret of the organism irresoluble in terms of lower categories. But we differ from him inasmuch as we believe that this admission is fatal to his formula of evolution, to his definition of life, and to the coherence of his *Synthetic Philosophy*.

CHAPTER IX

SPENCER AS BIOLOGIST: INDUCTIONS OF BIOLOGY

Growth—Development—Structure and Function—Waste and Repair—Adaptation—Cell-Life—Genesis—Nutrition and Reproduction—The Germ-Cells

Growth.—Perhaps the widest and most familiar induction of Biology, is that organisms grow. But there is growth in crystals, in terrestrial deposits, in celestial bodies; in fact, growth, as being an integration of matter, is the primary trait of evolution; it is universal, in the sense that all aggregates display it in some way at some period. "The essential community of nature between organic growth and inorganic growth is, however, most clearly seen on observing that they both result in the same way. The segregation of different kinds of detritus from each other, as well as from the water carrying them, and their aggregation into distinct strata, is but an instance of a universal tendency towards the union of like units and the parting of unlike units (*First Principles*, § 163). The deposit of a crystal from a solution is a differentiation of the previously mixed molecules; and an integration of one class of molecules into a solid body, and the other class into a liquid solvent. Is not the growth of an organism an essentially similar process? Around a plant there exist certain elements like the elements which form its substance; and its increase in size is effected by continually integrating these surrounding like elements with itself." And so on.

Passing over the far-fetched statement that the deposit of sediment in distinct strata illustrates the universal tendency towards the union of like units and the parting of unlike units, we must point out that Spencer begins his discussion of organic growth by describing it in such general terms that its essential characteristic is lost sight of. A minute crystal of alum is dropped into a saturated solution of alum, and it grows rapidly under our eyes out of material the same as its own, but the living creature grows larger at the expense of material *different* from its own. The grass grows at the expense of air, water, and salts, and the lamb grows at the expense of the grass. Though the living creature cannot, of course, transform one element into another, and must have carbon, hydrogen, oxygen, nitrogen, etc., in its food, it utilises materials chemically very different from its own complex compounds.

Spencer's inductions as to growth were the following:—

(1) The growth of an organism is dependent on the available supply of such environing materials as are of like natures with the matters composing the organism.

(2) Other things being equal, the degree of growth varies according to the surplus of nutrition over expenditure.

(3) In the same organism the surplus of nutrition over expenditure differs at different stages, and growth is unlimited or has a definite limit, according as the surplus does or does not rapidly decrease. There is almost unceasing growth in organisms that expend relatively little energy and definitely limited growth in organisms that expend much energy. [There are many difficulties here, *e.g.*, the apparent absence of a limit of growth in many very energetic fishes.]

(4) Among organisms which are large expenders of force, the size ultimately attained is, other things equal, determined by the initial size. [By initial size Spencer means the bulk of the organism when it begins to feed for itself.] A calf and a lamb commence their physiological transactions on widely different scales; their first increments of growth are similarly contrasted in their amounts; and the two diminishing series of such increments end at similarly-contrasted limits.

[But the further we penetrate into details, the more inevitable seems the conclusion that adult size is *an adaptive phenomenon*; in other words that growth has been punctuated by natural selection.]

(5) Where the likeness of other circumstances permits a comparison, the possible extent of growth depends on the degree of organization; an inference testified to by the larger forms among the various divisions and sub-divisions of organisms.

In connection with growth and its limit Spencer made a simple but shrewd observation, which seems also to have occurred to Prof. Leuckart and to Dr Alexander James. He pointed out, that in the growth of similarly shaped bodies the increase of volume continually tends to outrun the increase of surface. The volume of living matter must grow more than the surface through which it is kept alive, if the surface remain regular in contour. In spherical and all other regular units the volume increases as the cube of the radius, the surface only as the square of the radius. Thus a cell, for instance, as it grows, must get into physiological difficulties, for the nutritive necessities of the increasing volume are ever less adequately supplied by the less rapidly increasing absorbent surface. There is less and less opportunity for nutrition, respiration, and excretion. A nemesis of growth sets in, for waste gains upon, overtakes, balances, and threatens to exceed repair. Growth may cease at this limit, and a balance be struck; or the form of the unit may be altered and surface gained by flattening out, or very frequently by ramifying processes; or—and this the most frequent solution—the cell may divide, halving its volume, gaining new surface, and restoring the balance. In more general terms, growth expresses the preponderance of constructive processes or anabolism; increase of volume with less rapid increase of nutritive, respiratory, and excretory surface involves a relative predominance of katabolism; the limit of growth occurs when further increase of volume would prejudicially increase the ratio of katabolism to anabolism; at that point the cell restores the balance by dividing. And what is true of the unit applies also in a general way to organs, such as leaves which increase their surface by becoming much divided, and even to organisms which exhibit many adaptations for increasing their nutritive, respiratory, and excretory surfaces.

Development.—Growth is increase in bulk, development is increase in structure, and Spencer's chief induction in regard to development is that we see a change from an incoherent, indefinite homogeneity to a coherent, definite heterogeneity. "The originally like units called cells become unlike in various ways, and in ways more numerous and marked as the development goes on. The several tissues which these several classes of cells form by aggregation, grow little by little distinct from each other; and little by little put on those structural complexities that arise from differentiations among their component units. In the shoot, as in the limb, the external form, originally very simple, and having much in common with simple forms in general, gradually acquires an increasing complexity and an increasing unlikeness to other forms. Meanwhile, the remaining parts of the organism to which the shoot or limb belongs, having been severally assuming structures divergent from one another and from that of this particular shoot or limb, there has arisen a greater heterogeneity in the organism as a whole." Moreover, "whereas the germs of organisms are extremely similar, they gradually diverge widely in modes now regular and now irregular, until in place of a multitude of forms practically alike we finally have a multitude of forms most of which are extremely unlike." In other words, there is in individual development (ontogeny) some condensed recapitulation of the steps in racial evolution (phylogeny). Furthermore, in the progressing differentiation of each organism there is a progressing differentiation of it from its environment; it becomes freer from the environmental grip and more master of its fate. Here again there is an individual progress parallel to that seen in the course of historic evolution.

A general criticism must be made, that Spencer thought of the germ-cell much too simply. It is a microcosm full of intricacy; the nucleus is often exceedingly definite and coherent; the early cells are often from the first defined, with prospective values which do not change. The fertilised ovum has only apparent simplicity; it has a complex individualised organisation— often visible. No one can doubt that development is progressive differentiation, but it is rather a realisation of a complex inheritance of materialised potentialities than a change from an incoherent, indefinite homogeneity to a coherent, definite heterogeneity.

Structure and Function.—To the question, does Life produce Organisation, or does Organisation produce Life? Spencer answered that "structure and function must have advanced *pari passu*: some difference of function, primarily determined by some difference of relation to the environment, initiating a slight difference of structure, and this again leading to a more pronounced difference of function; and so on through continuous actions and reactions." As structure progresses from the homogeneous, indefinite, and incoherent, so does function, illustrating progressive division of labour. From an evolutionist point of view, Spencer argued that life necessarily comes before organisation; "organic matter in a state of homogeneous aggregation must precede organic matter in a stage of heterogeneous aggregation. But since the passing from a structureless state to a structured state is itself a vital process, it follows that vital activity must have existed while there was yet no structure: structure could not else arise. That function takes precedence of structure, seems also implied in the definition of Life. If Life is shown by inner actions so adjusted as to balance outer actions—if the implied energy is the *substance* of Life while the adjustment of the actions constitutes its *form*; then may we not say that the actions to be formed must come before that which forms them—that the continuous change which is the basis of function, must come before the structure which brings function into shape?"

But all such discussions of "structure" and "function" in the abstract tend to verbal quibbling. We cannot have activity without something to act, we cannot have metabolism without stuff. No one can tell what the first thing that lived on the earth was like, what organisation it had, or what it was able to do, but we may be sure that vital organisation and vital activity are only static and kinetic aspects of the same thing. It is quite probable, however, that there is no one thing that can be called protoplasm, for vital function may depend upon the inter-relations or inter-actions of several complex substances, none of which could by itself be called alive; which are, however, held together in that unity which makes an organism what it is. Just as the secret of a firm's success may depend upon a particularly fortunate association of partners, so it may be with vitality.[7]

[7] See J. Arthur Thomson's *Progress of Science in the Nineteenth Century*, 1903, p. 317, and E. B. Wilson's *The Cell in Development and Inheritance*, 1900.

Waste and Repair.—Organisms are systems for transforming matter and energy and the law of conservation holds good. "Each portion of mechanical or other energy which an organism exerts implies the transformation of as much organic matter as contained this energy in a latent state," and the waste must be made good by repair. We thus see why plants with an enormous income of energy and little expenditure of energy have no difficulty in sustaining the balance between waste and repair; we understand the relation between small waste, small activity, and low temperature in many of the lower animals; we understand conversely the rapid waste of energetic, hot- blooded animals. The deductive interpretation of waste is easy, but it is different with repair, for here the analogy between the organism and an inanimate engine breaks down. The living creature is a self-stoking, self- repairing, and also—it may be noted in passing—a self-reproducing engine. Spencer did not do more than restate the difficulty when he said that the component units of organisms have the power of moulding fit materials into other units of the same order.

In passing to consider the ability which an organism often has of recompleting itself when one of its parts has been cut off, just as an injured crystal recompletes itself, Spencer was led to the hypothesis that "the form of each species of organism is determined by a peculiarity in the constitution of its units—that these have a special structure in which they tend to arrange themselves; just as have the simpler units of inorganic matter." "This organic polarity (as we might figuratively call this proclivity towards a specific structural arrangement) can be possessed neither by the chemical units nor the morphological units, we must conceive it as possessed by certain intermediate units, which we may term *physiological*." But if in each organism the physiological units which result from the compounding of highly compound molecules have a more or less distinctive character, the germ-cell is not so very *indefinite* after all.

Many of the facts of regeneration are very striking. A crab may regrow its complex claw, a starfish arm may regrow an entire body. A snail has been known to regenerate an amputated eye-bearing horn twenty times in succession, a newt can replace a lost lens, a lizard can regrow its tail and part of its leg, a stork can regrow the greater part of its bill. In many cases, the surrender of parts which are afterwards regrown is exceedingly common, as in some worms and Echinoderms, and is a life-saving adaptation. Organically, though not consciously, the brainless starfish has learned that it is better that one member should perish than that the whole life should be lost. This regenerative capacity no doubt implies certain properties in the living matter and in the organism, but we are far from being able to picture how it comes about. What does seem clear is that the distribution and mode of occurrence of the regenerative capacity—in external organs often, but in internal organs very rarely; in most lizard's tails, but not in the chamæleon's; in the stork's bill but not in its toes—are *adaptive*, being related to the normal risks of life, as Réaumur, Lessona, Darwin, and Weismann have pointed out. According to Lessona's Law, which Weismann has elaborated, regeneration tends to occur in those organisms and in those parts of organisms which are in the ordinary course of nature most liable to injury. To which we must add two saving-clauses—(*a*) provided that the lost part is of some vital importance, and (*b*) provided that the wound or breakage is not in itself very likely to be fatal. In Weismann's words, the theory is, that "the power of regeneration possessed by an animal or by a part of an animal is regulated by adaptation to the frequency of loss and to the extent of the damage done by the loss."

Adaptation.—Wherever we look in the world of organisms we find examples of adaptation; we see form suited for different kinds of motion, organs suited for their uses, constitution suited to circumstances in such external features as colouring and in such internal adjustments as the regulation of temperature; we find effective weapons and effective armour, flowers adapted to insect visitors and insect visitors adapted to flowers, one sex adapted in relation to the other, the mother adapted to bearing and rearing offspring, the embryo adapted to its pre-natal life; everywhere there is adaptation in varying degrees of perfection. The adaptation is a fact, in regard to which all naturalists are agreed; difference of opinion arises when we ask how these adaptations have come to be.

In the chapter "Adaptation" Spencer practically restricted his attention to a certain kind of adaptation, namely the direct modifications which result from use or disuse, or from environmental influence. The blacksmith's arm, the dancer's legs, the jockey's crural adductors, illustrate direct results of practice; "à force de forger on devient forgeron." The skin forms protective callosities where it is much pressed or rubbed, as on the schoolboy's hands or the old man's toothless gums. The blood-vessels may respond by enlargement to increased demands made on them; the fingers of the blind become extraordinarily sensitive.

Spencer points to the general truth that extra function is followed by extra growth, but that a limit is soon reached beyond which very little, if any, further modification can be produced. Moreover, the limited increase of size produced in any organ by a limited increase of its function, is not maintained unless the increase of function is permanent. When the modifying influence is removed, the organism rebounds or tends to rebound. A lasting change of importance involves a re-organisation, a new state of equilibrium.

On inductive and deductive grounds, Spencer summed up in four conclusions:

—

(1) An adaptive change of structure will soon reach a point beyond which further adaptation will be slow.

(2) When the modifying cause has been but for a short time in action, the modification generated will be evanescent.

(3) A modifying cause acting even for many generations will do little towards permanently altering the organic equilibrium of a race.

(4) On the cessation of such cause, its effects will become unapparent in the course of a few generations.

But two cautions must be emphasised (*a*) that Spencer, in this discussion, dealt only with those direct adjustments which are referable to the action of use or disuse, or of surrounding influences; and (*b*) that we have no security in regarding these as being as such transmissible.

By adaptations biologists usually mean permanent adjustments, and there are two theories of the origin of these: (*a*) by the action of natural selection on inborn variations, or (*b*) by the inheritance of the directly acquired bodily modifications.

Cell-Life.—In this chapter, interpolated in the revised edition, Spencer summed up the main results of the study of the structural units or cells which build up a body. "Nature everywhere presents us with complexities within complexities, which go on revealing themselves as we investigate smaller and smaller objects." Thus protoplasm itself has a complicated structure; the nucleus of the cell is a little world in itself; and the cell-firm has other partners, such as the centrosome. When a cell divides, the readily stainable bodies or chromosomes, present in definite number within the nucleus, are divided, usually by a most intricate process, in such a manner that equal amounts are bequeathed by the mother-cell to each of the two daughter-cells. Spencer favoured the view that the chromatin, which "consists of an organic acid (nucleic acid) rich in phosphorus, combined with an albuminous substance, probably a combination of various proteids" may be peculiarly unstable and active.

"From the chromatin, units of which are thus ever falling into stabler states, there are ever being diffused waves of molecular motion, setting up molecular changes in the cytoplasm. The chromatin stands towards the other contents of the cell in the same relation that a nerve-element stands to any element of an organism which it excites." "We may infer that cell-evolution was, under one of its aspects, a change from a stage in which the exciting substance and the substance excited were mingled with approximate uniformity, to a stage in which the exciting substance was gathered together into the nucleus and finally into the chromosomes, leaving behind the substance excited, now distinguished as cytoplasm."

But the suggestion that chromosomes may be stimulating, change-exciting elements, does not, Spencer goes on to say, conflict with the conclusion that the chromosomes are the vehicles conveying hereditary traits. "While the unstable units of chromatin, ever undergoing changes, diffuse energy around, they may also be units which, under the conditions furnished by fertilisation, gravitate towards the organisation of the species. Possibly it may be that the complex combination of proteids, common to chromatin and cytoplasm, is that part in which constitutional characters inhere; while the phosphorised component, falling from its unstable union and decomposing, evolves the energy which, ordinarily the cause of changes, now excites the more active changes following fertilisation."

From this speculation Spencer passes to a brief consideration of what occurs before and during the fertilisation of the ovum. Before fertilisation is accomplished the nucleus of the ovum normally divides twice in rapid succession, and gives off two abortive cells—known as polar bodies—which come to nothing. The usual result of this "maturation," as it is called, is that the number of chromosomes in the ovum is reduced to a half of the normal number characteristic of the cells of the species to which it belongs. In the history of the male element or spermatozoon, there is an analogous reduction, so that when spermatozoon and ovum unite in fertilisation the normal number is restored. It is now recognised that the maturation-divisions are useful in obviating the doubling of the number of chromosomes which fertilisation would otherwise involve, and it has also been suggested that this continually recurrent elimination of chromosomes may be one of the causes of variation.

Spencer suggested another interpretation. He pointed out the general fact that sexual reproduction (gamogenesis) commonly occurs when asexual reproduction (agamogenesis) is arrested by unfavourable conditions, that failing asexual reproduction initiates sexual reproduction. Now as egg-cells and sperm-cells are the outcome of often long series of cell divisions (asexual multiplication), may not the polar bodies, which are aborted cells, indicate that asexual multiplication can no longer go on, and that the conditions leading to sexual multiplication have set in? "As the cells which become spermatozoa are *left* with half the number of chromosomes possessed by preceding cells, there is actually that impoverishment and declining vigour here suggested as the antecedent of fertilisation." In short, the germ-cells, separately considered, are cells in which the power of further asexual multiplication is exhausted, as it is known to become exhausted in Infusorians and such body-cells as nerve-cells; there arises a state which initiates a sexual union or amphimixis of the two kinds of germ-cells, and the decrease in the chromatin is an initial cause of that state.

We quote this speculation as a good instance of Spencer's continual endeavour to rationalise puzzling and exceptional facts by showing that there is a general principle underlying them. But the objections to his hypothesis are numerous. Mature ova or spermatozoa will not normally divide if left to themselves, but that is because they are specialised to secure amphimixis, not because their powers are in any way declining or impoverished. A parthenogenetic ovum gives off one polar body—though without reduction in the number of chromosomes—and then proceeds by asexual multiplication or ordinary cell division to build up a body. The spore of a fern or a moss has only half the number of chromosomes that the cells of its producer have, yet it proceeds by asexual multiplication or ordinary cell-division to build up the gametophyte or sexual generation.

Genesis.—Spencer attempted a classification of the various modes of reproduction that occur among organisms—asexual reproduction (agamogenesis) by fission and budding, sexual reproduction (gamogenesis) by specialised germ-cells usually involving fertilisation or amphimixis, and all the complications involved in "alternation of generations" (metagenesis), the development of eggs without fertilisation (parthenogenesis), and so on. But what gives particular importance to the chapter on genesis is not the discussion of the modes of reproduction, but the general conclusion that nutrition and reproduction are antithetic processes—a very fruitful idea in biology.

Where there is alternation of generation, sexual and asexual, we find that asexual reproduction continues as long as the forces which result in growth are greatly in excess of the antagonistic forces. Conversely the recurrence of sexual reproduction occurs when the conditions are no longer so favourable to growth. Similarly, where there is no alternation, "new individuals are usually not formed while the preceding individuals are still rapidly growing—that is, while the forces producing growth exceed the opposing forces to a great extent; but the formation of new individuals begins when nutrition is nearly equalled by expenditure."

In illustration Spencer points to facts like the following: "Uniaxial plants begin to produce their lateral, flowering axes, only after the main axis has developed the great mass of its leaves, and is showing its diminished nutrition by smaller leaves, or shorter internodes, or both"; "root-pruning" and "ringing," which diminish the nutritive supply, promote the formation of flower-shoots; high nutrition in plants prevents or arrests flowering.

Similarly, the aphides or green-flies, hatched from eggs in the spring, multiply by parthenogenesis throughout the summer; with extraordinary rapidity one generation follows on another; but when the weather becomes cold and plants no longer afford abundant sap, males reappear and sexual reproduction sets in. It has been shown that in the artificial summer of a green-house, parthenogenesis may continue for four years. In a large number of cases of ordinary reproduction, *e.g.* in birds, the connexion between cessation of growth and commencement of reproduction is very distinct.

It is not difficult to see the advantages in the postponement of sexual reproduction until the rate of growth begins to decline. "For so long as the rate of growth continues rapid, there is proof that the organism gets food with facility—that expenditure does not seriously check assimilation; and that the size reached is as yet not disadvantageous: or rather, indeed, that it is advantageous. But when the rate of growth is much decreased by the increase of expenditure—when the excess of assimilative power is diminishing so fast as to indicate its approaching disappearance—it becomes needful, for the maintenance of the species, that this excess shall be turned to the production of new individuals; since, did growth continue until there was a complete balancing of assimilation and expenditure, the production of new individuals would be either impossible or fatal to the parent. And it is clear that 'natural selection' will continually tend to determine the period at which gamogenesis commences, in such a way as most favours the maintenance of the race."

That natural selection punctuates the life to advantage does not imply that it works directly towards such a remote goal as species-maintaining; it means that the arrangements which do secure this end most effectively are those which tend to establish themselves. Those that do not secure this end are eliminated.

Nutrition and Reproduction.—Spencer's doctrine of the antithesis between Nutrition and Reproduction is of great importance in biology, and we must dwell on it a little longer.

The life of organisms is rhythmic. Plants have their long period of vegetative growth, and then suddenly burst into flower. Animals in their young stages grow rapidly, and as the growth ceases reproduction normally begins; or again, just as perennial plants are strictly vegetative through a great part of the year or for many successive years, but have their periodic recurrence of flowers and fruit, so it is with many animals which after remaining virtually asexual for prolonged periods, exhibit periodic returns of a reproductive or sexual tide. Foliage and fruiting, periods of nutrition and crises of reproduction, hunger and love, must be interpreted as life-tides, punctuated by the seasons and other circumstances through the agency of Natural Selection, but none the less as expressions of the fundamental organic rhythm between rest and work, upbuilding and expenditure, repair and waste, which on the protoplasmic plane are known as anabolism and katabolism.[8]

[8] P. Geddes and J. Arthur Thomson, *The Evolution of Sex*, revised edition, 1901, p. 238.

Anabolism and katabolism are the two sides of protoplasmic life, and the major rhythms of the respective preponderance of these give the antitheses of growth and multiplication, asexual and sexual reproduction. The contrasts of metabolism represent the swings of the organic see-saw; the periodic contrasts correspond to alternate weightings or lightenings of the two sides.

Spencer's induction that "an approach towards equilibrium between the forces which cause growth and the forces which oppose growth, is the chief condition to the recurrence of sexual reproduction," is an approximate answer to the question—*When* does sexual reproduction recur? But there remains, he says, the more difficult question—*Why* does sexual reproduction recur? *Why* cannot multiplication be carried on in all cases, as it is in many cases, by asexual reproduction?

As yet, he says, biology is not advanced enough to give a reply, but a certain hypothetical answer may be suggested. "Seeing, on the one hand, that gamogenesis recurs only in individuals which are approaching a state of organic equilibrium; and seeing, on the other hand, that the sperm-cells and germ-cells thrown off by such individuals are cells in which developmental changes have ended in quiescence, but in which, after their union, there arises a process of active cell-formation; we may suspect that the approach towards a state of general equilibrium in such gamogenetic individuals is accompanied by an approach towards molecular equilibrium in them; and that the need for this union of sperm-cell and germ-cell is the need for overthrowing this equilibrium, and re-establishing active molecular change in the detached germ —a result probably effected by mixing the slightly different physiological units of slightly different individuals."

Now, while Spencer was probably right in saying that fertilisation promotes change, we cannot think that he succeeded in finding what he was seeking, namely a primary physiological reason why sexual reproduction should occur. It may be pointed out that it is only in a limited sense that sperm-cells or egg-cells can be spoken of as in a state of "quiescence," and that it is only in a limited sense that the organism which has finished growing and is beginning to be sexual can be spoken of as in a state of general or molecular equilibrium. An egg-cell is quiescent, as a seed lying in the ground is quiescent, awaiting its stimulus of warmth and moisture; a sperm-cell is quiescent, as a spore floating in the air is quiescent, awaiting its appropriate soil. The egg-cells and sperm-cells cannot be very quiescent since they do so much when they unite. Moreover, we have simply to recall the facts of natural parthenogenesis on the one hand or of artificial parthenogenesis on the other, to see that the quiescence of the egg is a secondary restriction adapted to secure amphimixis. Moreover, the familiar external and internal changes which occur in the bodies of organisms when they are approaching sexual maturity suggest the very opposite of general or molecular equilibrium.

It may be pointed out that although asexual multiplication persists in many organisms both large and small, and is sometimes the only method of multiplication, yet it is apt to be a somewhat expensive process and would be difficult to arrange for in highly differentiated animals. On the other hand, asexual multiplication succeeds admirably in many cases; it does not imply degeneration; it is not inconsistent with the occurrence of variations; and it is *conceivable* that it might have been arranged for even in the highest animals. What other reason can there be why the circuitous process of sexual reproduction has been preferred? It may be said that the arrangement by which multiplication is secured through special germ-cells, more or less apart from the cells which build up the body, may be justified as an arrangement which prevents or tends to prevent the transmission of bodily modifications, many of which are detrimental. But as this cuts both ways, preventing or tending to prevent the transmission of useful modifications, there must be some other reason why the circuitous process of sexual reproduction has been preferred. We believe the answer to be that sexual reproduction is an adaptive process securing the benefits of amphimixis, for in amphimixis and in the changes preparatory to it, there is an important *source of variation*. In one of his essays Weismann wrote as follows:—

"Sexual reproduction is well known to consist in the fusion of two contrasted reproductive cells, or perhaps even in the fusion of their nuclei alone. These reproductive cells contain the germinal material or germ-plasm, and this again, in its specific molecular structure, is the bearer of the hereditary tendencies of the organisms from which the reproductive cells originate. Thus in sexual reproduction two hereditary tendencies are in a sense intermingled. In this mingling, I see the cause of the hereditary individual characteristics; and in the production of these characters, the task of sexual reproduction. It has to supply the material for the individual differences from which selection produces new species."

When we inquire into the reasons for the occurrence of a process such as sexual reproduction, there are four different questions which may be put: (1) We may inquire into the historical evolution of the process, so far as that can be legitimately imagined or inferred from still persistent grades. (2) We may try to discover what factors may have operated in the course of evolution in raising the process from one step of differentiation to another. (3) We may also try to show how the process is justified by its advantages either self-regarding or species-maintaining. (4) We may inquire into the physiological sequences in the internal economy of the individual organism which lead up to the process in question. There is no doubt always an immediate necessity for the occurrence of an organic process, but we are in many cases quite unable at present to do more than describe the series of events without understanding their causal nexus. The reason for this is apparent, since the organism is much more than a detached inanimate engine; it is a system which has summed up in it the long results of time, the history of ages. Its rhythms and periodicities and crises puzzle us because they originated under conditions which obtained untold millennia ago. Thus some processes in higher animals may have had originally a reference to tides from the reach of which their present possessors are far withdrawn.

We have entered on this digression partly for clearness sake, and partly to explain why Spencer had, as we think, very limited success in his answer to the question: Why does sexual reproduction occur? The curious reader may be referred to the discussion of these problems in *The Evolution of Sex*, Contemporary Science Series, Revised Edition, 1901.

The Germ-Cells.—But we cannot leave the interesting chapter on genesis without referring to another of Spencer's conclusions, which does not seem to us to be quite consistent with facts.

"The marvellous phenomena initiated by the meeting of sperm-cell and germ-cell, or rather of their nuclei, naturally suggest the conception of some quite special and peculiar properties possessed by these cells. It seems obvious that this mysterious power which they display of originating a new and complex organism, distinguishes them in the broadest way from portions of organic substance in general. Nevertheless, the more we study the evidence the more are we led towards the conclusion that these cells are not fundamentally different from other cells." The evidence he gives is: (1) that small fragments of tissue in many plants and inferior animals may develop into entire organisms; (2) that the reproductive organs producing eggs and sperms are organs of low organisation, with no specialities of structure "which might be looked for, did sperm-cells and germ-cells need endowing with properties unlike those of all other organic agents." "Thus, there is no warrant for the assumption that sperm-cells and germ-cells possess powers fundamentally unlike those of other cells."

To this it must be answered: (1) though sperm-cells and egg-cells, being living units, cannot be "*fundamentally* unlike" other living units, such as ordinary body-cells, yet they may be very unlike them; (2) that the germ-cells are very unlike ordinary body-cells is shown by the fact that they can do what no single body-cell can do, build up a whole organism; (3) so specific are germ-cells that in certain cases and in favourable conditions a small fraction of an egg, bereft of its own nucleus, may, if fertilised, develop into an entire and normal larva; (4) it is quite consistent with the idea of evolution that in lower organisms the contrast between body-cells and germ-cells should be less pronounced than in higher forms. But the fundamental answer is found when we inquire into the history of the germ-cells. In many cases, and the list is being added to, the future reproductive cells are segregated off at an early stage in embryonic development. Even before differentiation sets in, the future reproductive cells may be set apart from the body-forming cells. The latter develop in manifold variety into skin and nerve, muscle and blood, gut and gland; they differentiate, and may lose almost all protoplasmic likeness to the mother ovum. But the reproductive cells are set apart; they take no share in the differentiation, but remain virtually unchanged, continuing unaltered the protoplasmic tradition of the original fertilised ovum. After a while their division-products will be liberated as functional reproductive cells or germ- cells, handing on the tradition intact to the next generation.

An early isolation of the reproductive cells has been observed in the harlequin fly (*Chironomus*) and in some other insects, in the aberrant worm-type *Sagitta*, in leeches, in thread-worms, in some Polyzoa, in some small Crustaceans known as Cladocera, in the water-flea *Moina*, in some Arachnoids (Phalangidæ), in the bony fish *Micrometrus aggregatus*, and in other cases. In the development of the threadworm of the horse according to Boveri, the very first cleavage of the ovum establishes a distinction between somatic and reproductive cells. One of the first two cells is the ancestor of all the cells of the body; the other is the ancestor of all the germ-cells. "Moreover, from the outset the progenitor of the germ-cells *differs from the somatic cells not only in the greater size and richness of the chromatin of its nucleus, but also in its mode of mitosis (division)*, for in all those blastomeres (segmentation-cells) destined to produce somatic cells a portion of the chromatin is cast out into the cytoplasm, where it degenerates, and *only in the germng-cells is the sum-total of the chromatin retained*" (E. B. Wilson, *The Cell in Development and Inheritance*, 1896, p. 111).

In the majority of cases, we admit, the reproductive cells *are not to be seen* in early segregation, and the continuous lineage from the fertilised ovum cannot be traced. In the majority of cases, the germ-cells are seen as such after considerable differentiation has gone on, and although they are linear descendants of the ovum, their special lineage cannot be traced. But it seems legitimate to argue from the clear cases to the obscure cases, and to say that the germ-cells are those cells which retain the complete complement of heritable qualities. Adopting the conception of the germ-plasm as the material within the nucleus which bears all the properties transmitted in inheritance, we may still say, in Weismann's words, "In every development a portion of this specific germ-plasm, which the parental ovum contains, is unused in the upbuilding of the offspring's body, and is reserved unchanged to form the germ-cells of the next generation.... The germ-cells no longer appear as products of the body, at least not in their more essential part—the specific germ-plasm; they appear rather as something opposed to the sum-total of body-cells; and the germ-cells of successive generations are related to one another like generations of Protozoa." In terms of this conception, which fits many facts, we may say that in plants and lower animals the distinction between germ-plasm and somato-plasm has not been much accentuated, and that in some organisms the body-cells retain enough undifferentiated germ- plasm to enable them in small or large companies to regrow an entire organism.

It may be said that Spencer must also have regarded the germ-cells as containing the whole complement of hereditary qualities. *It must be so.* The point is that he rejected the theory which gives a rational account of how the germ-cells have this content and their power of developing into an organism, like from like. The sentence in which he points out that the reproductive organs have "none of the specialities of structure which might be looked for, did the sperm-cells and germ-cells need *endowing with properties* unlike those of all other organic agents," shows how far he deliberately stood from the conception we have outlined.

> Here we may note that the "Inductions" regarding Heredity are discussed in our eleventh chapter, and those regarding Variation in our twelfth chapter. We have not dealt with the suggestive concrete sections which deal with structural and functional evolution, partly because they are too concrete to be dealt with briefly, and partly because they are saturated with the hypothesis of the transmission of acquired characters. Spencer's most important conclusion in regard to the Laws of Multiplication is

referred to under the heading Population.

95

CHAPTER X

HERBERT SPENCER AS CHAMPION OF THE EVOLUTION-IDEA

*The Evolution-Idea—Spencer's Historical Position—Von Baer's Law—
Evolution and Creation—Arguments for the Evolution-Doctrine*

Spencer has been called "the philosopher of the Evolution-movement," but the appropriateness of this description depends on what is meant by philosopher. What is certain is that he championed the evolutionist interpretation at a time when it was as much tabooed as it is now fashionable; that he showed its applicability to all orders of facts—inorganic, organic, and super-organic; that he threw some light on various factors in the evolution- process, and that he attempted to sum up in a universal formula what he believed to be the common principle of all evolutionary change. In judging of what he did it must be remembered that he was pre-Darwinian, and that chemistry and physics, biology and psychology have made enormous strides since he wrote his *First Principles* in 1861-2.

The Evolution-Idea.—The general idea of evolution, like many other great ideas, is essentially simple—that the present is the child of the past and the parent of the future. It is the idea of development writ large and historically applied. It is the same as the scientific conception of human history. In general terms, a process of Becoming everywhere leads, through the interaction of inherent potentialities and environmental conditions, to a new phase of Being. The study of Evolution is a study of *Werden und Vergehen und Weiterwerden.*

Stated concretely in regard to living creatures, the general doctrine of organic evolution suggests, as we all know, that the plants and animals now around us —with all their fascinating complexities of structure and function, of life-history, behaviour, and inter-relations—are the natural and necessary results of long processes of growth and change, of elimination and survival, operative throughout practically countless ages; that the forms we know and admire are the lineal descendants of ancestors on the whole somewhat simpler except when we have to deal with retrogressive or degenerative series; that these ancestors are descended from yet simpler forms, and so on backwards, till we lose our clue in the unknown, but doubtless momentous vital events of pre-Cambrian ages, or, in other words, in the thick mist of life's beginnings. Though the general idea of organic evolution is simple, it has been slowly evolved both as regards concreteness and clarity; it has gradually gained content as research furnished fuller illustration, and clearness as criticism forced it to keep in touch with facts. It has slowly developed from the stage of suggestion to that of verification; from being an *a priori* anticipation it has become an interpretation of nature; and from being a modal interpretation of the animate world it is advancing to the rank of a causal interpretation.

The evolution-idea is perhaps as old as clear thinking, which we may date from the (unknown) time when man discovered the year—with its marvellous object-lesson of recurrent sequences—and realised that his race had a history. Whatever may have been its origin, the idea was familiar to several of the ancient Greek philosophers, as it was to Hume and Kant; it fired the imagination of Lucretius and linked him to another poet of evolution—Goethe; it persisted, like a latent germ, through the centuries of other than scientific preoccupation; it was made actual by the pioneers of modern biology—men like Buffon, Lamarck, Erasmus Darwin and Treviranus;—and it became current intellectual coin when Spencer, Darwin, Wallace, Haeckel and Huxley, with united but varied achievements, won the conviction of the majority of thoughtful men.[9]

[9] See J. Arthur Thomson, *The Science of Life* (1899), chapter xvi., "Evolution of Evolution Theory"; and *The Study of Animal Life* (1892), chapter xviii., "The Evolution of Evolution Theories."

Spencer's historical position in regard to the Evolution-Idea.—In 1840, when Herbert Spencer was twenty, he bought Lyell's *Principles of Geology*—then recently published. His reading of Lyell was a fortunate incident, for one of the chapters, devoted to a refutation of Lamarck's views concerning the origin of species, had the effect of giving Spencer a decided leaning to them.

"Why Lyell's arguments produced the opposite effect to that intended, I cannot say. Probably it was that the discussion presented, more clearly than had been done previously, the natural genesis of organic forms. The question whether it was or was not true was more distinctly raised. My inclination to accept it as true in spite of Lyell's adverse criticisms, was, doubtless, chiefly due to its harmony with that general idea of the order of Nature towards which I had, throughout life, been growing. Super-naturalism, in whatever form, had never commended itself. From boyhood there was in me a need to see, in a more or less distinct way, how phenomena, no matter of what kind, are to be naturally explained. Hence, when my attention was drawn to the question whether organic forms have been specially created, or whether they have arisen by progressive modifications, physically caused and inherited, I adopted the last supposition; inadequate as was the evidence, and great as were the difficulties in the way. Its congruity with the course of procedure throughout things at large gave it an irresistible attraction; and my belief in it never afterwards wavered, much as I was in after years ridiculed for entertaining it" (*Autobiography*, i. p. 176).

Thus early convinced, Spencer did not remain a mute evolutionist. The idea was a seed-thought in his mind, and eventually it became the dominant one, bearing much fruit. In his early letters to the "Nonconformist" in 1842 on "The Proper Sphere of Government," "the only point of community with the general doctrine of Evolution is a belief in the modifiability of human nature through adaptation to conditions, and a consequent belief in human progression." But in his *Social Statics* (1850) there "may be seen the first step toward the general doctrine of Evolution." Thus he says, "The development of society as well as the development of man and the development of life generally, may be described as a tendency to individuate—*to become a thing*. And rightly interpreted, the manifold forms of progress going on around us are uniformly significant of this tendency."

It was a great moment in Herbert Spencer's intellectual life when in 1851 (*ætat.* 31) he first came across von Baer's formula "expressing the course of development through which every plant and animal passes—the change from homogeneity to heterogeneity." At the close of his *Social Statics* Spencer had indicated that progress from low to high types of society or organism implied an advance "from uniformity of composition to multiformity of composition." "Yet this phrase of von Baer, expressing the law of individual development, awakened my attention to the fact that the law which holds of the ascending stages of each individual organism is also the law which holds of the ascending grades of organisms of all kinds. And it had the further advantage that it presented in brief form, a more graphic image of the transformation, and thus facilitated further thought. Important consequences eventually ensued."

Von Baer's formula of embryonic development, which he regarded as a progress from the apparently simple to the obviously complex, and as the individual's condensed and modified recapitulation of racial history, accentuated and stimulated a thought already existing in Spencer's mind, and in part expressed. It gave objective vividness to the concept of development which Spencer had already realised in regard to societary forms. In 1864 he wrote to G. H. Lewis, "If anyone says that had von Baer never written I should not be doing that which I now am, I have nothing to say to the contrary —I should reply it is highly probable."

Herbert Spencer spoke of his early recognition of von Baer's law as one of the moments in his intellectual development. He realised objectively and vividly that out of an apparently simple and homogeneous stage of development, there is developed by division of labour and other processes, a wondrous complexity of nervous, muscular, glandular, skeletal, and connective tissues or organs, as the case may be. Organic development is not like crystallisation; it is heteromorphic crystallisation, so to speak. From a group of apparently similar cells, heterogeneous tissues and organs are developed. Thus von Baer as an embryologist gave Spencer as a general evolutionist a concrete basis for the concept of development which was simmering in his mind.

Von Baer's Law.—It does not appear, however, that Spencer ever read von Baer's embryological memoirs, else he might have been less well-satisfied with summing up individual development as a progress from homogeneity to heterogeneity. Von Baer was much more cautious than some of his followers and expositors, and subsequent research has justified his caution. The once popular "Recapitulation Doctrine" that a developing organism "climbs up its own genealogical tree," that "ontogeny recapitulates phylogeny," is now seen to be true only in a very general way, and with many saving clauses. The germ is now known as a unified mosaic of ancestral contributions, as a multiplex of potentialities; it is even visibly very complex and anything but homogeneous or "simple"; and the individual recapitulation of racial history is verifiable rather in the stages of organogenesis than in the history of the embryo as a whole. Thus while all are agreed that there is a gradual emergence of the obviously complex from the apparently simple, that development means progressive differentiation and integration, and that past history is *in some measure* resumed in present development, it must also be allowed that germ-cells are microcosms of complexity, that development is the realisation of a composite inheritance, the cashing of ancestral cheques, and that the "minting and coining of the chick out of the egg" is not adequately summed up as "a progress from homogeneity to heterogeneity."

But although embryology does not appear to us to give unequivocal support to Spencer's formula of progress from the homogeneous to the heterogeneous, it seemed all plain sailing to him, and he proceeded to illustrate the utility of his formula by applying it to all orders of facts. In a famous passage in the essay on "Progress: its Law and Cause" (*Essays*, vol. i., 1883, p. 30) he wrote as follows:—

"We believe we have shown beyond question that that which the German physiologists (von Baer, Wolff, and others) have found to be the law of organic development (as of a seed into a tree and of an egg into an animal) is the law of all development. The advance from the simple to the complex, through a process of successive differentiations (i.e. the appearance of differences in the parts of a seemingly like substance), is seen alike in the earliest changes of the Universe to which we can reason our way back; and in the earlier changes which we can inductively establish; it is seen in the geologic and climatic evolution of the Earth, and of every simple organism on its surface; it is seen in the evolution of Humanity, whether contemplated in the civilised individual, or in the aggregation of races; it is seen in the evolution of Society in respect alike of its political, its religious, and its economical organisation; and it is seen in the evolution of all those endless concrete and abstract products of human activity which constitute the environment of our daily life. From the remotest past which Science can fathom up to the novelties of yesterday, that in which Progress essentially consists is the transformation of the homogeneous into the heterogeneous." This was written in 1857.

As far back as 1852 Spencer contributed to the 'Leader' an essay on the 'Development Hypothesis' which is one of the most noteworthy of the pre-Darwinian presentations of the general idea of evolution. Supposing that there are some ten millions of species, extant and extinct, he asks "which is the most rational theory about these ten millions of species? Is it most likely that there have been ten millions of special creations? or is it most likely that by continual modifications, due to change of circumstances, ten millions of varieties have been produced, as varieties are being produced still?… Even could the supporters of the Development Hypothesis merely show that the origination of species by the process of modification is conceivable, they would be in a better position than their opponents. But they can do much more than this. They can show that the process of modification has effected, and is effecting, decided changes in all organisms subject to modifying influences…. They can show that in successive generations these changes continue, until ultimately the new conditions become the natural ones. They can show that in cultivated plants, domesticated animals, and in the several races of men, such alterations have taken place. They can show that the degrees of difference so produced are often, as in dogs, greater than those on which distinctions of species are in other cases founded. They can show, too, that the changes daily taking place in ourselves—the facility that attends long practice, and the loss of aptitude that begins when practice ceases—the strengthening of passions habitually gratified, and the weakening of those habitually curbed—the development of every faculty, bodily, moral, or intellectual according to the use made of it—are all explicable on this same principle. And thus they can show that throughout all organic nature there *is* at work a modifying influence of the kind they assign as the cause of these specific differences; an influence which, though slow in its action, does, in time, if the circumstances demand it, produce marked changes—an influence which, to all appearance, would produce in the millions of years, and under the great varieties of condition which geological records imply, any amount of change."

While Spencer did not discern the modifying influence of Natural Selection, which it was reserved for Darwin and Wallace to disclose, his clear presentation of the general doctrine of evolution seven years before the publication of the "Origin of Species" (1859) should not be forgotten.

In other essays before 1858 and in his *Principles of Psychology* (1855), Spencer championed the evolutionist position, and the first programme of his "Synthetic Philosophy" was drawn up in January 1858.

Arguments for the Evolution-Doctrine.—The idea that the present is the child of the past and the parent of the future, that what we see around us is the long result of time, that there has been age-long progress from relatively simple beginnings—the evolution-formula in short—is now part of the intellectual framework of most educated men with a free mind. We no longer trouble to argue about it; like wisdom it is justified of its children. It has afforded a modal interpretation of the world's history, an interpretation that works well, which no facts are known to contradict. It has been the most effective organon of thought that the world has known; it is becoming organic in all our thinking.

We cannot indeed give an evolutionary account of the origin of life, or of consciousness, or of human reason; we cannot read the precise pedigree of many of the forms of life; we are in great doubt as to the *modus operandi* by which familiar results have been brought about, but all this ignorance does not diminish our confidence in the scientific value of the general evolution-idea. It may be that there are some primary facts, such as life and consciousness, which we must be content to postulate as at present irresoluble data, but it is also certain that our inquiry into the *factors of evolution* is still very young. So much has been done in half a century, since serious ætiology began, that it is premature to say *ignorabimus* where we must confess *ignoramus*.

It seems possible to give a provisional evolutionist account of so many of "the wonders of life," as Haeckel calls them, that there are few nowadays who will maintain that, given certain postulates, a scientific interpretation of nature is impossible. This is what the doctrine of special creation or creations implies; it means an abandonment of the scientific interpretation of nature as a hopeless task.

If the evolution key failed to open the doors to which we apply it, then there would be justification for a rehabilitation of the creationist doctrine, but the reverse is the case. To some minds, notably Mr Alfred Russel Wallace, the problems of the origin of life, of consciousness, and of man's higher qualities seem so hopelessly far from scientific interpretation, that a combination of evolutionism with a moiety of creationism appears necessary. But as we are only beginning to know the scope and efficacy of the factors of evolution, and are not without hope of discovering other factors, this dualism seems premature.

Evolution and Creation.—But while the Evolution-Doctrine is now admitted as a valid and useful genetic formula, it was far otherwise when Spencer was writing his *Principles of Biology* (1864-6). Then the doctrine of descent was struggling for existence against principalities and powers both temporal and spiritual, and then it was still relevant to pit it against the theory of special creations. Yet for a younger generation it is difficult to appreciate the warmth of Spencer's chapter on the Special-Creation hypothesis (§ 109-§ 115 of vol. i. of the original edition of *The Principles of Biology*).

"The belief in special creations of organisms is a belief that arose among men during the era of profoundest darkness; and it belongs to a family of beliefs which have nearly all died out as enlightenment has increased. It is without a solitary established fact on which to stand; and when the attempt is made to put it into definite shape in the mind, it turns out to be only a pseud-idea. This mere verbal hypothesis, which men idly accept as a real or thinkable hypothesis, is of the same nature as would be one, based on a day's observation of human life, that each man and woman was specially created—an hypothesis not suggested by evidence, but by lack of evidence—an hypothesis which formulates absolute ignorance into a semblance of positive knowledge."…

"Thus, however regarded, the hypothesis of special creations turns out to be worthless—worthless by its derivation; worthless in its intrinsic incoherence; worthless as absolutely without evidence; worthless as not supplying an intellectual need; worthless as not satisfying a moral want. We must therefore consider it as counting for nothing, in opposition to any other hypothesis respecting the origin of organic beings."

The appreciation of the evolution-formula in the minds of thoughtful men has been greatly modified—for the better—since the early Darwinian days of hot-blooded controversy, when Spencer was a prominent champion of the new way of looking at things. The special-creation hypothesis has almost ceased to find advocates who know enough about the facts to bring forward arguments worthy of consideration, and by a legitimate change of front on the part of theologians it has come to be recognised that the evolution-formula is not antithetic to any essential transcendental formula. Naturalists, on the other hand, recognise that the Evolution-formula is no more than a genetic description, that it does not pretend to give any ultimate explanations, that as such it has nothing whatever to do with such transcendental concepts as almighty volition, and that it has no quarrel with the modern theological view of creation as the institution of the primary order of nature—the possibility of natural evolution included. Thus Spencer's destructive attack on the Special-Creation hypothesis has now little more than historical interest. And for this result, we have in part to thank Spencer himself, who made the precise point at issue so definitely clear.

The general theory of organic evolution—the theory of Descent—tacitly makes the assumption, which is the basal hope of all biology, that it is not only legitimate but promiseful to try to interpret scientifically the history of life upon the earth. It formulates the idea that the present phase of being is the natural and necessary outcome of a previous, on the whole, simpler phase of being, and so on, backwards and forwards in time, under the operation of more or less clearly discernible natural factors and conditions—notably variation and heredity, selection and isolation. Tested a thousand times, the general evolution-formula seems to cover the facts, it gives them a new rationality, it applies to minutiose details as well as to the general progress of life, it even affords a basis for verified prophecy. The formula is a key that fits all locks, though it has not yet, because of our fumbling fingers, opened all.

But just here, as Spencer pointed out, there is a parting of the ways, and there is no *via media*, no compromise. Is there no hopefulness in trying to give a scientific account of the nature and history and genesis of the confessedly vast and perplexing orders of facts which we call Physical Nature, Animate Nature, and Human Nature?—then let us become agnostics pure and simple, or let us remain philosophers or theologians, poets or artists, and sigh over an impetuous science which started so much in debt that its bankruptcy was a foregone conclusion!

On the other hand, if the scientific attempt at interpretation is legitimate, and if it has already made good progress (considering its youth), and if its results, achieved piecemeal, always make for greater intelligibility, then let us give the scientific, *i.e.*, evolutionist formulation its due; let us rigidly exclude from our science all other than scientific interpretations; let us cease from juggling with words in attempting a mongrel mixture of scientific and transcendental formulation; let us stop trying to eke out demonstrable factors, such as variation and selection, by assuming alongside of these, "ultra-scientific causes," "spiritual influxes," *et hoc genus omne*; let us cease writing or reading books such as *God or Natural Selection*, whose titular false antinomy is an index of the bathos of their misunderstanding. To place scientific formulæ in opposition to transcendental formulæ is to oppose "incommensurables," and to display an ignorance of what the aim of science really is.

Logically, the antithesis is between the possibility or the impossibility of giving a scientific interpretation of the world around us (and ourselves). The hypothesis of special creations is irrelevant until the scientific interpretation is shown to be inadequate or fallacious.

Arguments for the Evolution-Doctrine.—But what, it may be asked, is the evidence substantiating the formula of organic evolution, and compelling us to accept it? To this question, we propose to give in brief resumé Spencer's answer, but it is impossible to refrain from observing that the question involves some measure of misunderstanding. The evolution theory, as a modal formula, is just a particular way of looking at things; it is justified wherever it is applied; it makes for progress whenever it is utilised; but it cannot be proved by induction or experiment like the law of gravitation or the doctrine of the conservation of energy. Fritz Müller said that he would be content to stake the evolution theory on a study of butterflies alone, and he was right. The formula is justified by its detailed applicability; there are not any special evidences of evolution; any set of facts in regard to organisms well worked-out illustrates the general thesis. At the same time, it is possible to classify the different ways in which the Evolution-Idea fits the facts, and this is what Spencer did in his presentation of the "arguments for evolution"—a presentation which has never been surpassed in clearness, though every illustration has been multiplied many times since 1866.

I. The Arguments from Classification. Spencer started with the fact that naturalists have utilised resemblances in structure and development as a basis for the orderly classification of organisms in groups within groups—varieties, species, genera, families, races, and so on. But "this is the arrangement which we see arises by descent, alike in individual families and among races of men." "Where it is known to take place evolution actually produces these feebly-distinguished small groups and these strongly-distinguished great groups." "The impression made by these two parallelisms, which add meaning to each other, is deepened by the third parallelism, which enforces the meaning of both—the parallelism, namely, that as, between the species, genera, orders, classes, etc., which naturalists have formed, there are transitional types; so between the groups, sub-groups, and sub-sub-groups, which we know to have been evolved, types of intermediate values exist. And these three correspondences between the known results of evolution (as in human races, domesticated animals, and cultivated plants) and the results here ascribed to evolution have further weight given to them by the fact, that the kinship of groups through their lowest members is just the kinship which the hypothesis of evolution implies." "Even in the absence of these specific agreements, the broad fact of unity amid multiformity, which organisms so strikingly display, is strongly suggestive of evolution. Freeing ourselves from pre-conceptions, we shall see good reason to think with Mr Darwin, "that propinquity of descent—the only known cause of the similarity of organic beings—is the bond, hidden as it is by various degrees of modification, which is partly revealed to us by our classifications" (*Principles of Biology*, Rev. Ed. vol. i. p. 448).

II. Arguments from Embryology. Organisms may be arranged on a tree which symbolises their structural affinities and divergences. On the evolutionist interpretation this is an adumbration of the actual genealogical tree or *Stammbaum*. But when we consider the facts of embryology we find that the developing organism advances from stage to stage by steps which are more or less comparable to the various levels and branchings of the classificatory tree. There is a resemblance, sometimes a parallelism, between individual development and the grades of organisation which have or have had persistent stability as living creatures. "On the hypothesis of evolution this parallelism has a meaning—indicates that primordial kinship of all organisms, and that progressive differentiation of them which the hypothesis alleges. On any other hypothesis the parallelism is meaningless." It is true that there are nonconformities to the general law that individual development tends to recapitulate racial history, or that ontogeny tends to recapitulate phylogeny. There may be in the individual development condensations or telescopings of the presumed ancestral stages, and there may be an interpolation of developmental stages which are adaptive to peculiar conditions of juvenile life and have no historical import, but the deviations are such as may be readily interpreted on the evolution-hypothesis (*Principles of Biology*, i. pp. 450-467).

III. Arguments from Morphology. In back-boned animals from frog to man there is a great variety of fore-limb, adapted for running, swimming, flying, grasping, and so forth, but throughout there is a unity of structure and development. There are the same fundamental bones and muscles, nerves and blood vessels, and the early stages are closely similar. So it is throughout organic nature; there is unity of type, maintained under extreme dissimilarities of form and mode of life. This is "explicable as resulting from descent with modification; but it is otherwise inexplicable." "The likenesses disguised by unlikenesses, which the comparative anatomist discovers between various organs in the same organism, are worse than meaningless if it be supposed that organisms were severally framed as we now see them; but they fit in quite harmoniously with the belief that each kind of organism is a product of accumulated modifications upon modifications. And the presence, in all kinds of animals and plants, of functionally-useless parts corresponding to parts that are functionally-useful in allied animals and plants, while it is totally incongruous with the belief in a construction of each organism by miraculous interposition, is just what we are led to expect by the belief that organisms have arisen by progression."

IV. Arguments from Distribution.—"Given that pressure which species exercise on one another, in consequence of the universal overfilling of their respective habitats—given the resulting tendency to thrust themselves into one another's areas, and media, and modes of life, along such lines of least resistance as from time to time are found—given besides the changes in modes of life, hence arising, those other changes which physical alterations of habitats necessitate—given the structural modifications directly or indirectly produced in organisms by modified conditions; and the facts of distribution in space and time are accounted for. That divergence and re-divergence of organic forms, which we saw to be shadowed forth by the truths of classification and the truths of embryology, we see to be also shadowed forth by the truths of distribution. If that aptitude to multiply, to spread, to separate, and to differentiate, which the human races have in all times shown, be a tendency common to races in general, as we have ample reason to assume; then there will result those kinds of spacial relations and chronological relations among the species, and genera, and orders, peopling the Earth's surface, which we find exist. The remarkable identities of type discovered between organisms inhabitating one medium, and strangely modified organisms inhabiting another medium, are at the same time rendered comprehensible. And the appearances and disappearances of species which the geological record shows us, as well as the connections between successive groups of species from early eras down to our own, cease to be inexplicable" (*Principles of Biology*, i. p. 489).

"Thus," Spencer concludes, "of these four groups each furnished several arguments which point to the same conclusion; and the conclusion pointed to by the arguments of any one group, is that pointed to by the arguments of every other group. This coincidence of coincidences would give to the induction a very high degree of probability, even were it not enforced by deduction. But the conclusion deductively reached is in harmony with the inductive conclusion."

CHAPTER XI

AS REGARDS HEREDITY

Problems of Heredity—Physiological Units—A Digression—The Germ-Cells—Transmission of Acquired Characters—Inconceivability—A Priori Argument—Practical Conclusion

Heredity is the relation of genetic continuity which links generation to generation. An inheritance is all that the organism is or has to start with on its life-journey in virtue of the hereditary relation to parents and ancestors. In all ordinary cases, the inheritance has its initial material basis in the egg-cell and the sperm-cell which unite in fertilisation at the beginning of a new life, and these two kinds of germ-cells, which bear the maternal and the paternal contributions, have their peculiar virtue of reproducing like from like, just because they are the unchanged or very slightly changed cell-descendants of the fertilised ova from which the parents arose. A bud or a cutting separated off from a living creature—tiger-lily or potato, polyp or worm—reproduces an entire organism like the parent, if the appropriate nurture-conditions are available; and it can do so because it is a fair sample of the parental organisation. Similarly a germ-cell or two germ-cells in conjunction can develop into a creature like the parent or parents, in virtue of being the condensed essence of the parental organisation. And the germ-cell is this because of its direct continuity through undifferentiating cell-divisions with the original germ-cell from which the parental body developed.

Even in ancient times men pondered over the resemblances and differences between children and their parents—for like only *tends* to beget like—and wondered as to the nature of the bond which links generation to generation. But although the problems are old, the precise study of them is altogether modern. The first great step towards clearness was the formulation of the cell-theory by Schwann and Schleiden (1838-9), by Goodsir and Virchow, which made it clear that all but the simplest organisms are built up of cells or modifications of cells, and that the individual life usually begins as a fertilised egg-cell which proceeds by division and re-division, by differentiation and integration, to develop a more or less complex "body." It has become gradually clear that while the fertilised egg-cell gives rise to body-cells which become specialised, it also gives rise to unspecialised descendant-cells, which take no share in body-making, but become the germ-cells—the potential starting-points of another generation. A second great step was the accumulation of facts of inheritance showing that all sorts of qualities innate or inborn in the parents, essential and trivial, normal and abnormal, bodily and mental, may be transmitted to the offspring as part of the organic heritage. A third great step was implied in the acceptance which Darwin in particular won for the general idea of descent, for it is hardly too much to say that the scientific study of the problems of heredity began when it was recognised that heredity is a fundamental condition of evolution.

Problems of Heredity.—In regard to Heredity there are three large problems which tower above the crowd of more detailed problems. The *first* is: In what way are the germ-cells peculiar, how do they differ from ordinary cells, what gives them their unique reproductive power, how do they come to be such marvellous units that their development results in a new organism? Only two answers have been suggested: (1) that the germ-cells become receptacles of representative samples from the different parts of the body (the pangenetic theory), and (2) that the germ-cells owe their unique character to the fact that they are, along lines of undifferentiated cell-lineage, the direct descendants of the fertilised ova of the parents (the theory of germinal continuity). Thanks, largely, to Weismann, the second view has prevailed over the first, for which there is little factual basis.

The *second* large problem is as to the way in which it may be supposed that the hereditary qualities are represented in the germ-cell. Is the germ-cell an extremely complex chemical mixture without pre-formed architecture, which, as it lives and grows, gradually gives rise to heterogeneous elements, differentiating along diverse lines according to their diverse relations to one another and to their surrounding conditions? Or is it from the first a complex architecture, an intricate organisation of a large number of items representing particular qualities, a mosaic of inheritance-bearers?

The *third* large problem is as to the modes in which the inheritance, normally bi-parental, and in some sense always a mingling of ancestral contributions, can express itself. Sometimes the expression is one-sided, sometimes it is a blend. The mother may look out of one eye, and the father out of another, or the grandfather may be re-incarnated. By inter-breeding hybrids pure types may be got, *or* reversions, *or* "an epidemic of variations." This is the problem of the diverse modes of hereditary transmission, which we know in some cases to be expressible in a formula, such as Mendel's law or Galton's law, and for which we can sometimes hazard a hypothetical physiological interpretation.

Physiological Units.—To each of these three problems Spencer made a contribution. He started with the legitimate and fertile hypothesis of "physiological units"—the ultimate life-bearing elements, intermediate between the chemical molecules and the cell. Just as the same kinds and even the same number of atoms compose by different arrangements numerous quite different chemical molecules, *e.g.* in the protein-group, so out of similar molecules diversely grouped an immense variety of "physiological units" may be evolved. Out of the same pieces of coloured glass one may get in the kaleidoscope a very large number of distinct patterns, so in the course of nature similar molecules, grouping themselves differently, have formed a very large number of distinct "physiological units." The grouping is not merely positional and static as in the kaleidoscope; it is dynamic and vital. Since Spencer sketched his idea in 1864 many biologists have thought of units intermediate between the chemical molecules and the cell, and the number of different names which have been bestowed upon them is extraordinary, each voyager re-naming his discovery, ignorant of or ignoring those who had previously sailed the same seas. This recognition of "physiological units" was a natural step in analysis as soon as it began to be recognised that the cell was a little world in itself, a "firm" with many partners. While we cannot agree with Delage that "Spencer est le vrai père de la conception initiale," since Brücke expressed the same idea in 1861, Spencer's exposition in 1864 was quite independent, and it has not found the recognition it deserved.

It should be noted that the "gemmules" which Darwin assumed in his provisional hypothesis of pangenesis to be given off by the various cells of the body, were supposed to be of innumerable unlike kinds, whereas in Spencer's argument "the implication everywhere is that the physiological units are all of one kind."

It is admitted that the molecules of a crystallisable substance have more or less mysterious relations to one another—"polarities" as we call them—which result in definite crystalline forms appearing in definite conditions, with a certain amount of diversity as everyone may see in snow-crystals, and as is more precisely known in the case of certain substances which have several forms of crystallisation. But just as chemical molecules have in virtue of their organisation (always dynamic as well as static) certain prescribed modes of relating themselves to others like themselves, and building up a beautiful integrate, a crystal, so, as Spencer pointed out, the "physiological units" have their "polarities," *i.e.* their inherent constitutional tendencies to build up forms along with their fellows. Here we have two useful suggestions, (1) that development is like an elaborate organic crystallisation, only much more energetically dynamic, and (2) that the big fact of heredity—that like tends to beget like—has its parallel in the way in which a minute fragment of a crystal can in the appropriate environment of a solution of the same substance build up a crystal like the original form from which it was separated. Germ-cells are potential samples of the organisation which is expressed in the parent, but Spencer did not advance to the more distinctively modern position which recognises that they are separated off rather from the fertilised ovum which gave rise to the parent's body than from that body itself. The parental body is the trustee rather than the producer of the germ-cells.

A Digression.—Here we must digress a little to compare Spencer's conception of physiological or constitutional units with Weismann's conception of the Germ-Plasm. According to Weismann, there is in the nuclei of the germ-cells a distinctive physical basis of inheritance, the germ-plasm. It is the vehicle of the hereditary qualities, the architectural substance which enables the germ-cell to build up an organism; it has an extremely complex and at the same time persistent structure. Following a hypothesis of De Vries, he supposed that the readily stainable nuclear bodies (the chromosomes or idants) consist of a colony of invisible self-propagating vital units or *biophors*, each of which has the power of expressing in development some particular quality. He supposed that these biophors are aggregated into units of a higher order, known as *determinants*, one for each structure of the body which is capable of independent variation. These determinants are supposed to be grouped together in *ids*, each of which is supposed to possess a complete complement of the specific characters of the organism and also to have an individual character. The *ids* are arranged in linear series to form the visible *idants* or chromosomes, which will be slightly different from one another according to the individualities of the component ids. When the fertilised egg- cell develops, it gives rise (1) to *somatic* cells which carry with them part of the germ-plasm, and differentiate to form the body, and (2) to the *germ* cells which reserve part of the germ-plasm in an unchanged state, and eventually give rise in appropriate conditions to new individuals *and their germ-cells*.

Spencer refused to accept the contrast between *body*-cells and *germ*-cells as expressing a fact, and referred for his reasons to the numerous cases in which small pieces of a plant or polyp may grow into an entire organism. But when he represented Weismann as maintaining that the "soma contains in its components none of those latent powers possessed by those of the germ-plasm," he did not do justice to the comprehensive theory of the "Germ-plasm." For Weismann assumes that in certain cases the body-cells, even though differentiated, may carry with them some residual unused-up germ-plasm.

When a lizard regrows a lost tail—effectively responding to a casualty which has been common for untold generations—Weismann interprets the mechanism of this as due to a reserve of tail-determinants resident at or near the place of breakage, and localised there as the result of a long-continued process of selection. A chamæleon does not regenerate its tail, and this may be interpreted in terms of the selection-theory, since the chamæleon with its tail coiled up or embracing a branch has not been, in the course of its evolution, subjected to the frequently recurrent casualty which has beset most other lizards. Spencer said, "We cannot arbitrarily assume that wherever a missing organ has to be reproduced there exists the needful supply of determinants representing that organ," but Weismann made no such arbitrary assumption. Many organs are lost which are not regenerated, even when, as far as materials or differentiation are concerned, it would be easy to replace them. Why the everywhere present uniform physiological units that Spencer believed in should not replace them, we do not know; but if the distribution of regenerative determinants has been wrought out by selection, we understand the facts.

Spencer said that the hypothesis of a supply of determinants lying latent at or near the seat of injury, and able to reproduce the missing part in all its details, and to do this several times over, was "a strong supposition." We venture to think that the hypothesis that the same result is achieved by the "physiological units," which are all of the same kind, is a weak supposition. Spencer said: "Reproduction of the lost part would seem to be a normal result of the proclivity towards the form of the entire organism." But it is difficult to see why "proclivity of the physiological units towards the form of the entire organism" should bring about the regeneration of a tail here and a head there, a claw here and an eye there. But Spencer was too acute a thinker not to feel that if the theory of regenerative determinants was "incompetent," his own theory, which interpreted regeneration as due to the activity of physiological units, "with a proclivity towards the organic form of the species," did not cover the facts; *e.g.* the establishment of "false-joints," where the ends of a broken bone failing to unite remain movable one upon the other. Therefore he suggested a qualification of his hypothesis.

In "the social organism," it is often seen that the components of an aggregate "have their activities and arrangements mainly settled by local conditions." "A local group of units, determined by circumstances towards a certain structure, coerces its individual units into that structure." In an emigrant settlement, "individuals are led into occupations and official posts, often quite new to them, by the wants of those around—are now influenced and now coerced into social arrangements which, as shown perhaps by gambling saloons, by shootings at sight, and by lynchings, are scarcely at all affected by the central government. Now the physiological units in each species appear to have a similar combination of capacities. Besides their general proclivity towards specific organisation, they show us abilities to organise themselves locally; and these abilities are in some cases displayed in defiance of the general control, as in the supernumerary finger or the false joint. Apparently each physiological unit, while having in a manner the whole organism as the structure which, along with the rest, it tends to form, has also an aptitude to take part in forming any local structure, and to assume its place in that structure under the influence of adjacent physiological units" (*Principles of Biology*, revised edition, i. p. 364).

The experiments of Born and others have shown that fragments of a young tadpole may go on developing to some extent after they are cut off, and that the undifferentiated rudiment of a limb may be successfully grafted on to another tadpole. "In brief, we may say that each part is in chief measure autogenous." "Though all parts are composed of physiological units of the same nature, yet everywhere, in virtue of local conditions and the influence of its neighbours, each unit joins in forming the particular structure appropriate to its place." This conclusion is very interesting when compared with that reached more inductively by many embryologists (of the so-called epigenetic school), namely, that what a blastomere or cleavage-cell of an egg does, is determined by its intra-embryonic environment, by its relations, both statical and dynamical, to the whole organisation of which it forms a part. As Driesch puts it: "The relative position of a blastomere in the whole determines in general what develops from it; if its position be changed, it gives rise to something different; in other words, its prospective value is a function of its position." But those who assume heterogeneous determinants do not thereby exclude what truth there may be in this view that what an early blastomere does is a function of its inter-relations.

But let us consider how much Spencer puts to the credit of his "constitutional units." (1) They carry within them the traits of the species and even some of the traits of the ancestors of the species, the traits of the parents and even some of the traits of their immediate ancestors, and the congenital idiosyncrasies of the individual itself. In this they resemble the germ-plasm.
(2) They "must be at once in some respects fixed and in other respects plastic; while their fundamental traits, expressing the structure of the type, must be unchangeable, their superficial traits must admit of modification without much difficulty; and the modified traits, expressing variations in the parents and immediate ancestors, though unstable, must be considered as capable of becoming stable in course of time." Again they resemble the germ-plasm. (3) Once more, "we have to think of these physiological units (or constitutional units as I would now re-name them) as having such natures that while a minute modification, representing some small change of local structure, is inoperative on the proclivities of the units throughout the rest of the system, it becomes operative in the units which fall into the locality where that change occurs." Here they part company from the germ-plasm, except in so far as it may be said that the development of the distributed determinants is in part dependent on local conditions. (4) Finally, since Spencer supposed "an

unceasing circulation of protoplasm throughout an organism," such that "in the course of days, weeks, months, years, each portion of protoplasm visits every part of the body"—a wild assumption—"we must conceive that the complex forces of which each constitutional unit is the centre, and by which it acts on other units while it is acted on by them, tend continually to re-mould each unit into congruity with the structures around: superposing on it modifications answering to the modifications which have arisen in these structures. Whence is to be drawn the corollary that in the course of time all the circulating units—physiological, or constitutional if we prefer so to call them—visit all parts of the organism; are severally bearers of traits expressing local modifications; and that those units which are eventually gathered into sperm-cells and germ-cells also bear these superposed traits."

This theory—which is not unlike a combination of Darwin's pangenesis with De Vries's neo-pangenesis—is very significant, for it discloses Spencer's hypothesis as to the *modus operandi* of the transmission of acquired characters. But there is unfortunately no factual warrant for the assumption that the constitutional units visit one another in various corners of the body, getting impressions as they go, or for the assumption that they are eventually gathered into the germ-cells—an assumption which shows how far Spencer deliberately stood from the conception of the continuity of the germ-plasm. Even if we suppose an organism to undergo numerous modifications in different parts of its body, as a plant may do when it is transferred from the Alps to the lowlands; even if we suppose the constitutional units—which are all of one kind—to circulate and become bearers of the traits expressing local modifications, we have to face other questions: do they all become remoulded in relation to all the modifications? or do some become remoulded in relation to one modification and some in relation to another? or do all the modifications so hang together that one kind of alteration impressed upon the constitutional units covers them all? The difficulties of the conception of constitutional-units certainly do not seem less than the difficulties of the conception of specific determinants.

Even to the general reader, who is not concerned with the problem of the mechanism of inheritance and development, who has a shrewd suspicion that it is one of those things no fellow can understand, our digression should be interesting, for it illustrates Spencer's fertility of invention and his adroitness in lugging in one hypothesis after another to eke out a theory which in its first statement appears to be very simple. It is instructive to observe how the constitutional units at first so harmlessly simple, grow under the conjurer's hands until they become more marvellous than Clerk Maxwell's "sorting demons."

But it is more instructive still to hear the conclusion of the whole matter. "At last then we are obliged to admit that the actual organising process transcends conception. It is not enough to say that we cannot know it; we must say that we cannot even conceive it. And this is just the conclusion which might have been drawn before contemplating the facts. For if, as we saw in the chapter on "the Dynamic Element in Life," it is impossible for us to understand the nature of this element—if even the ordinary manifestations of it which a living body yields from moment to moment are at bottom incomprehensible; then still more incomprehensible must be that astonishing manifestation of it which we have in the initiation and unfolding of a new organism." "Thus all we can do is to find some way of symbolising the process so as to enable us most conveniently to generalise its phenomena; and the only reason for adopting the hypothesis is that it best serves this purpose."

But the hypothesis only serves the purpose because the constitutional units are gradually invested with the powers of effective response, co-ordination, and the like which remain the secret of the organism as a whole—the secret of life, which many think will never be read until we recognise that it is also the secret of mind.

The Germ-Cells.—According to Spencer, "sperm-cells and germ-cells are essentially nothing more than vehicles in which are contained small groups of the physiological units in a fit state for obeying their proclivity towards the structural arrangement of the species they belong to," and "if the likeness of offspring to parents is thus determined, it becomes manifest, *a priori*, that besides the transmission of generic and specific peculiarities, there will be a transmission of those individual peculiarities which, arising without assignable causes, are classed as spontaneous." Not only are the main characters transmitted, the same may be true of even minute details—varietal characters, like the taillessness of Manx cats, and individual congenital peculiarities such as a sixth finger; normal qualities such as swiftness in race- horses, abnormal qualities such as nervousness in man. Here Spencer was of course at one with all biologists.

Transmission of Acquired Characters.—He went on, however, to try to substantiate the proposition, which has been the subject of so much discussion, that modifications or acquired bodily characters are also transmissible, and we must follow his argument carefully.

He first points out that when a structure is altered by a change of function the modification is often unobtrusive, and its transmission consequently difficult to detect. "Moreover, such specialities of structure as are due to specialities of function, are usually entangled with specialities which are, or may be, due to selection, natural or artificial. In most cases it is impossible to say that a structural peculiarity which seems to have arisen in offspring from a functional peculiarity in a parent, is wholly independent of some congenital peculiarity of structure in the parent, whence this functional peculiarity arose. We are restricted to cases with which natural or artificial selection can have had nothing to do, and such cases are difficult to find. Some, however, may be noted."

When a plant is transferred from one soil to another it undergoes "a change of habit"; its leaves may become hairy, its stem woody, its branches drooping. "These are modifications of structure consequent on modifications of function that have been produced by modifications in the actions of external forces. And as these modifications reappear in succeeding generations, we have, in them, examples of functionally-established variations that are hereditarily transmitted." But this is a *non sequitur*, since the modifications may reappear merely *because they are re-impressed directly* on each successive generation.

Spencer notes that in the domestic duck the bones of the wing weigh less and the bones of the leg more in proportion to the whole skeleton than do the same bones in the wild duck; that in cows and goats which are habitually milked the udders are large; that moles and many cave-animals have rudimentary eyes, and so on. But all these results may be readily interpreted as due to selection of germinal variations.

The best examples of inherited modifications occur, he says, in mankind. "Thus in the United States the descendants of the immigrant Irish lose their Celtic aspect, and become Americanised.... To say that 'spontaneous variation' increased by natural selection can have produced this effect is going too far." But if the vague statement as to the Americanisation of the Irishman be correct, and if it be true that intermarriage is rare, it remains probable that the Americanisation is a modificational veneer impressed afresh on each successive generation.

"That large hands are inherited by those whose ancestors led laborious lives, and that those descended from ancestors unused to manual labour commonly have small hands, are established opinions." But if we accept the fact, it is easy to interpret the size of the hands as a stock-character correlated with a muscularity and vigour, and established by selection. The prevalence of short-sightedness among the "notoriously studious" Germans is a singularly unfortunate instance to give in support of the inheritance of functional modifications, for there is no reason to believe that short-sightedness is primarily an acquired character. Nor is it confined to readers.

Spencer twits those who are sceptical as to the transmission of acquired modifications, for assigning the most flimsy reasons for rejecting a conclusion they are averse to; but when Spencer cites the inheritance of musical talent and a liability to consumption as evidence of the transmission of functional modifications, we are reminded of the pot calling the kettle black.

Spencer made his position stronger by adducing what he calls *negative* evidence, namely those "cases in which traits otherwise inexplicable are explained if the structural effects of use and disuse are transmitted."

(1) First he refers to the co-adaptation of co-operative parts. With the enormous antlers of a stag there is associated a large number of co-adaptations of different parts of the body, and similarly with the giraffe's long neck and the kangaroo's power of leaping. Spencer argued that the co-adaptation of numerous parts cannot have been effected by natural selection, but might be effected by the hereditary accumulation of the results of use. The difficulty is to discover how much deep-seated co-adjustment can be effected by exercise even in the course of a long time, and the theory requires such data before it can be more than a plausible interpretation, with certain *a priori* difficulties against it. If an animal suddenly takes to leaping many individual adjustments to the new exercise will arise; if the animals of successive generations leap yet more freely, they will individually acquire more thorough adjustments up to a certain limit; meanwhile there may arise constitutional variations making towards adaptation to the new habit, and under the screen of the individual modifications these may increase from minute beginnings till they acquire selection-value. Professors Mark Baldwin, Lloyd Morgan, and Osborn, have all made the same useful suggestion that adaptive modifications acquired individually may act as the fostering nurses of constitutional variations in the same direction until these coincident variations are large enough in amount to be themselves effective.

(2) Secondly, Spencer dwelt upon the notably unlike powers of tactile discrimination possessed by the human skin, and sought to show that while these could not be interpreted on the hypothesis of natural selection or on the correlated hypothesis of panmixia, they could be interpreted readily if the effects of use are inherited. But the difficulty again is to get secure data. It is uncertain how much of the inequality in tactile sensitiveness is due to individual exercise and experience, though it is certain that tactility in little-used parts can be greatly increased by use. Nor is it certain how much of the apparent unlikeness in tactility is due to unequal distribution of peripheral nerve-endings and how much to specialised application of the power of central perception. As Prof. Lloyd Morgan says: "We do not yet know the limits within which education and practice may refine the application of central powers of discrimination within little-used areas. The facts which Mr Spencer

adduces may be in large degree due to individual experience; discrimination being continually exercised in the tongue and finger-tips, but seldom on the back or breast. We need a broader basis of assured fact." Nor, it may be added, is the action of selection to be excluded.

(3) Spencer's third set of negative evidences was based on rudimentary organs which, like the hind limbs of the whale, have nearly disappeared. Dwindling by natural selection is here out of the question; and dwindling by panmixia, i.e. the diminution of a structure when natural selection ceases to affect its degree of development, "would be incredible, even were the assumptions of the theory valid." But as a sequence of disuse the change is clearly explained. Prof. Lloyd Morgan replies: "Is there any evidence that a structure really dwindles through disuse in the course of individual life? Let us be sure of this before we accept the argument that vestigial organs afford evidence that this supposed dwindling is inherited. The assertion may be hazarded that, in the individual life, what the evidence shows is that, without due use, an organ does not reach its full functional or structural development. If this be so, the question follows: How is the mere absence of full development in the individual converted through heredity into a positive dwindling of the organ in question?" Moreover, the convinced Neo-Darwinian is not in the least prepared to abandon the theory of dwindling in the course of panmixia, especially in the light which Weismann's conception of Germinal Selection has thrown on this process.

The inductive evidence in support of the conclusion that bodily modifications due to use or disuse or environmental influence can be as such or in any representative degree transmitted, is very weak. The so-called evidences are often anecdotal and vague, often irrelevant and fallacious, and those Spencer adduced are by no means convincing. Let us consider the question briefly from the *a priori* side.

The general argument *against* the hypothesis rests on a realisation of the continuity of the germ-plasm. For if the germ-plasm, or the material basis of inheritance within the germ-cells, be somewhat apart from the general life of the body, often segregated at an early stage, and in any case not directly sharing in the every day metabolism, then there is a presumption against the likelihood of its being readily affected in a specific manner by changes in the nature of the body-cells. The germ-cell is in a sense so apart that it is difficult to conceive of the mechanism by which it might be influenced in a specific or representative manner by changes in the cells of the body.

On the other hand, in many plants and lower animals, the distinction between body-cells and germ-cells is far from being demonstrably marked, and even in higher animals we cannot think of the germ-cells as if they led a charmed life uninfluenced by any of the accidents and incidents in the daily life of the body which is their nurse, though not exactly their parent. No one believes this, Weismann least of all, for he finds one of the chief sources of germinal variation in the nutritive stimuli exerted on the germ-plasm by the varying state of the body. The organism is a unity; the blood and lymph and other body-fluids form a common internal medium; various poisons may affect the whole system, germ-cells included; and there are real though dimly understood correlations between the reproductive system and the rest of the organism.

There are some who pretend to find in this admission "a concealed abandonment of the central position of Weismann," for if, they say, the germ-plasm is affected by changes in nutrition in the body, and if acquired characters affect changes in nutrition, then "acquired characters or their consequences will be inherited." But it is a quite illegitimate confusion of the issue to slump acquired characters and their consequences as if the distinction was immaterial. The illustrious author of the *Germ-Plasm* has made it quite clear that there is a great difference between admitting that the germ-plasm has no charmed life, insulated from bodily influences, and admitting the transmissibility *of a particular acquired character*, even in the faintest degree. The whole point is this: Does a change in the body, induced by use or disuse or by a change in surroundings, influence the germ-plasm in such a specific or representative way that the offspring will exhibit the same modification which the parent acquired, or even a tendency towards it? Even when we fully recognise the unity of the organism, or recognise it as fully as we know how, it is difficult to suggest any *modus operandi* whereby a particular modification in, say, the brain or the thumb can specifically affect the germinal material in such a way that the modification or a tendency towards it becomes part of the inheritance. Did we accept Darwin's provisional hypothesis of pangenesis according to which the parts of the body give off gemmules which are carried as samples to the germ-cells, the possibility of transfer might seem more intelligible. But Darwin's suggestion remains a pure hypothesis, and is admitted by none except in extremely modified form. In fairness, however, we must note how little we understand of the *modus operandi* of influences which certainly pass in the other direction, from the reproductive organs to the body; we must recall Prof. Lloyd Morgan's warning that although we cannot conceive how a modification might as such saturate from body to germ-cells, this does not exclude the possibility that it may actually do so.

As a matter of fact, Spencer has himself suggested a *modus operandi*—as already outlined. The constitutional units are supposed to circulate; when they come to a modified organ and visit its modified constitutional units, they are supposed to be themselves impressed; they are supposed to be "eventually gathered into sperm-cells and germ-cells," which thus come to bear the "superposed traits" resulting from modification. But, as we have seen, the difficulty is to find any basis in fact on which these assumptions can rest. Indeed, they are contradictory to well-established physiological facts.

Inconceivability.—In reference to the difficulties which beset theories of heredity, Spencer remarks:—

"If it is said that the mode in which functionally-wrought changes, especially in small parts, so affect the reproductive elements as to repeat themselves in offspring, cannot be imagined—if it be held inconceivable that those minute changes in the organ of vision which cause myopia can be transmitted through the appropriately modified sperm-cells or germ-cells; then the reply is that the opposed hypothesis presents a corresponding inconceivability. Grant that the habit of a pointer was produced by selection of those in which an appropriate variation in the nervous system had occurred; it is impossible to imagine how a slightly different arrangement of a few nerve-cells and fibres could be conveyed by a spermatozoon. So too it is impossible to imagine how in a spermatozoon there can be conveyed the 480,000 independent variables required for the construction of a single peacock's feather, each having a proclivity towards its proper place. Clearly the ultimate process by which inheritance is effected in either case passes comprehension; and in this respect neither hypothesis has an advantage over the other."

Let us consider what Spencer has said in regard to "inconceivability." Most ova are very minute cells, often microscopically minute, and a spermatozoon may be only 1/100,000th of the ovum's size—inconceivably minute, but yet exceedingly real and potent. We cannot conceive how a complex inheritance made up of numerous contributions is potentially contained in such small compass, and yet in some form it must be. Similarly, we cannot conceive how the pin-head like brain of the ant contains all the ant's "wisdom."

Those who find it difficult to believe that items so minute as the germ-cells can have room for the complexity of hereditary organisation which seems to be a necessary postulate may be reminded of three things: (1) They should recall what students of physics have told us in regard to the fineness, or, from another point of view, the coarse-grainedness of matter. They tell us that the picture of a Great Eastern filled with framework as intricate as that of the daintiest watches does not exaggerate the possibilities of molecular complexity in a spermatozoon, whose actual size is usually very much less than the smallest dot on the watch's face.

(2) It should be remembered that in development one step conditions the next, and one structure grows out of another, so that there is no need to think of the microscopic germ-cells as stocked with more than *initiatives*. (3) It should be remembered that every development implies an interaction between the growing organism and a complex environment without which the inheritance would remain unexpressed, and that the full-grown organism includes much that was not as such inherited, but has been individually acquired as the result of nurture or external influence.

Now, returning to Spencer, we find that by an extraordinary argument he concludes that the number of determinants required for the development of a single feather in the peacock's tail must be 480,000, and he points to the inconceivability of these being contained, along with much else of course, in the spermatozoon. We are not at present concerned with the precise number of determinants, but we can see no reason why a spermatozoon should not contain millions if they were needed. The inconceivability is a general one; it is due to the difficulty of imaging the complexity of matter.

But the inconceivability of a particular modification of the nose affecting the germ-cells in a specific and representative way is a different kind of inconceivability. It is due to our being unable to imagine any reasonable *modus operandi* consistent with our knowledge of the structure and metabolism of the organism. As we have seen and emphasised Spencer does himself suggest a *modus operandi*, but it seems to us to make unwarranted assumptions, and is for that reason to us "inconceivable."

A Priori Argument.—But Spencer advanced an *a priori* argument to strengthen the position which he felt bound to hold—the transmissibility of acquired characters. "That changes of structure caused by changes of action must be transmitted, however obscurely, appears to be a deduction from first principles—or if not a specific deduction, still, a general implication. For if an organism A, has, by any peculiar habit or condition of life, been modified into the form A', it follows that all the functions of A', reproductive function included, must be in some degree different from the functions of A." [This, we venture to think, must depend on the nature and amount of the modification.] "An organism being a combination of rhythmically-acting parts in moving equilibrium, the action and structure of any one part cannot be altered without causing alterations of action and structure in all the rest." [The appreciability of the change will depend on the amount and nature of the modification, and on the intimacy of the correlation subsisting in the organism. Dislodging a rock may alter the centre of gravity of the earth, but it does not do so appreciably.] "And if the organism A, when changed to A', must be changed in all its functions; then the offspring of A' cannot be the same as they would have been had it retained the form A." [Assuming that is to say that the change in the physiological units of the body affects the physiological units in the germ-cells.] "That the change in the offspring must, other things equal, be in the same direction as the change in the parent, appears implied by the fact that the change propagated throughout the parental system is a change towards a new state of equilibrium—a change tending to bring the actions of all organs, reproductive included, into harmony with these new actions." [It seems to us to pass the wit of man to conceive how or why an improved equilibrium in the use of the hand should involve any corresponding or representative change of equilibrium in the germ-cells.]

Spencer seems to have seen the matter quite clearly. If the physiological units in the germ-cell mould the aggregate organism, the organism modified by incident actions will impress some corresponding modifications on the structures and polarities of its units. And if the physiological units are in any degree so remoulded as to bring their polar forces towards equilibrium with the forces of the modified aggregate, then, when separated in the shape of reproductive centres, these units will tend to build themselves up into an aggregate modified in the same direction.

The drawback to abstract biology based on first principles is that it enables its devotee to develop arguments which seem plausible until they are reduced to the concrete. Why had Herbert Spencer small hands? Because his grandfather and father were schoolmasters who did little from day to day but wield the pen and sharpen the pencil! Through disuse of the sword and the spade their hands were directly equilibrated towards smallness. But since Mr Spencer senior, was "a combination of rhythmically-acting parts in moving equilibrium," the dwindling of the hands and the moulding of the physiological units thereof reverberated through the whole aggregate; a change towards a new state of equilibrium "was propagated throughout the parental system—a change tending to bring the actions of all organs, reproductive included, into harmony with these new actions," or inactions. The modified aggregate impressed some corresponding modification on the structures and polarities of the germ-units. And this was why Herbert Spencer had small hands. At least so he tells us, for the instance is his own.

Practical Conclusion.—It is obvious that we have not in these pages attempted to give an adequate discussion of an extremely difficult problem. We have endeavoured to give a fair statement of Spencer's position in regard to a question which appeared to him of "transcendent importance." "A right answer to the question whether acquired characters are or are not inherited, underlies right beliefs, not only in Biology and Psychology, but also in Education, Ethics, and Politics." "A grave responsibility rests on biologists in respect of the general question; since wrong answers lead, among other effects, to wrong beliefs about social affairs and to disastrous social actions."

It cannot be an easy question this, when we find Spencer on one side and Weismann on the other, Haeckel on one side and Ray Lankester on the other, Turner on one side and His on the other. Therefore while it seems to us that the transmission of acquired characters as strictly defined is non-proven, and while there seems to us to be a strong presumption that they are not transmitted, the scientific position should remain one of active scepticism— leading on to experiment.

And if there is little scientific warrant for our being other than sceptical at present as to the transmission of acquired characters, this scepticism lends greater importance than ever, on the one hand, to a good "nature," to secure which is the business of careful mating; and, on the other hand, to a good "nurture," to secure which for our children is one of our most obvious duties, the hopefulness of the task resting upon the fact that, unlike the beasts that perish, man has a lasting external heritage, capable of endless modification for the better, a heritage of ideas and ideals embodied in prose and verse, in statue and painting, in Cathedral and University, in tradition and convention, and above all in society itself.

CHAPTER XII

FACTORS OF ORGANIC EVOLUTION

Variation—Selection—Isolation—Spencer's   Contribution—External Factors—Internal Factors—Direct Equilibration—Indirect Equilibration

Darwin rendered three great services to evolution-doctrine, (1) By his marshalling of the evidences which suggest the doctrine of descent, he won the conviction of the biological world. (2) He applied the evolution-idea to various sets of facts, not only to the origin of species in general, but to the difficult case of Man; not only to the origin of the countless adaptations with which organic nature is filled, but to particular problems such as the expression of the emotions; and in so doing he corroborated the evolution- formula by showing what a powerful organon it is. (3) Along with Alfred Russel Wallace, he elaborated the theory of natural selection, which disclosed one of the factors in the evolution-process.

As we have seen, Herbert Spencer preceded Darwin in his championing of the doctrine of descent, to which the natural mood of his mind, and the influences of Lamarck and von Baer had led him to give his adhesion. He also applied the evolution-formula to an even wider series of facts than Darwin ventured to touch, viz., to the inorganic world and to psychological and sociological facts. It remains to be seen what his position was in regard to the Factors of Organic Evolution.

Spencer's position may be more clearly defined if we first sketch the answer which most biologists would at present give to the question—What are the factors of Organic Evolution?

Variation.—Postulating the powers of growing and reproducing, of acting on and reacting to the environment, postulating also heredity without which no organic evolution is possible, biologists distinguish two sets of factors in the evolution process. On the one hand there are *originative factors* which produce those changes in living creatures which make them different from their fellows. These changes or observed differences are of two kinds—(*a*) they may have their origin in the arcana of the germ and be inborn *variations* (germinal, constitutional, endogenous, etc.), or (*b*) they may be acquired *modifications* wrought on the body of the individual by environmental influences or by use and disuse (somatic, acquired, exogenous, etc.). Thus "modifications" or "acquired characters" may be defined as structural changes in the body of the individual organism, directly induced by changes in the environment or in the function, and such that they transcend the limit of organic elasticity and persist after the inducing causes have ceased to operate. Merely transient changes which disappear soon after their cause has ceased to operate may be conveniently called "adjustments." Now when we subtract from the total of observed differences between individuals of the same stock, all the modifications and adjustments which we can distinguish as such by their being causally related to some alteration in function or environment, we have a remainder which we call "variations." We cannot causally relate them to differences in habit or surroundings, they are often hinted at even before birth, and they are not alike even among forms whose conditions of life seem absolutely uniform. This distinction between *modifications* and *variations*, though clear in theory, is not always readily drawn in practice, but it is of great importance, for while all innate variations, except complete sterility, are transmissible, and thus may form the raw materials of progress, there is no secure evidence that acquired characters or somatic modifications are transmissible. Therefore, the latter, though very important for the individual, and indirectly important for the race, cannot be assumed (without further proof) as directly important in the transmutation of species.

As to the nature and frequency of inborn variations, Biology has recently begun to accumulate precise observations, and has renounced the bad habit of simply postulating variability without statistically or otherwise defining it. Life is so abundant and so Protean that biologists have tended to draw cheques upon Nature as if they had unlimited credit, scarce waiting in their impetuosity to see whether these are honoured, but the very title—*Biometrika*
—of a new journal shows that the science is emerging from the slough of vagueness in which, to the physicists' contempt, it has so long floundered. All science begins with measurement, and one of the great steps that have been made of recent years is in the tedious, but necessary task of recording the variations which do actually occur. From these we can argue with a clear intellectual conscience back to what may have been. One result is plain, that variation is a very general fact of life; whenever we settle down to measure we find that specific diagnoses are averages, that specific characters require a curve of frequency for their expression, that a living organism is usually like a Proteus. There are no doubt long-lived, non-plastic, conservative types, such as Lingula, where no visible variability can be detected (even in untold ages if we consider the hard parts preservable as fossils), but to judge from these as to the rate of evolutionary change is like estimating the rush of a river from the eddies of a sheltered pool. Another result is that it becomes possible to distinguish between *continuous* variations, which are just like stages in continuous growth, in which the descendant has a little more or a little less of a given character than its parents had, and *discontinuous* variations in which a

new combination appears suddenly without gradational stages, and with no small degree of perfection. Although there is truth in Lamarck's dictum that "Nature is never brusque," although Jack-in-the-box phenomena are rare, the evidence, *e.g.* of Bateson and De Vries, as to the frequent occurrence of discontinuous variations appears conclusive. Such words as "freaks" and "sports" express a truth, suggested by Mr Galton's phrase "transilient variations," that organisms may pass with seeming abruptness from one form of equilibrium to another. There is evidence that these sudden and discontinuous variations—"mutations" many of them are called—are often very heritable, that when they appear they come to stay; and it seems likely, especially from facts of breeding and cultivation, that these mutations, rather than the minute "fluctuating" variations, have supplied the raw material on which selection has chiefly operated in the evolution of species.

It also becomes more and more evident that the living creature may vary as a unity, so that if there is more of one character there is less of another, and so that one change brings another in its train. It seems as if the organism as a whole—through its germinal organisation, of course—may suddenly pass from one position of organic equilibrium to another. Thus we are not shut up to the assumption of the piecemeal variation of minute parts; there is greater definiteness and less fortuitousness in variation than was previously supposed. We begin, from actual data, to see the truth of the view which Goethe and Nägeli suggested, that the evolution of organisms is pre- eminently a story of self-differentiating and self-integrating growth,— cumulative, selective, definite, and harmonious—like crystallisation. As to the *origin* of variations, it must be admitted that until we know the actual facts better, we cannot expect to know much in regard to their antecedents. Many suggestions have been made, some of which may be summarised.

There is something comparable to the First Law of Motion to be read out of the persistence of characteristics from generation to generation. Like tends to beget like. But while the relation of genetic continuity which links generation to generation tends to ensure this persistence, it presents no more than a curb to the occurrence of variation. While complete and perfect inheritance and complete and perfect expression of that inheritance in development would mean the absence of variation, there are many reasons why this completeness of hereditary resemblance is rare. For the inheritance seems to consist of sets of hereditary qualities not in duplicate merely but in multiplicate; they are not all of equal strength or of equal stability; there may be a struggle amongst them; and they are subject to changes induced by the changes in the complex nutritive supply which the parental body—their bearer—affords.

A variation, which makes its possessor different from the parents, is often interpretable as due to some incompleteness of inheritance or in the *expression* of the inheritance. It seems as if the entail were sometimes broken in regard to a particular characteristic. Oftener, perhaps, as the third generation shows, the inheritance has been complete enough potentially, but the young creature has been prevented from realising its entire legacy. Contrariwise, it may be that the novelty of the newborn is seen in an intensifying of the inheritance, for the contributions from the two parents may, as it were, corroborate one another.

But in many cases a variation turns up which we must call *novel*, some peculiar mental pattern, it may be, which spells originality, some structural change which suggests a new departure. We tentatively interpret this as due to some fresh permutation or combination of the complex substances which form the material basis of inheritance, and are mingled from two sources at the outset of every life sexually reproduced. It is not merely in an intermingling of maternal and paternal contributions that a life begins, but of legacies through the parents from remoter ancestors. The permutations and combinations may be due to a struggle between the elements which are the bearers of the heritable qualities, or they may be due to fluctuations in the nutritive stream which the body supplies to its germ-cells. It must be remembered that the hereditary material is very complex, and that it has a complex environment within the parental body. In spite of its essential architectural stability, it may have a tendency to instability as regards minor details, and we may perhaps find the change-exciting stimuli in the ceaseless nutritive oscillations within the body, while the mode of restoring a disturbed equilibrium may be through a germinal struggle among the different sets of minute elements which we may call the heritage-bearers. The idea of germinal selection has been elaborated with great subtlety by Prof. Weismann.

Nor does it seem to us legitimate to exclude the possibility that the germ-cell, or the germ-plasm as the essential part of it, may *grow* into a slightly more differentiated and integrated unity before it begins its task of development. For the power of growth is characteristic of everything living. Enough has been said, however, to indicate how uncertain is the voice of biology in answering the fundamental questions as to the nature and origin of variations.

Selection.—The first and most important of the *directive factors* is natural selection, and the most distinctive contribution which Darwin and Wallace made to ætiology was to show how selection works and what it can effect. The process admits of brief statement.

Variability is a fact of life, the members of a family or species are not born alike; some may have qualities which give an advantage both as to hunger and love; others are relatively handicapped. But a struggle for existence, as

Malthus called it, is also a fact of life, necessitated especially by two facts—first, that two parent organisms usually produce many more than two children organisms, and that population thus tends to outrun the means of subsistence; and, secondly, that organisms are at the best only relatively well-adapted to the complex and changeful conditions of their life. This struggle expresses itself not merely as an elbowing and jostling around the platter of subsistence, but at every point where the effectiveness of the response which the living creature makes to the stimuli playing upon it, is of critical moment. As Darwin said, though many seem to have forgotten, the phrase "struggle for existence" must be used "in a wide and metaphorical sense." It includes much more than an internecine scramble for the necessities of life; it includes all endeavours for and all changes that make towards preservation and welfare, not only of the individual, but of the offspring as well. In many cases, indeed, the struggle for existence both among men and beasts is fairly described as an endeavour after well-being, and what may have been primarily self-regarding impulses become replaced by others which are distinctively species- maintaining, the self failing to find full realisation apart from its kin and society.

Now, in this struggle for existence, which has so many expressions, the relatively less fit to the present conditions tend to be eliminated. Though the process may work out progress, as measured by degree of differentiation and integration, by increasing freedom and fullness of life, and has doubtless done so, yet until we come to its highest forms in subjective and finally rational selection, it works not towards an ideal but towards a relative fitness to present conditions. And this may spell degeneration, as in parasites, when an extrinsic standard is used. Tapeworms may be just as fit to survive as golden eagles. Again, the process of elimination does not necessarily mean that the handicapped variants come at once to a violent end, as when rat devours rat, or the cold decimates a flock of birds in a single night; it often simply means that the less fit die before the average time, and are less successful than their neighbours as regards pairing and having offspring. Moreover, although the selective process is primarily eliminative or destructive, like thinning turnips or pruning fruit-trees, we cannot separate its positive and negative aspects. That nothing succeeds like success is continually verifiable in nature, the fit variant gets a start just as surely as the unfit variant is handicapped; there is favouring and fostering just because there is sifting and singling.

Given variations and given some mode of selection in the manifold struggle for existence, the argument continues, then the result will be in Spencer's phrase "the survival of the fittest." And since many variations are transmitted from generation to generation, and may, through the pairing of similar or suitable mates, be gradually increased in amount and stability, the eliminative or selective process works towards the establishment of new adaptations and the origin of new species.

Darwin thought chiefly of the struggle between individuals—either between fellows of the same kin or between fellow-kin and foreign foes—and of the struggle between organisms and the inanimate environment. He also emphasised the sexual selection which occurs (*a*) when rival males fight or otherwise compete for the possession of a desired mate or mates, and in so doing reduce the leet, and (*b*) when the females appear to choose their mates from amid a crowd of suitors. While many now doubt if the range and effectiveness of preferential mating is so great as Darwin believed, there seems no reason to doubt that this mode of selection has been a factor in evolution. There are facts which warrant us in saying that *das ewig weibliche* plays a part in the upward march of life, that Cupid's darts as well as Death's arrows have evolutionary significance.

Even more important, however, are other extensions of the selection-idea. There may be struggle between groups as well as between individuals, as when one ant-colony goes to war with another, and there may be struggle of the parts within the organism just as there is struggle between organisms. There is struggle when one ovum survives in an ovary by devouring all its sister-cells, as in the case of *Hydra* and *Tubularia*, and, after allowing a wide margin for chance, there may be some form of selection among the crowd of spermatozoa encompassing the egg which only one will fertilise, just as there is some form of selection among the many drones which pursue the queen- bee in her nuptial flight. Weismann has carried the selection-idea to a logical finesse in his theory that there may be a struggle between the different sets of hereditary qualities in the germ-cell, or that there is a process of "germinal selection" at the very beginning of the individual life. There are, we admit, great differences between the struggle of hereditary items and the struggle of large parts within the organism; between intra-organismal and inter- organismal struggle; between the competition of individuals and the struggle against physical nature; between personal selection and the conflict of races; between objective and subjective selection; but, as it seems to us, they may be all expressed in the same formula if it is useful so to do.

Isolation.—In organic evolution variation supplies the materials which some form of selection sifts. But besides selection another directive factor has been indicated in what is called the theory of isolation. A formidable objection to the Darwinian doctrine, first clearly stated by Professor Fleeming Jenkin, is that variations of small amount and sparse occurrence would tend to be swamped out by inter-crossing before they had time to accumulate and gain stability. In artificial selection, the breeder takes measures to prevent this swamping-out by deliberately pairing similar or suitable forms together, or by deliberately removing unsuitable mateable forms; but what in Nature corresponds to the breeder?

It may be that similar variations occur in many individuals at once and many times over; it may be that many variations are not at first small in amount, but express big steps in organisation, as in Bateson's instances of Discontinuous Variation or in De Vries's instances of Mutation; it may be that many variations are not from the first unstable, but express changes of organic equilibrium which have come to stay if they get a chance at all; and it may be that the supposed swamping effects of inter-crossing are in part illusory, as is strongly suggested by some of the facts summed up in Mendel's Law; but there seems to be still room and need for the theory of Isolation worked out by Romanes, Gulick, and others.

They point out the great variety of ways in which, in the course of nature, the range of inter-crossing is restricted—*e.g.* by geographical barriers, by differences in habit, by psychical likes and dislikes, by reproductive variation causing mutual sterility between two sections of a species living on a common area, and so on. According to Romanes, "without isolation, or the prevention of free inter-crossing, organic evolution is in no case possible." The supporting body of illustrative facts is still unsatisfactorily small, but there seems sound sense in the idea.

An interesting corollary has been recently indicated by Professor Cossar Ewart. Breeding within a narrow range often occurs in nature, and often in human kind, being necessitated by geographical and other barriers. In artificial conditions, this in-breeding often results in the development of what is called prepotency. This means that certain forms have an unusual power of transmitting their peculiarities, even when mated with dissimilar forms, or, in other words, that some variations have a strong power of persistence. Therefore, wherever through in-breeding (which implies some form of isolation) prepotency has developed, there is no difficulty in understanding how even a small idiosyncrasy may come to stay, even although the bridegroom does not meet a bride endowed with a peculiarity like his own. Similarly, Dr A. Reibmayr has argued that the establishment of a successful human tribe or race involves periods of in-breeding (*i.e.*, marriage within a limited range of relationship), with the effect of "fixing" constitutional characteristics, and periods of cross-breeding (*i.e.* marriage between members of distinct stocks), with the effect of promoting a new crop of variations or initiatives.

Spencer's contribution.—Spencer was led to become an evolutionist by the workings of his own mind, influenced by Laplace's Nebular Hypothesis, by the transformist theory of Lamarck, by von Baer's law of individual development, and by Malthus's recognition of the struggle for existence in mankind. On the whole, it may be said that he came to the theory of organic evolution from above, rather than from below, from his studies on the intellectual and social evolution of man rather than from acquaintance with the biological data. Not unnaturally, therefore, he was to begin with a Lamarckian, believing in the cumulative transmission of the transforming results of use and disuse and of environmental influences.

In the essay on "a theory of Population" (1852) Spencer was within sight of one of the great doctrines of Darwinism. "From the beginning," he said, "pressure of population has been the proximate cause of progress." "The effect of pressure of population, in increasing the ability to maintain life, and decreasing the ability to multiply, is not a uniform effect, but an average one.... All mankind in turn subject themselves more or less to the discipline described; they either may or may not advance under it; but, in the nature of things, only those who *do* advance under it eventually survive.... For as those prematurely carried off must, in the average of cases, be those in whom the power of self-preservation is the least, it unavoidably follows that those left behind to continue the race, are those in whom the power of self-preservation is the greatest— are the select of their generation."

Here Spencer recognised the eliminative and selective effect of struggle in mankind. Why was he "blind to the fact," as he afterwards said, "that here was a universally-operative factor in the development of species"? In his *Autobiography* he gives two reasons for his oversight, one was his Lamarckian preconception that the inheritance of functionally-produced modifications sufficed to explain the facts of evolution. The other was, that he "knew little or nothing about the phenomena of variation," that "he had failed to recognise the universal tendency to vary."

Similarly, in his essay on "Progress: its Law and Cause" (1857), he still "ascribed all modifications to direct adaptations to changing conditions; and was unconscious that in the absence of that indirect adaptation effected by the natural selection of favourable variations, the explanation left the larger part of the facts unaccounted for" (*Autobiography*, i. p. 502).

In his article "Transcendental Physiology" (1857), Spencer advanced a step beyond the position occupied in his essay on "Progress." He showed that with advance in the forms of life there is an increasing differentiation of them from their environments, that integration as well as differentiation is part of the developmental process, but the leading conception of the essay was "the instability of the homogeneous." This was recognised, like "the multiplication of effects," as a cause of progress, as "a principle holding not among organic phenomena only, but among inorganic and super-organic phenomena." It was in this essay also that he began to use the word "evolution" in place of the more teleological word "progress."

In the same year (1857) Spencer again approached the idea of selection as a directive factor in evolution. In an essay on "State Tamperings with Money and Banks" he gave among other reasons for reprobating grandmotherly legislation, that "such a policy interferes with that normal process which brings benefit to the sagacious and disaster to the stupid." "The ultimate result of shielding men from the effects of folly, is to fill the world with fools." "This was a tacit assertion, recalling like assertions previously made, that the survival of the fittest operates beneficially in society."

Darwin's *Origin of Species* appeared in 1859, and marked another step in Spencer's evolutionism. Hitherto, though he had several times approached the idea of Natural Selection, he had "held that the sole cause of organic evolution is the inheritance of functionally-produced modifications"; now it became clear to him that he was wrong, and that the larger part of the facts cannot be due to any such cause (*Autobiography*, ii. 50).

In 1864 Spencer definitely sought to assimilate the Darwinian idea of Natural Selection into his system. He had become convinced that the hereditary accumulation of functional modifications could not be the sole factor in organic evolution; he had recognised the importance and efficacy of Natural Selection as a directive agency thinning and "singling" the crop of variations which is always abundant; but he had not seen how to absorb "Natural Selection" into his general physical theory of evolution. It seemed "to stand apart as an unrelated process."

"The search for congruity led first of all to perception of the fact that what Mr Darwin called 'natural selection,' might more literally be called survival of the fittest. But what is survival of the fittest, considered as an outcome of physical actions?"

Spencer's answer was that the changes constituting evolution tend ever towards a state of equilibrium; on the way to this there are stages of "moving equilibrium"; some organisms have their moving equilibrium less easily overthrown than others; these are the fittest which survive; they are, in Darwin's language, the select which nature preserves; and thus "the survival and multiplication of the select becomes conceivable in purely physical terms, as an indirect outcome of a complex form of the universal redistribution of matter and motion" (*Autobiography*, ii. pp. 100-1). In short, natural selection is part of the universal process towards more stable equilibrium.

When formulating his views on the classification of the sciences and his reasons for dissenting from the philosophy of Comte, Spencer pointed out that all the concrete sciences under their most general aspects give accounts of the redistributions of matter and motion; and he asked the question, What is the universal trait of all such redistributions? His answer was that "increasing integration of matter necessitates a concomitant dissipation of motion, and that increasing amount of motion implies a concomitant disintegration of matter." Thus Evolution and Dissolution appeared "under their primordial aspects," and differentiations, with resulting increase of heterogeneity, were seen to be secondary not primary traits of evolution. So he arrived at his famous definition of evolution:— *"Evolution is an integration of matter and concomitant dissipation of motion, during which the matter passes from an indefinite, incoherent homogeneity to a definite, coherent heterogeneity; and during which the retained motion undergoes a parallel transformation"* (*First Principles*, p. 396).

Having illustrated the evolution of the evolution-theory in Spencer's mind, we pass to his final statement of the factors of organic evolution.

(1) *External Factors.*—He begins by pointing out that living creatures are in the grip of a complex environment, which acts on them and to which they react. And whether we think of the seasons or the climate, the soil or the sea, we find that this environment is intricately variable. Every kind of plant and animal may be regarded as for ever passing into a new environment, and with increasing fullness of life there is additional complexity in the incidence of external forces. Every increase of locomotive power, for instance, increases the multiplicity and multiformity of action and reaction between organism and environment. There are chemical, mechanical, dynamic, and animate influences which modify organisms, and as the actions of these several orders of factors are compounded, there is produced a geometric progression of changes increasing with immense rapidity. All through the ages living creatures have as it were been passing over a series of anvils on which the hammers of external forces play, with tunes of ever-increasing complexity.

(2) *Internal Factors.*—Passing to internal factors, Spencer started from the fact that organic matter is built up of very unstable complex molecules. "But a substance which is beyond all others changeable by the actions and reactions of the forces liberated from instant to instant within its own mass, must be a

substance which is beyond all others changeable by the forces acting on it from without." In any aggregate "the relations of outside and inside, and of comparative nearness to neighbouring sources of influences, imply the reception of influences that are unlike in quantity, or quality, or both; and it follows that unlike changes will be produced in the parts thus dissimilarly acted on." Thus arise differentiations of structure, a transition from a uniform to a multiform state, a passage from homogeneity to heterogeneity, and this must go on cumulatively. For "the more strongly contrasted the parts of an aggregate become, the more different must be their reactions on incident forces, and the more unlike must be the secondary effects which these initiate. This multiplication of effects conspires, with the instability of the homogeneous, to work an increasing multiformity of structure in an organism." Thus, if the head of a bison becomes much heavier, what a multiplication of effects— mechanical and physiological—must ensue on muscles and bones and blood-vessels. One modification brings another in its train; there are secondary and tertiary effects. And as the increasing assemblage of individuals arising from a common stock is thus liable to lose its original uniformity and to grow more pronounced in its multiformity, indirect effects follow from inter-crossing and from altered competitive conditions. Moreover, as times and seasons and ages pass, the environment goes on changing, and on previous complications wrought by incident forces, new complications are continually superimposed by new incident forces. Thus there is an almost continuous movement towards heterogeneity. But how is that kind of heterogeneity insured which is required to carry on life? How is the evolution directed?

(3) *Direct Equilibration.*—How is it that action and reaction between the organism and its environment bring about *effective adaptations*? Spencer's answer is that every change is towards a balance of forces, and can never cease until a balance of forces is reached. "Any unequilibrated force to which an aggregate is subject, if not of a kind to overthrow it altogether, must continue modifying its state until an equilibrium is brought about." Thus "there go on in all organisms, certain changes of function and structure that are directly consequent on changes in the incident forces—inner changes by which the outer changes are balanced, and the equilibrium restored." "That a new external action may be met by a new internal action, it is needful that it shall either continuously or frequently be borne by the individuals of the species, without killing or seriously injuring them; and shall act in such a way as to affect their functions." But as many of the environing agencies to which organisms have to be adjusted, either do not immediately affect the functions at all, or else affect them in ways that prove fatal, there must be at work some other process which equilibrates the actions of organisms with the actions

they are exposed to.

(4) *Indirect Equilibration.*—There are many very precise adaptations, *e.g.* in the not-living hard parts of many animals, which no ingenuity can interpret as the directly equilibrated results of incident forces. To interpret mimicry as due to direct equilibration is hopeless. Therefore, Spencer passed to what he called "indirect equilibration."

"Besides those perturbations produced in any organism by special disturbing forces there are ever going on many others—the reverberating effects of disturbing forces previously experienced by the individual, or by ancestors; and the multiplied deviations of function so caused implied multiplied deviations of structure." A directly induced modification induces correlated secondary and tertiary perturbations, and when two differently endowed parents are mated they will bequeath to their joint offspring "compound perturbations of function and compound deviations of structure, endlessly varied in their kinds and amounts." In short, Spencer postulated variations as indirect results of the action of incident forces.

As the individuals of a species are thus necessarily made unlike in countless ways and degrees, then amongst them "some will be less liable than others to have their equilibria overthrown by a particular incident force previously unexperienced... Inevitably, some will be more stable than others when exposed to this new or altered factor. That is to say, those individuals whose functions are most out of equilibrium with the modified aggregate of external forces, will be those to die; and those will survive whose functions happen to be most nearly in equilibrium with the modified aggregate of external forces. But this survival of the fittest implies the multiplication of the fittest. Out of the fittest thus multiplied there will, as before, be an overthrowing of the moving equilibrium wherever it presents the least opposing force to the new incident force. And by the continual destruction of the individuals least capable of maintaining their equilibria in presence of this new incident force, there must eventually be reached an altered type completely in equilibrium with the altered conditions." In short, Spencer incorporated the characteristic Darwinian idea of Natural Selection operating upon a crop of variations, and thus securing by the survival of the fittest an indirect equilibration.

In an ingenious way, to which we have already alluded, Spencer assimilated the theory of Natural Selection with his own formula of evolution. Let us recapitulate his argument. All the processes by which organisms are refitted to their ever-changing environments must be equilibrations of one kind or another, for change of every order is towards equilibrium, and life itself is a moving equilibrium between inner and outer actions—a continual adjustment of internal relations to external relations. The process called Natural Selection is literally a survival of the fittest; and "that is a maintenance of the moving equilibrium of the functions in presence of outer actions; implying the possession of an equilibrium which is relatively stable in contrast with the unstable equilibria of those which do not survive." ... "The conception of Natural Selection is manifestly one not known to physical science: its terms are not of a kind physical science can take cognisance of. But here we have found in what manner it may be brought within the realm of physical science."

It is to be feared that Spencer deluded himself as to the success of his *tour de force*. For he did not show that there is in inanimate nature anything corresponding to the struggle for existence, nor did he give any instances where the degree of effectiveness of response is of critical value in determining the survival of competing inanimate systems.

After pointing out that the various factors in organic evolution must be thought of as co-operating, Spencer considered their respective shares in producing the total result. Briefly stated, his conclusions were the following:

—

At first, the direct action of the physical environment was the only cause of change. "But as, through the diffusion of organisms and consequent differential actions of inorganic forces, there arose unlikenesses among them, producing varieties, species, genera, orders, classes, the actions of organisms on one another became new sources of organic modifications." The mutual actions of organisms became more and more influential, and eventually became the chief factors.

"Always there must have been, and always there must continue to be, a survival of the fittest: natural selection must have been in operation at the outset, and can never cease to operate! While organisms had small abilities of co-ordinating their actions and actively adjusting themselves, natural selection worked almost alone in moulding and remoulding organisms into fitness for their changing environments, but as activity increased and brains grew, the power of varying actions to fit varying requirements became considerable." "As fast as essential faculties multiply, and as fast as the number of organs which co-operate in any given function increases, indirect equilibration through natural selection becomes less and less capable of producing specific adaptations; and remains capable only of maintaining the general fitness of constitution to conditions. The production of adaptations by direct equilibration then takes the first place: indirect equilibration serving to facilitate it. Until at length, among the civilised human races, the equilibration becomes mainly direct: the action of natural selection being limited to the destruction of those who are too feeble to live, even with external aid."

Returning to our scheme of Originative and Directive Factors, let us inquire into Spencer's views regarding Variation and Selection.

Spencer recognised three causes of variation. *First* there is heterogeneity among progenitors which "generates new deviations by composition of forces"; in other words new patterns arise from the mingling of diverse hereditary contributions in fertilisation. *Secondly*, functional variation in the parents produces unlikeness in the offspring; those begotten under different constitutional states are different. In other words, fluctuations of nutrition in the parental body may cause variations in the germ-plasm. [In mammals there are also *modifications* produced during the pre-natal life of the offspring which are congenital in the sense that they are present at birth in latent or patent form, which do not, however, really affect the germ-plasm since they disappear in the third generation.] *Thirdly*, an organism exposed to a marked change of external conditions, may have its equilibrium altered, and the offspring may be influenced. "The larger functional variations produced by greater external changes, are the initiators of those structural variations which, when once commenced in a species, lead by their combinations and antagonisms to multiform results. Whether they are or are not the direct initiators, they must still be the indirect initiators."

But Spencer admitted that there were numerous minor so-called "spontaneous" variations, which could not be referred to the causes noticed above. He attributed these to the fact that no two ova, no two spermatozoa, can be identical, since the process of nutrition cannot be absolutely alike. Minute initial differences in the proportions of the physiological units will lead, during development, to a continual multiplication of differences. "The insensible divergence at the outset will generate sensible divergences at the conclusion." This is not different from the general idea that nutritive fluctuations in the body provoke variations in the complex germ-plasm, "still it may be fairly objected that however the attributes of the two parents are variously mingled in their offspring, they must in all of them fall between the extremes displayed in the parents. In no characteristic could one of the young exceed both parents, were there no cause of "spontaneous variation" but the one alleged. Evidently, then, there is a cause yet unfound."

Spencer's further answer was that the sperm-cells or egg-cells which any organism produces will differ from each other not quantitatively only but qualitatively, because inheritance is multiple. In some the paternal units, in another the maternal units, in another the grand-paternal or the grand- maternal units will give the impress. "Here, then, we have a clue to the multiplied variations, and sometimes extreme variations, that arise in races which have once begun to vary. Amid countless different combinations of units derived from parents, and through them from ancestors, immediate and remote—and the various conflicts in their slightly different organic polarities, opposing and conspiring with one another in all ways and degrees, there will from time to time arise special proportions causing special deviations. From the general law of probabilities it may be concluded that while these involved influences, derived from many progenitors, must, on the average of cases, obscure and partially neutralise one another; there must occasionally result such combinations of them as will produce considerable divergences from average structures; and at rare intervals, such combinations as will produce very marked divergences. There is thus a correspondence between the inferable results and the results as habitually witnessed."

In conclusion, after his wonted manner, Spencer pointed out that Variation, like everything else, is necessitated by the Persistence of Force. "The members of a species inhabiting any area cannot be subject to like sets of forces over the whole of that area. And if, in different parts of the area, different kinds or amounts or combinations of forces act on them, they cannot but become different in themselves and in their progeny. To say otherwise, is to say that differences in the forces will not produce differences in the effects; which is to deny the persistence of force."

Selection.—As we have seen, Spencer incorporated into his scheme the Darwinian concept of Selection, and sought to show that it could be included under the general concept of Evolution as "a continuous redistribution of matter and motion." "That natural selection is, and always has been, operative is incontestable.... The survival of the fittest is a necessity, its negation is incontestable."

That he did not take a narrow view of the process of Selection, which has so many forms and operates at so many levels, will be admitted; and we may illustrate this by showing that he had a prevision of what Roux called "intra-individual selection" or "intra-selection."

In his essay on "The Social Organism" (1860), he wrote:—

> "The different parts of a social organism, like the different parts of an individual organism, compete for nutriment; and severally obtain more or less of it according as they are discharging more or less duty." (See also *Essays*, i. 290.) And, again, in 1876, in his *Principles of Sociology*, he amplified his statement thus: "All other organs, therefore, jointly and individually, compete for blood with each organ,... local tissue formation (which under normal conditions measures the waste of tissue in discharging function) is itself a cause of increased supply of

materials… the resulting competition, not between units simply, but between organs, causes in a society, as in a living body, high nutrition and growth of parts called into the greatest activity by the requirements of the rest." And once more: "For clearly, if the survival of the fittest among organisms is a process of equilibration between actions in the environment and actions in the organism; so must the local modifications of their parts, external and internal, be regarded as survivals of structures, the reactions of which are in equilibrium with the actions they are subject to." Clearly Spencer had a prevision of what Roux calls "*Der Kampf der Theile im Organismus*" (The struggle of parts within the organism), and we have here another example of his biological insight. That Spencer was not far from the idea of a struggle between hereditary units, we see from the following passage: "In the fertilised germ we have two groups of physiological units, slightly different in their structures. These slightly different units severally multiply at the expense of the nutriment supplied to the unfolding germ—each kind moulding this nutriment into units of its own type. Throughout the process of development the two kinds of units, mainly agreeing in their proclivities and in the form which they tend to build themselves into, but having minor differences, work in unison to produce an organism of the species from which they were derived, but work in antagonism to produce copies of their respective parent-organisms. And hence ultimately results an organism in which traits of the one are mixed with traits of the other; and in which, according to the predominance of one or other group of units, one or other sex with all its concomitants is produced" (*Principles of Biology*, vol. i., revised ed., p. 315).

While Spencer had this wide appreciation of the scope of selection, he firmly held that biologists burdened it unjustifiably by disbelieving in the transmission of acquired characters, and, as we have seen, he gave a number of examples of phenomena which he believed the Darwinian theory minus the Lamarckian factor was quite inadequate to interpret. He went the length of saying: "Either there has been inheritance of acquired characters or there has been no evolution." Spencer indicated three general difficulties or limitations besetting the theory of Natural Selection.

(1) "The general argument proceeds upon the analogy between natural selection and artificial selection. Yet all know that the first cannot do what the last does. Natural Selection can do nothing more than preserve those of which the *aggregate* characters are most favourable to life. It cannot pick out those possessed of one particular favourable character, unless this is of extreme importance."

[It is admitted that we cannot prove that Natural Selection effected this or that result in the distant past, but we know that a process of discriminate elimination is a fact of life, and we argue from the present to the past. Given variations enough and time enough, it is difficult to put limits to the efficacy of selection. If in a race of birds fairly well adapted to the conditions of their life, variations occur in the length of wing, there is no theoretical difficulty in supposing that if a longer wing is advantageous, this particular favourable character may in the course of time become through selection the property of the whole race.]

(2) "In many cases a structure is of no service until it has reached a certain development; and it remains to account for that increase of it by natural selection which must be supposed to take place before it reaches the stage of usefulness."

[One variation is often correlated with another, and the stronger variation may afford *point d'appui* for the action of natural selection, and thus act as a cover for the incipient variation until that reaches the stage of usefulness and becomes itself of selection-value. What Spencer himself says in regard to the selection of aggregates rather than items, seems half the answer to his difficulty.

It has also been suggested that adaptive modifications may act as fostering nurses of germinal variations in the same direction. Let us suppose a country in which a change of climate made it year by year of the utmost importance that the inhabitants should become swarthy. Some individuals with a strong innate tendency in this direction would doubtless exist, and on them and their similarly endowed progeny, the success of the race would primarily, and might wholly depend. At the same time, there might be many individuals in whom the constitutional tendency in the direction of swarthiness was too weak and incipient to be of use. If these, or some of them, made up for their lack of natural swarthiness by a great susceptibility to acquired swarthiness, to becoming tanned by the sun, it is conceivable that this modification, though never taking organic root, might serve as a life-saving screen until coincident congenital variations in the direction of swarthiness had time to grow strong and become of selection value. We can also imagine that a stock without great mental ability might succeed, in conditions where a premium was put on brains, by their application and docility, till eventually innate variations in the direction of real cleverness became established in the stock. Similarly, many animals by increased 'will-power' or intelligence may survive until bodily variations of an adaptive kind arise to economise the higher energies. Here and everywhere we venture to say that the more anthropomorphic we can *reasonably* make our conception of organic evolution the truer it is likely to be.

A third answer to Spencer's second difficulty is afforded by Weismann's subtle theory of Germinal Selection.]

(3) "Advantageous variations, not preserved in nature as they are by the breeder, are liable to be swamped by crossing or to disappear by atavism."

[We have already referred to various answers to this difficulty—in terms of Isolation, Prepotency, and other conceptions. But the answer which will occur to everyone at the present time is in terms of "Mendelism," into a discussion of which we cannot enter. Suffice it to say, that for the cases with which he dealt, Mendel has given evidence that variations which arise suddenly and are discontinuous—mutations, as De Vries calls them—are not likely to be swamped by in-breeding with the normal form, and that he has given a reason why this swamping does not occur.]

In regard to the second directive factor—Isolation, Spencer had no criticism to offer. It seemed to him that "in whatever way effected, the isolation of a group subject to new conditions and in course of being changed, is requisite as a means to permanent differentiation."

But after allowing full play to variation and modification, selection and isolation, Spencer felt that "though all phenomena of organic evolution must fall within the lines indicated, there remain many unsolved problems." "We can only suppose that as there are devised by human beings many puzzles apparently unanswerable till the answer is given, and many necromantic tricks which seem impossible till the mode of performance is shown; so there are apparently incomprehensible results which are really achieved by natural processes. Or, otherwise, we must conclude that since Life itself proves to be in its ultimate nature inconceivable, there is probably an inconceivable element in its ultimate workings."

CHAPTER XIII

EVOLUTION UNIVERSAL

*The Starting-point—Inorganic Evolution—What Spencer tried to do—
Summary of his Evolutionism—Notes and Queries—The Origin of Life—
Evolution of Mind—Ascent of Man—The Scientific Position*

Every attempt to describe how our world has come to be as it is must begin somewhere. It must postulate an initial state of Being from which to start any particular chapter in the story of Becoming. How the simplest conceivable raw material began—if it ever began—the evolutionist cannot tell.

The Starting-point.—Spencer began as far back as his scientific imagination could take him—with "formless diffused matter." With this to start with, he utilised the "Nebular Hypothesis" of Laplace, which showed how the planetary system may have arisen by the diffused matter becoming aggregated through the force of attraction into different centres. This theory has been corroborated and improved by subsequent researches in thermodynamics and spectroscopy, and in a modified form it is very generally accepted. The researches of Sir Norman Lockyer on "Inorganic Evolution" (1900) and of M. Faye (Sur l'origine du monde, 2nd. ed., Paris 1885) have strengthened and broadened the foundation of Spencer's Evolutionism; many inquiries point to the idea that matter has a homogeneous constitution; and the recent revolutionary discoveries centred in "radio-activity" have given new life to the view that the eighty odd elements of the chemist have had a long history behind them, and have evolved from simple homogeneous units. The alchemists' dream seems to be coming true, for we hear whispers of the transmutation of elements. "It may be true," as Prof. R. K. Duncan says in his *New Knowledge* (1905) "that all bodily existence is but the manifestation of units of negative electricity lying embosomed in an omnipresent ether of which these units are, probably, a conditioned part."

Inorganic Evolution.—We cannot follow this fascinating new story of inorganic evolution, but we wish to point out that the progress of science since Spencer wrote his *First Principles* has tended to justify him in beginning with formless diffused homogeneous matter. Were that work being written to-day, it would have to be entirely recast. It would probably begin (as Prof. Duncan sketches) with units of negative electricity, assuming motion and carrying with them bound portions of the ether in which they are bathed, becoming corpuscles endowed with the primary qualities of matter superimposed upon those of electricity. "Corpuscles congregating into groups or various configurations constitute essentially the atoms of the chemical elements, locking up in these configurations super-terrific energies, and leaving but "a slight residual effect" as chemical affinity or gravitation with which we attempt to carry on the work of the world. These atoms, congregating in their turn as nebulæ and under the slight residual force of gravitation condense into blazing suns. The suns decay in their temperature and become ever more and more complex in their constitution as the atoms lock themselves into multiple forms. We then see these multiple atoms developing up into the molecules of matter to form a world. We see the molecules growing ever more and more complex as the world grows colder until we attain to organic compounds. We see these organic compounds united to form living beings and we see these living beings developing into countless forms, and, after æons of time, evolving into a dominant race which is Us" (*The New Knowledge*, pp. 252-3). Of course there is both imagination and faith in Prof. Duncan's "We see," but no one at all aware of recent advances will doubt that the scientific cosmogony is evolving rapidly, and that its movement is towards a fuller revelation of the Unity of Nature.

What Spencer tried to do.—Spencer's aim was to show that "our harmonious Universe once existed potentially as formless diffused matter, and has slowly grown into its present organised state." He sought to account for its growing "in terms of Matter, Motion, and Force." Of course he was careful to explain that "the interpretation of all phenomena in terms of Matter, Motion, and Force, is nothing more than the reduction of our complex symbols of thought, to the simplest symbols; and when the equation has been brought to its lowest terms the symbols remain symbols still." His common denominator for all phenomena was "Matter, Motion, and Force," but he also recognised a greatest common measure—"the unknown Cause co-extensive with all orders of phenomena," "the unknown Reality which underlies all things," "a Power of which the nature remains for ever inconceivable," and of which phenomena are merely the manifestations. But while he was technically an abstract Monist, he was practically a "mechanist," believing that it was feasible to redescribe all evolution in terms of mechanical categories. The scientific ideal to which he looked forward is expressed in the sentence: "Given the Persistence of Force, and given the various derivative laws of Force, and there has to be shown not only how the actual existences of the inorganic world necessarily exhibit the traits they do, but how there necessarily result the more numerous and involved traits exhibited by organic and super-organic existences—how an organism is evolved, what is the genesis of human intelligence, whence social progress arises?" (*First Principles*, p. 555). He looked forward to a unification of knowledge, to "*one science*, which has for its object-matter the continuous transformation which the universe undergoes." "Evolution being a universal process, one and continuous throughout all forms of existence, there can be no break, no change from one group of concrete phenomena to another without a bridge of intermediate phenomena."

Summary of Spencer's Evolutionism.—Spencer drew up the following summary for publication in Appleton's *American Cyclopædia.*[10]

[10] Quoted from Prof. W. H. Hudson's *Introduction to the Philosophy of Herbert Spencer*.

1. Throughout the universe, in general, and in detail, there is an unceasing redistribution of matter and motion.

2. This redistribution constitutes evolution where there is a predominant integration of matter and dissipation of motion, and constitutes dissolution where there is a predominant absorption of motion and disintegration of matter.

3. Evolution is simple when the process of integration, or the formation of a coherent aggregate, proceeds uncomplicated by otherprocesses.

4. Evolution is compound when, along with this primary change from an incoherent to a coherent state, there go on secondary changes, due to differences in the circumstances of the different parts of the aggregate.

5. These secondary changes constitute a transformation of the homogeneous into the heterogeneous—a transformation which, like the first, is exhibited in the universe as a whole and in all (or nearly all) its details—in the aggregate of stars and nebulæ; in the planetary system; in the earth as an inorganic mass; in each organism, vegetal or animal (von Baer's law); in the aggregate of organisms throughout geologic time; in the mind; in society; in all products of social activity.

6. The process of integration, acting locally as well as generally, combines with the process of differentiation to render this change, not simply from homogeneity to heterogeneity, but from an indefinite homogeneity to a definite heterogeneity; and this trait of increasing definiteness, which accompanies the trait of increasing heterogeneity, is, like it, exhibited in the totality of things, and in all its divisions and sub-divisions down to the minutest.

7. Along with this redistribution of the matter composing any evolving aggregate there goes on a redistribution of the retained motion of its components in relation to one another; this also becomes, step by step, more definitely heterogeneous.

8. In the absence of a homogeneity that is infinite and absolute, this redistribution, of which evolution is one phase, is inevitable. The causes which necessitate it are:—

9. The instability of the homogeneous, which is consequent upon the different exposures of the different parts of any limited aggregate to incident forces. The transformations hence resulting are complicated by

10. The multiplication of effects: every mass and part of a mass on which a force falls sub-divides and differentiates that force, which thereupon proceeds to work a variety of changes; and each of these becomes the parent of similarly multiplying changes: the multiplication of these becoming greater in proportion as the aggregate becomes more heterogeneous. And these two causes of increasing differentiations are furthered by—

11. Segregation, which is a process tending ever to separate unlike units, and to bring together like units, so serving continually to sharpen or make definite differentiations otherwise caused.

12. Equilibration is the final result of these transformations which an evolving aggregate undergoes. The changes go on until there is reached an equilibrium between the forces which all parts of the aggregate are exposed to, and the forces these parts oppose to them. Equilibration may pass through a transition stage of balanced motions (as in a planetary system), or of balanced functions (as in a living body), on the way to ultimate equilibrium; but the state of rest in inorganic bodies, or death in organic bodies, is the necessary limit of the changes constituting evolution.

13. Dissolution is the counterchange which sooner or later every evolved aggregate undergoes. Remaining exposed to surrounding forces that are unequilibrated, each aggregate is ever liable to be dissipated by the increase, gradual or sudden, of its contained motion; and its dissipation, quickly undergone by bodies lately animate, and slowly undergone by inanimate masses, remains to be undergone at an indefinitely remote period by each planetary and stellar mass, which, since an indefinitely remote period in the past, has been slowly evolving: the cycle of its transformations being thus completed.

14. This rhythm of evolution and dissolution, completing itself during short periods in small aggregates, and in the vast aggregates distributed through space completing itself in periods which are immeasurable by human thought, is, so far as we can see, universal and eternal: each alternating phase of the process predominating—now in this region of space, and now in that—as local conditions determine.

15. All these phenomena, from their great features down to their minutest details, are necessary results of the persistence of force under its forms of matter and motion. Given these in their known distributions through space, and their quantities being unchangeable, either by increase or decrease, there inevitably result the continuous redistributions distinguishable as evolution and dissolution, as well as all

those special traits above enumerated.

16. That which persists, unchanging in quantity, but ever-changing in form, under these sensible appearances which the universe presents to us, transcends human knowledge and conception; is an unknown and an unknowable power, which we are obliged to recognise as without limit in space, and without beginning or end in time.

And the universal formula of Evolution stands thus: "Evolution is an integration of matter and concomitant dissipation of motion; during which the matter passes from an indefinite, incoherent homogeneity to a definite, coherent heterogeneity; and during which the retained motion undergoes a parallel transformation" (*First Principles*, p. 396).

Notes and Queries.—(1) It should be noted that Spencer never suggested that he had explained the origin of things. On the contrary, "While the genesis of the Solar System, and of countless other systems like it, is thus rendered comprehensible, the ultimate mystery remains as great as ever. The problem of existence is not solved: it is simply moved further back." What he offered was a genetic description, and that is all that the scientific evolutionist ever offers.

(2) In the strict sense Spencer was no materialist. "Though the relation of subject and object renders necessary to us these antithetical conceptions of Spirit and Matter, the one is no less than the other to be regarded as but a sign of the Unknown Reality which underlies both." "Matter, Motion, and Force are but symbols of the Unknown Reality." "Only in a doctrine which recognises the Unknown Cause as co-extensive with all orders of phenomena, can there be a consistent Religion, or a consistent Philosophy." "Were we compelled to choose between the alternatives of translating mental phenomena into physical phenomena, or of translating physical phenomena into mental phenomena, the latter alternative would seem the more acceptable of the two."

It is one of the difficulties of Spencer's system that even when he is using physical concepts he is thinking of these not merely as symbols by which to formulate the routine of our sense-experience, but as symbols of the reality behind matter and motion of which we do not know anything. He works with the concept which he calls "the persistence of force," and when the reader is feeling its inadequacy to meet the situation, he is bluffed by the reminder —"By persistence of force we really mean the persistence of some Power which transcends our knowledge and conception": "Asserting the persistence of Force is but another mode of asserting an Unconditioned Reality without beginning or end."

(3) When an investigator in giving an account of a process insists on using higher categories than the sequences appear to require, he is guilty of "*a transcendentalism*," e.g., if he says that an instinctive action is rational, or that digestion is a psychical process. Similarly, when an investigator in giving an account of a process insists on using lower categories than the sequences appear to require, he is guilty of "*a materialism*," e.g., if he says that a rational act is simply a higher reflex, or that digestion is simply a chemical reaction. Therefore, although Spencer was not a materialist, we think that he was guilty of gross "materialisms," of attempting to give a false simplicity to the facts, e.g., in his attempt to trace the evolution of mind in terms of the evolution of the nervous system, and in his universal evolution-formula which is wholly in terms of Matter and Motion.

(4) By keeping throughout to mechanical categories, Spencer gives a semblance of simplicity and precision to his evolutionism, and his skill is such that the unwary reader is led gently on from orders of facts where mechanical categories (if not Spencer's) do certainly suffice, to other orders of facts—in immaterial evolution—where they seem strangely irrelevant. But if the reader, having his suspicions aroused by sundry jolts and jars in the onward sweep of the chariot of First Principles, begins to inquire into the reality of the apparent mechanical precision, he is likely to be disillusioned. Thus, at an early stage, he may discover that Spencer uses the word "force" without special definition in at least five senses,[11] which is not reassuring.

[11] See Karl Pearson. *The Grammar of Science*, p. 329.

As we have no expertness in these matters, we would submit the verdict of a recognised authority, Prof. Karl Pearson. One of Spencer's principles is "the redistribution of force," which he states in the following words:—

"A decreasing quantity of motion, sensible or insensible, always has for its concomitant an increasing aggregation of matter, and conversely an increasing quantity of motion, sensible or insensible, has for its concomitant a decreasing aggregation of matter."

In regard to this Prof. Pearson remarks: "This principle has, so far as I am aware, no real foundation in physics... it seems, so far as I can grasp it at all, to flatly contradict the modern principle of the conservation of energy"... the keystone of Spencer's system.

(5) What has taken place since Spencer stereotyped his *First Principles* seems to us to have rendered it almost useless to attempt a detailed criticism of his scheme of evolution—wonderful and stimulating as it was and is. He spoke of his delight in "intellectual hunting," and a great huntsman he certainly was,

but the *venue* has changed since his day. He did not fully nor always rightly utilise the chemistry and physics of his time, and we have now to deal with a new chemistry and a new physics.

Mr J. B. Crozier speaks of Spencer as "of all thinkers ancient or modern the one whose power of analysing, decomposing, and combining the complex web of Matter, Motion, and Force is the most incontestable and assured." He describes Spencer's system as "No mere logical castle built of air and definitions, and assuming in its premises, like the systems of the metaphysicians, the very difficulties to be explained, but a great granite pile sunk deep in the bed-rock of the world, each stone a scientific truth, and all so compacted and dove-tailed together that it was difficult to find anywhere a logical flaw among their seams."

This is one view, but another will be found in Prof. James Ward's Gifford Lectures on "Naturalism and Agnosticism," in Mr Malcolm Guthrie's three volumes of criticism, and in several luminous papers by Principal James Iverach.

When we think of the evolution of the world and all that is therein—of a universal process of Becoming—we recognise that at an uncertain time the earth was framed, that living organisms appeared by and by, that by and by some of these exhibited mental as well as bodily life, and that finally man emerged, a rational and social person. This is a convenient and unified retrospect, but when we go further and say that all this evolution is expressible in one descriptive formula whose terms are mechanical, we are going further than our present knowledge warrants. Even Spencer did not really carry his evolution-formula throughout, for he admitted that "the development of Mind itself cannot be explained by a series of deductions from the Persistence of Force," though he covered his retreat by the suggestion that Mind is the subjective concomitant of the objective nervous system which has been evolved according to formula. But even if this *tour de force* seemed legitimate, we should still be unable to accept a universal formula of Evolution in terms of mechanism. For we are not at present able to think of the facts of bodily life in terms of mechanical categories. Thus, in short, when we enter the chariot of Spencer's Evolution-formula, and attempt to make an intellectual journey— "one and continuous" from the primitive nebula to human society, we confess to suffering serious joltings. We must admit that on that chariot at least we have never been able to arrive. Let us refer briefly to three of the worst jolts—at the origin of Life, at the origin of Mind, at the origin of Man.

Origin of Life.—It is much to be regretted that Spencer "had to omit that part of the System of Philosophy, which deals with Inorganic Evolution. Two volumes are missing." The closing chapter of the second volume was to have dealt with "the evolution of organic matter—the step preceding the evolution of living forms." It is tantalising to learn that he habitually carried with him in thought the contents of this unwritten chapter, for it would certainly have been interesting reading. He did, however, give us some hint of his views.

First of all negatively, Spencer did not believe in any alleged cases of spontaneous generation; he did not believe that any creature like an Infusorian could arise from not-living matter; he did not believe in an "absolute commencement of organic life," or in a "first organism." But just as the chemist is able to build up complex organic compounds from simple substances, so Spencer supposed that organic compounds were evolved in nature. He supposed the evolution of some substance like protein, which is capable of existing in many isomeric forms, and of forming with itself and other elements, substances yet more intricate in composition. "To the mutual influences of its metamorphic forms under favouring conditions, we may ascribe the production of the still more composite, still more sensitive, still more variously-changeable portions of organic matter, which, in masses more minute and simpler than existing Protozoa, displayed actions verging little by little into those called vital." By a continuance of the process, the nascent life displayed became gradually more pronounced.

No one who is aware of recent achievements in chemical synthesis, or of the recent "vitalising" of the concept of matter, or of the apparent simplicity of life in its humblest expressions, will seek to foreclose the question of the possible origin of living matter from not-living matter. The conclusion which most biologists accept is, that while there is no known evidence of not-living matter giving origin to living organisms, this does not exclude (*a*) the possibility that this once took place, or (*b*) the possibility that it may be made to take place again. It must always be remembered, however, that there is a great gap between a drop of living matter and an integrated living organism. We may firmly say that if living matter was once evolved from not-living matter, it must have been the outcome of long preparatory processes, that if it occurred, we cannot at present suggest "how" except in the vaguest way, and that if we knew it had occurred we should still be unable to *explain the organism* in terms of its antecedents.

Evolution of Mind.—Spencer speaks of the evolution-process as one and continuous throughout, but he felt, as other thorough-going evolutionists feel, that the emergence of psychical phenomena is a difficulty in the way of unified formulation.

"Let it be granted that all existence distinguished as objective, may be resolved into the existence of units of one kind. Let it be granted that every species of objective activity may be understood as due to the rhythmical motions of such ultimate units; and that among the objective activities so understood, are the waves of molecular motion propagated through nerves and nerve-centres. And let it further be granted that all existence distinguished as subjective, is resolvable into units of consciousness similar in nature to those which we know as nervous shocks; each of which is the correlative of a rhythmical motion of a material unit, or group of units. Can we then think of the subjective and objective activities as the same? Can the oscillation of a molecule be represented in consciousness side by side with a nervous shock, and the two be recognised as one? No effort enables us to assimilate them. That a unit of feeling has nothing in common with a unit of motion, becomes more than ever manifest when we bring the two into juxtaposition" (*Principles of Psychology*, i. p. 158).

He concluded that "there is not the remotest possibility of interpreting Mind in terms of Matter." Since our "ideas of Matter and Motion, merely symbolic of unknowable realities, are complex states of consciousness built out of units of feeling," "it seems easier to translate so-called Matter into so-called Spirit, than to translate so-called Spirit into so-called Matter, which latter is, indeed, wholly impossible."

The obvious difficulty, of which Spencer was well aware, is "how mental evolution is to be affiliated on Evolution at large, regarded as a process of physical transformation?

"Specifically stated, the problem is to interpret mental evolution in terms of the redistribution of Matter and Motion. Though under its subjective aspect Mind is known only as an aggregate of states of consciousness, which cannot be conceived as forms of Matter and Motion, and do not therefore necessarily conform to the same laws of redistribution; yet under its objective aspect, Mind is known as an aggregate of activities manifested by an organism—is the correlative, therefore, of certain material transformations, which must come within the general process of material evolution, if that process is truly universal. Though the development of Mind itself cannot be explained by a series of deductions from the Persistence of Force, yet it remains possible that its obverse, the development of physical changes in a physical organ, may be so explained; and until it is so explained, the conception of mental evolution as a part of Evolution in general, remains incomplete" (*Principles of Psychology*, i. p. 508).

Therefore Spencer passes to discuss the genesis of nervous systems and nervous functions, and by treating Mind as a mere aspect or epiphenomenon, eventually gets "an adequate explanation of nervous evolution, and the concomitant evolution of Mind," the Ultimate Reality being always postulated as the amalgam.

"See then our predicament. We can think of Matter only in terms of Mind. We can think of Mind only in terms of Matter, when we have pushed our explorations of the first to the uttermost limit, we are referred to the second for a final answer; and when we have got the final answer of the second, we are referred back to the first for an interpretation of it. We find the value of x in terms of y; then we find the value of y in terms of x; and so on we may continue for ever without coming nearer to a solution. The antithesis of subject and object, never to be transcended while consciousness lasts, renders impossible all knowledge of that Ultimate Reality in which subject and object are united" (*Principles of Psychology*, i. 627).

Ascent of Man.—Spencer was careful to say that it is not necessary to suppose "an absolute commencement of social life" or "a first social organism." But an ascent has to be accounted for however gradual the inclined plane may be, and like the origin of life, and the evolution of mind, the ascent of man to the level of a rational and social person is a very difficult problem, to the solution of which Spencer paid relatively little attention.

From our frankly biological point of view there seems considerable warrant for the suggestion that Man arose as a saltatory or transilient variation or "sport" in a gregarious Simian stock, which was not too hard-pressed by a struggle for subsistence either as regards food or climate, which was not too severely menaced by ever-persecuting stronger foes, which lived in conditions implying some measure of temporary isolation, in-breeding, and daily "brain-stretching" education. It seems likely that the transilient advance was in the direction of increased cerebral complexity, associated with greater freedom of speech, and a strengthened sense of kinship. It may be imagined that the advance occurred in times of relative peace and in a stimulating environment, where the seasons were well-defined, or where recurrent vicissitudes gave an advantage to memory and capacity for prevision.

Various useful suggestions have been made as to the possible factors in the evolution of man. (*a*) When the incipient man with his growing brain got on to his hind-legs, and walked more or less erect upon the earth, the new attitude, however prompted, would leave the hands more free for manipulation, for using a stone, a tool, or a weapon, for feeling round things and appreciating their three dimensions, it would react on other parts of the body, such as the spinal column, the pelvis, and perhaps even the larynx. In his address to the Anthropological Section of the British Association in 1893, Dr Robert Munro directed attention to three propositions: (1) the mechanical and physical advantages of the erect position, (2) the consequent differentiation of the limbs into hands and feet, and (3) the causal relation between this and the development of the brain.

(b) Fiske and others have called attention to the prolonged helpless infancy, so characteristic of human offspring, and illustrated in a less marked degree among Simian races. It would tend, in conditions not too severe, to tighten the family bond, and to evolve gentleness and a habit of altruistic outlook. It should also be remembered that the type of brain which characterises man is marked by its relative poverty in inherited instinct and by its eminent educability.

(c) The influence of the family was probably an important factor, fostering sympathy and mutual aid, prompting talk and division of labour. Even in early days, children would educate their parents. It must be remembered that many animals exhibit family life, and also pairing for prolonged periods or for life.

(d) If we grant the incipient man a growing, plastic, and restless brain, a strong feeling of kinship, some family ties, an erect attitude, the habit of using his hands and voice, all of which the anthropoid analogy suggests, and if we deny him sufficient physical strength to keep his foothold by virtue of that alone, then it seems more than a platitude to say that natural selection would favour the development of wits, and not only of wits, but in the widest sense (partly through sexual selection) of "love," which became a new source of strength.

(e) With the development of tool-using and sentence-making, with recognition of the seasons as a fundamental illustration of the uniformity of nature, with the gaining of a firmer foothold in the struggle for existence, with slowly increasing altruism and sociality, and with the occasional emergence of the genius, there might gradually arise—in permanent products, in symbols and songs, in traditions and customs—an external heritage, which, it appears to us, has been the most potent factor in securing and furthering human evolution.

Ignorant as we are as to the factors in human evolution, there is a convergence of various lines of evidence towards the conclusion that man must have come of a social stock. It is difficult to conceive of his survival on any other supposition. In a deeper sense, perhaps, than Rousseau thought of, it seems true that Man did not make Society, Society (pre-human) made Man.

By some means or other, probably along various paths—through kinship-sympathies, through linguistic bonds, for economic or life-and-death reasons, man became definitely social, and a new order of things began, which Spencer has pictured with great skill. Just as it was a new event in the history of Hymenopterous insects when ants made an ant-hill, or bees a natural hive, so it was a new event in the history of Man when unified societary groups came into being.

Now all this is vague, and, it may be, unconvincing; but we are not aware that Spencer had any further light to throw on the problem—a problem so difficult that Alfred Russel Wallace, the Nestor among living evolutionists, has declared his conviction that the development of man's higher qualities cannot be conceived without postulating "spiritual influx." Our point at present is that the difficulties are greater than Spencer publicly recognised, and that his formula of evolution is not only too remotely abstract to be relevant, but that it is in its mechanical phrasing quite inapplicable.

The Scientific Position.—The idea of organic evolution suggests—that the forms of life have had a natural history, that they have descended from a far-distant relatively simple ancestry, that they have risen from level to level throughout many millions of years just as individual animals in their development rise from level to level in a few days or months or years. It is the only scientific conception we have of the Becoming of the world of life.

The theory of organic evolution raises this modal interpretation into a causal interpretation by disclosing the factors—such as Variation and Selection—in the long process. To some minds, the known factors appear inadequate to describe the process, especially in relation to the emergence of mental life and the ascent of man. Thus an attempt is often made to sit on both sides of the fence, accepting scientific factors for what they are worth, but eking them out by postulating "ultra-scientific" causes. This procedure, however, lands in mental confusion; it is like trying to speak two languages at once. It is also very premature.

When we extend the concept of evolution to the inorganic world, we find that it applies there also, that it enables us to resume the history of the solar system as a whole, and of the earth in particular in a convenient formula. Here again we are aware of factors of evolution, which enable us to give a causal interpretation of how the inanimate world came to be as it is. The factors are not the same as those verifiable in organic evolution; they are in terms of the laws of motion and other physical concepts.

Again the idea of evolution may be applied to the forms of mental life and to the forms of social life, and in these realms the factors are not the same as those used in interpreting the history of organisms (objectively considered) or the history of inanimate systems.

In all cases the general concept of evolution is the same—the idea of natural progressive change—but the factors are different. The reason for this is that the organism is very different from a planet or a crystal, that mind is quite different from metabolism, that a society is more than the sum of its parts.

It is quite plain that the sociological evolutionist will not advance far if he disregards the concept of the social organism, if he shuts his eyes to the fact that a societary form, however simple, is an integrate; not a mere congeries of persons, but a unity with a life and mind of its own. Yet he may quite consistently try to trace the emergence of societary forms from a simply gregarious stock, and that again from entirely non-social organisms.

In the same way the psychological evolutionist will not advance far if he disregards the distinctiveness of mental life, with principles of its own quite different from those of the bodily life with which it is inextricably associated. That is to say he must be more than a physiologist of the nervous system.

So, the biological evolutionist must admit that he cannot trace the evolution of organisms in terms of the concepts which suffice for inanimate systems. In so doing he does not dogmatically say that the activity of organisms *cannot* be described in terms of mechanism, he only says that it has not been done; he only says that neither physics nor physiology is at present within sight of deducing the laws of motion of organic corpuscles from the laws of motion of other corpuscles.

There is no reason why he should stand aloof from the theory that inorganic and organic evolution are continuous, in other words from the theory of the spontaneous generation of living matter at an appropriate time in the Earth's history—a theory which is suggested by many facts. If that is a legitimate theory it increases our respect for what we call the inanimate, but it does not make our biological evolutionism any easier, nor are we any nearer explaining life. The organism remains what it is, a living creature with a behaviour which we are unable to redescribe in terms of mechanism. And inanimate matter remains what it is, except that we should be able to say definitely that it had once given origin to living matter and might conceivably do so again. There would be no gain in adding to the properties of matter a mysterious "capacity-of-sharing-in-the-spontaneous-generation-of-life."

Let us state the position once more. When one of the higher animals, in the course of its development, reaches a certain, or rather uncertain, degree of differentiation, its functioning becomes behaviour; its activities are such that we cannot interpret them without using psychical terms, such as awareness or intelligence. This expression of fuller life is associated with the increased development of the nervous system, and we have no knowledge of any psychical life apart from nervous metabolism. Yet we remain quite unable to think of any way by which the metabolism of nerve-cells gives rise to what we know in ourselves as sensations or perceptions, ideas or feelings. Therefore while we see no reason to doubt the continuity of the individual development, we recognise as fact of experience that the merely sentient embryo becomes a thoughtful child, whose behaviour cannot be formulated in terms of our present biological or our present mechanical categories.

And as it is with the individual development, so it is with the evolution of organisms; when they exhibit a certain, or rather uncertain, degree of differentiation they behave in a way which we cannot interpret without using psychical terms. We know of very simple forms whose whole behaviour seems to be summed up in one reflex action, at least if there is more we cannot detect it; we know of other unicellular animals whose behaviour is such that we are forced to say that they seem to pursue the method of trial and error; and from that level we know of a long inclined plane leading up to very alert intelligence. Again we see no reason to doubt the continuity of the process, though we recognise that at a certain level of organisation the biological categories of metabolism and the like are no longer sufficient to formulate the facts. How it is that the activity of the nervous system does express itself in such a way, that we must use a new set of terms—psychical ones—to cover the facts of behaviour, no one has at present any conception. A living creature behaves in such a way that we cannot interpret what it does in terms of the motions of the organic corpuscles which compose it. We do not know how to formulate in physical terms its growth, its development, its power of effective response, its co-ordination of activities. Therefore we introduce a special series of biological concepts, without denying that a greater unity of formulation may some day be attained either by a further simplification of the biological concepts or by some change in the physical concepts, such as, indeed, seems coming about at present.

But again, a living creature behaves in such a way that our biological concepts are insufficient to formulate its behaviour. We do not know how to interpret what it does without psychological concepts of thinking, feeling, and willing. It is possible that here, too, a greater unity of formulation may some day be attained either by a further simplification of the psychological concepts or by some change in the biological concepts. But sufficient unto the day is the science thereof.

CHAPTER XIV

PSYCHOLOGICAL

Evolution of Mind—Body and Mind—Experience and Intuitions—Test of Truth

In seeking to appreciate Spencer's contributions to Psychology, it seems necessary to distinguish between what he tried to do and his success in doing it. For an attempt, especially a pioneer attempt, may have great historical importance although it is only to a limited degree successful. The attempts to cross a continent, or to scale a mountain, to make a flying machine, or to discover the nature of protoplasm, may be relative failures, but even the attempts may spell progress. They may offer clues for other attempts, or they may show that certain ways of attacking the problem are unpromising. And so while the doctors of philosophy differ as to the value of many of Spencer's psychological essays, there are few who go the length of denying their historical interest and importance.

(1) *Evolution of Mind.*—In his imaginary review of his *Principles of Psychology*, which is not without a grim humour, Spencer supposes the critic to begin by saying: "Our attitude towards this work is something like that of the Roman poet to whom the poetaster brought some verses with the request that he would erase any parts he did not like, and who replied—one erasure will suffice. We reject absolutely the entire doctrine which the book contains; and for the sufficient reason that it is founded on a fallacy." The fallacy was, of course, the evolution-idea, and it was Spencer's chief contribution to Psychology that he insisted on regarding the human mind as a product, the outlines of whose history could be more or less clearly descried. In other words, he attempted a genetic interpretation of our mental life in the light of antecedent simpler expressions of mentality in the child and in the animal world. In so doing he was a pioneer, and he doubtless made a pioneer's mistakes. None the less he helped to effect for psychology the transition from a static and morphological mode of interpretation to one which is distinctively kinetic, physiological, and historical. That this is nowadays the mood of all psychologists is well-known. Thus one of our leading modern exponents says, "We may define psychology as the science of the development of mind."[12]

[12] G. F. Stout, *Analytic Psychology*, vol. i., 1896, p. 9.

Spencer sought to make mental processes more intelligible by disclosing the gradualness of their evolution. "It is not more certain that, from the simple reflex action by which the infant sucks, up to the elaborate reasoning of the adult man, the progress is by daily infinitesimal steps, than it is certain that between the automatic actions of the lowest creatures and the highest conscious actions of the human race, a series of actions displayed by the various tribes of the animal kingdom may be so placed as to render it impossible to say of any one step in the series, Here intelligence begins." Objectively, with data drawn from the animal world and from child-study, he attempted to trace the evolution of mind from reflex action through instinct to reason, memory, feeling, and will, by the interaction of the nervous system with its gradually widening environment. Subjectively, in his analytic task, he endeavoured to show that all mental states are referable to primitive elements of consciousness or units of feeling, which he called nervous or psychical shocks.

Spencer's general position is thus summed up:—

"The Law of Evolution holds of the inner world as it does of the outer world. On tracing up from its low and vague beginnings the intelligence which becomes so marvellous in the highest beings, we find that under whatever aspect contemplated, it presents a progressive transformation of like nature with the progressive transformation we trace in the Universe as a whole, no less than in each of its parts. If we study the development of the nervous system, we see it advancing in integration, in complexity, in definiteness. If we turn to its functions, we find these similarly show an ever-increasing inter-dependence, an augmentation in number and heterogeneity, and a greater precision. If we examine the relations of these functions to the actions going on in the world around, we see that the correspondence between them progresses in range and amount, becomes continually more complex and special, and advances through differentiations and integrations like those everywhere going on. And when we observe the correlative states of consciousness, we discover that these, too, beginning as simple, vague, and incoherent, become increasingly numerous in their kinds, are united into aggregates which are larger, more multitudinous, and more multiform, and eventually assume those finished shapes we see in scientific generalisations, where definitely-quantitative elements are co-ordinated in definitely-quantitative relations" (*Principles of Psychology*, i. p. 627).

In Spencer's system mind is a secondary and derivative expression of life; it emerges after corporeal evolution has made some strides; it is always dependent on the development of the nervous system. This is an inference from the facts of individual development and racial evolution, which clearly show that mental life emerges from antecedent stages in which only bodily life can be discerned. And if mental life were a merely incidental quality, like the possession of red blood, there would be no objection to the inference. But since mental life is almost from the first a necessary postulate—wherever we have to deal with behaviour—and as we are quite unable to suggest how it can arise out of metabolism, it seems more scientific, at present, to regard the potentiality of mind as being just as primitive as metabolism. It should be noted that the most recent researches[13] on the behaviour of the simplest animals disclose something more than reflex actions, namely a pursuit of the method of trial and error, involving some of the fundamental qualities seen in higher animals.

[13] H. S. Jennings, "Publications of Carnegie Institute," Washington, No. 16 (1904), pp. 1-256.

Just as inorganic evolution must have made many advances before organisms became possible, so organic evolution must have made many advances before the mental side of life could find distinct expression. But as we cannot retranslate the daily activities of even a very simple animal into chemico-physical language, we are forced at present to conclude that what is called inanimate matter has somehow wrapped up with it the potentiality of life; and as we cannot retranslate behaviour into the metabolism of nerve-cells, we are forced at present to conclude that life has somehow wrapped up with it the potentiality of mind. In other words, what is called the evolution of mind is a genetic description of the stages in its emergence from its state of universal potentiality.

(2) *Body and Mind.*—A second service Spencer rendered to Psychology was that of linking it to Biology. He gave clear expression to the doctrine, which many workers had been reaching towards, of the correlation of mind and body. Although sagacious thinkers at many different dates had pointed out that the flesh not only wars against the spirit, but in a humiliating way conditions its activity, the recognition of the intimate correlation of body and mind was still requiring its advocate when Spencer wrote his *Psychology.* Ignoring what had been clearly shown even by Descartes and the truth in Hartley's *Observations on Man* (1749), there was still a school who practically dealt with the mind and its faculties on the one side, the body and its functions on the other side, as entirely independent existences. The old idea that character inheres in the ghost, and that the body is merely the ghost's house, having no causal relation to it, still lingered in more or less refined form when Spencer set himself to show "that, in both amounts and kinds, mental manifestations are in part dependent on bodily structures. Mind is not as deep as the brain only, but is, in a sense, as deep as the viscera." In a detailed way, he sought to show that "the amounts and kinds of the mental actions constituting consciousness vary, other things equal, according to the

rapidity, the quantity, and the quality, of the blood-supply; and all these vary according to the sizes and proportions of the sundry organs which unite in preparing blood from food, the organs which circulate it, and the organs which purify it from waste products." To put it concretely, he contended that when we consider Handel, for instance, "so wonderfully productive, so marvellous for the number and vigour of his musical compositions," we must also remember that he had an unusually active digestion. "And not the quantity of mind only, but the quality of mind also, is in part determined by these psycho-physical connections. Amount and structure of brain being the same, not only may the totality of feelings and thoughts be greater or less according as this or that viscus is well or ill-developed, but the feelings and thoughts may also be favourably or unfavourably modified in their kinds." So morality, as well as mind, is as deep as the viscera.

Here again the general truth which Spencer forcibly expounded, though it was not of course peculiarly his, is one that has met with almost universal recognition. As Prof. G. F. Stout says:—

"The life of the brain is part of the life of the organism as a whole, and inasmuch as consciousness is the correlate of brain-process, it is conditioned by organic process in general. It is clear that the unity and connection of psychical states cannot be clearly conceived without taking into account the unity and connection of the processes of the organism as a whole."[14]

As Prof. James Ward says[15]:—

[14] *Op. cit.*, p. 27.

[15] *Naturalism and Agnosticism*, 1899, vol. i. p. 10.

"Modern science is content to ascertain co-existences and successions between facts of mind and facts of body. The relations so determined constitute the newest of the sciences, psychophysiology or psychophysics. From this science we learn that there exist manifold correspondences of the most intimate and exact kind between states and changes of consciousness on the one hand, and states and changes of brain on the other. As respects complexity, intensity, and time-order, the concomitance is apparently complete. Mind and brain advance and decline *pari passu*; the stimulants and narcotics that enliven or depress the action of the one tell in like manner upon the other. Local lesions that suspend or destroy, more or less completely, the functions of the centres of sight and speech, for instance, involve an equivalent loss, temporary or permanent, of words and ideas."

Experience and Intuitions.—The history of psychology discloses a long drawn-out dispute between schools of "empiricists," who said "all our knowledge is derived from experience," and schools of "intuitionalists," who said, "Nay, but we have innate ideas or intuitions which transcend experience." A parallel dispute was long continued in regard to moral ideas. Between the disputants Spencer appeared as a peace-maker, and the reconciliation he proposed was in terms of evolution. We can best express it by a sentence from a letter to John Stuart Mill:—

> "Just in the same way that I believe the intuition of space, possessed by any living individual, to have arisen from organised and consolidated experiences of all antecedent individuals who bequeathed to him their slowly-developed nervous organisations—just as I believe that this intuition, requiring only to be made definite and complete by personal experiences, has practically become a form of thought, apparently quite independent of experience; so do I believe that the experiences of utility, organised and consolidated through all past generations of the human race, have been producing corresponding nervous modifications, which, by continued transmission and accumulation have become in us certain faculties of moral intuition—certain emotions responding to right and wrong conduct, which have no apparent basis in the individual experiences of utility."

In short, Spencer maintained that intellectual and moral intuitions had arisen from gradually organised and inherited experience. "What the transcendentalist called a *priori* principles the evolutionist regards as *a priori* indeed to the individual, but *a posteriori* to the race; that is as race experiences which in the individual appear as intuitions."[16]

[16] W. H. Hudson, Introduction to the Philosophy of Herbert Spencer.

This was an ingenious *eirenicon*, but it does not seem to satisfy all the philosophers, those namely who feel that intuitions—both intellectual and moral—have a validity, universality, and compelling necessity which cannot be accounted for if they are simply the outcome of race-experience. The only alternative seems to be to say that their validity depends on the nature of mind itself, or, what comes to the same thing, because they are in harmony with the spiritual principle in nature.

Nor are the biologists quite satisfied with Spencer's reconciliation, between empiricism and apriorism, for, in the form he gave it, there is the tacit assumption that results of experience are as such transmissible. But this is biologically a hazardous assumption. The only alternative would be to suppose that the advance to rational intuitions came about by the selection of variations towards that type of mental constitution which rational and moral intuitions express—a probably very slow process which would be sheltered by the individual moulding himself to the social heritage in which many results of experience are registered and entailed independently of any germ- plasm. It is possible that there has been an underestimate of the extent to which what are regarded as intuitions are sustained by tradition in the widest sense, and an underestimate of the extent to which they are individually acquired by each successive generation.

When we speak of either instincts or intuitions arising by the selection of variations, we need not think of such wonderful results as originating in fortuitous mental sports; we are quite entitled to think of definiteness in mental (at the same time neural) variation as in bodily variation; we are quite entitled to think of mental (at the same time neural) 'mutations' as well as bodily 'mutations'; we do not require to burden natural selection with more than the pruning off of irrationalities, instabilities, disharmonies, and imbecilities. Thus even biologically we may admit that the validity of intuitions depends on the nature of mind itself, socially confirmed from age to age.

Test of Truth.—Spencer took great stock in "intuitions," especially in his *First Principles*, and yet he believed in their empirical origin; and this leads us to ask what his test of truth was. It may be summed up in the phrase "the inconceivability of the opposite." After a curiously self-contradictory attempt to show by reasoning that "a certainty greater than that which any reasoning can yield has to be recognised at the outset of all reasoning," he states the "universal postulate": "The inconceivableness of its negation is that which shows a cognition to possess the highest rank—is the criterion by which its insurpassable validity is known."

He admitted, however, that there were limitations to the utility of this test of truth. "That some propositions have been wrongly accepted as true, because their negations were supposed inconceivable when they were not, does not disprove the validity of the test, for these reasons: (1) That they were complex propositions, not to be established by a test applicable only to propositions no further decomposable; (2) that this test, in common with any test, is liable to yield untrue results, either from incapacity or from carelessness in those who use it." In regard to which Prof. Sidgwick says:[17] "These two qualifications surely reduce very much the practical value of the criterion. For how are we to proceed if philosophers disagree about the application of the criteria? How are we to test 'undecomposability'? For notions which on first reflection appear to us simple are so often found on further reflective analysis to be composite. Which conclusion, then, are we to trust, the earlier or the later? This seems to me a serious dilemma for Mr Spencer; whichever way he answers he is in a difficulty."

It would seem then that Spencer did not get much further than others who have tried to answer the question: *What is the test of truth?* Nor for our part can we supply the deficiency. It is probably more profitable, as Sidgwick says, "to turn from infallible criteria to methods of verification, from the search after an absolute test of truth to the humbler task of devising modes of excluding error." "These verifications are based on experience of the ways in which the human mind has actually been convinced of error, and been led to discard it; *i.e.*, three modes of conflict, conflict between a judgment first formed, and the view of this judgment taken by the same mind on subsequent reconsideration; conflict between two different judgments, or the implications of two partially different judgments formed by the same mind under different conditions; and finally, conflict between the judgments of different minds." In other words, what is true for us is that which survives these conflicts, but the conflict is unceasing.

[17] *The Philosophy of Kant and other Lecturers*, 1905, p.319

CHAPTER XV

SOCIOLOGICAL

What Sociology is—Criticism of Sociology—Sociology and History—Spencer's Sociological Data—Central Ideas of Spencer's Sociology—The Idea of the Social Organism—Parallelisms between a Society and an Individual Organism

While Spencer had little agreement with Comte, he was at one with him in regarding Sociology as a possible science and as the crowning science.

What Sociology is.—By sociology is meant the study of the structure and activity, development and evolution of social groups, which have sufficient integration or unity to justify their being regarded as "organisms," with a life —and a mind—of their own. That many active-minded people persist in looking askance at sociology—as "a mass of facts about society," and "no science," is not unnatural, since the science is still very young and its definition is still elastic. At certain points it necessarily comes in contact with biology, *e.g.* in the study of heredity and eugenics; with psychology, *e.g.* in the study of tradition and religion; with anthropology and history; with economics and politics. But it has a distinctive place to fill as the study of human integrates, of groups capable of acting, consciously or unconsciously, as unities, as more than the sum of their parts. When it has grown up and done more work, it will be justified, like Wisdom in general, of its children, and any discussion of its claims to be a "science" will be an anachronism. Meanwhile, though the youngest of the sciences is still struggling for existence, we need not fear for its safety—it is a Hercules in the cradle.

Criticism of Sociology.—The distrust which many thoughtful minds have of "Sociology" is well expressed by Prof. Henry Sidgwick in one of his essays:

—

"It is not necessary to show that if we could ascertain from the past history of human society the fundamental laws of social evolution as a whole, so that we could accurately forecast the main features of the future state with which our present social world is pregnant—it is not needful, I say, to show that the science which gave this foresight would be of the highest value to a statesman, and would absorb or dominate our present political economy. What has to be proved is that this supremely important knowledge is within our grasp; that the sociology which professes this prevision is really an established science."[18]

[18] "The Scope and Method of Economic Science," *Miscellaneous Essays and Addresses*, 1904, p. 193.

He goes on to say that there are two simple tests of the establishment of a science, recognised by Comte in his discussion of this very subject, which can be quickly and decisively applied to the claims of existing sociology. These tests may be characterised as (1) Consensus or Continuity, and (2) Prevision. The former Sedgwick explains in Comte's own words: "When we find that recent works, instead of being the result and development of what has gone before, have a character as personal as that of their authors, and bring the most fundamental ideas into question—then," says Comte, "we may be sure we are not dealing with any doctrine deserving the name of positive science." [The validity of Comte's criterion seems very doubtful, but let that pass.]

"Now," Sidgwick continues, "if we compare the most elaborate and ambitious treatises on sociology, of which there happens to be one in each of the three leading scientific languages—Comte's *Politique Positive*, Spencer's *Sociology*, and Schäffle's *Bau und Leben des socialen Körpers*—we see at once that they exhibit the most complete and conspicuous absence of agreement or continuity in their treatment of the fundamental questions of social evolution." Sidgwick illustrates this, in the first place, by taking the exceedingly difficult question of the future of religion, and shows easily enough how the three doctors differ. Perhaps it would have been fairer to have selected a less difficult problem.

It seems profitable to follow Sidgwick's contrast since it brings out some of Spencer's characteristic doctrines.

"If we inquire after the characteristics of the religion of which their science leads them to foresee the coming prevalence, they give with nearly equal confidence answers as divergent as can be conceived. Schäffle cannot comprehend that the place of the great Christian Churches can be taken by anything but a purified form of Christianity; Spencer contemplates complacently the reduction of religious thought and sentiment to a perfectly indefinite consciousness of an Unknowable and the emotion that accompanies this peculiar intellectual exercise; while Comte has no doubt that the whole history of religion—which, as he says, 'should resume the entire history of human development,' has been leading up to the worship of the Great Being, Humanity, personified domestically for each normal male individual by his nearest female relatives. It would seem that the science which allows these discrepancies in its chief expositors must be still in its infancy." "I do not doubt that our sociologists are sincere in setting before us their conception of the coming social state as the last term of a series of which the law has been discovered by patient historical study; but when we look closely into their work it becomes only too evident that each philosopher has constructed on the basis of personal feeling and experience his ideal future in which our present social deficiencies are to be remedied; and that the process by which history is arranged in steps pointing towards his Utopia bears not the faintest resemblance to a scientific demonstration."

The remark on the influence of "personal feeling and experience" recalls the interesting sentence in the preface to Spencer's *Autobiography*, "One significant truth has been made clear—that in the genesis of a system of thought the emotional nature is a large factor: perhaps as large a factor as the intellectual nature." One cannot but ask if Sidgwick supposed that his own contributions were uninfluenced by his "personal feeling and experience." Is it not almost a truism that until science reaches the stage of measurement or other modes of direct perceptual verification, it must be tinctured with personal feeling?

Sidgwick goes on to point out that similar discrepancies are evident "when we turn from religion to industry, and examine the forecasts of industrial development offered to the statesman in the name of scientific sociology as a substitute for the discarded calculations of the mere economist. With equal confidence, history is represented as leading up, now to the naïve and unqualified individualism of Spencer, now to the carefully guarded and elaborated socialism of Schäffle, now to Comte's dream of securing seven-roomed houses for all working men—with other comforts to correspond—solely by the impressive moral precepts of his philosophic priests. Guidance, truly, is here enough and to spare: but how is the bewildered statesman to select his guidance when his sociological doctors exhibit this portentous disagreement?" "Nor is it only that they adopt diametrically opposed conclusions: we find that each adopts his conclusion with the most serene and complete indifference to the line of historical reasoning on which his brother sociologist relies."

Now this is wholesome criticism, but its force is due to the fact that sociology is still very young. It would be equally easy to discredit evolution-lore by showing the discrepancies between the ætiology of Darwin and Wallace, or Spencer and Weismann. But it must not be imagined that Sidgwick was opposed to Sociology or doubted its validity; he was simply advocating caution. "There is no reason to despair of the progress of general sociology;

but I do not think that its development can be really promoted by shutting our eyes to its present very rudimentary condition." He evidently looked forward with hope to a time "when the general science of society has solved the problems which it has as yet only managed to define more or less clearly—when for positive knowledge it can offer us something better than a mixture of vague and variously applied physiological analogies, imperfectly verified historical generalisations, and unwarranted political predictions—when it has succeeded in establishing on the basis of a really scientific induction its forecasts of social evolution." The recently established "Sociological Society"[19] has in its first volume of publications suggested many ways in which those interested can assist in the development of this new science, and already as one of its indirect fruits we can point to the establishment of well defined courses of Sociology in the University of London.

[19] For a discussion of the validity and scope of Sociology we may refer to the following papers: "On the Origin and Use of the word Sociology," "Note on the History of Sociology," by Mr Victor V. Branford; "The Relation of Sociology to the Social Sciences and to Philosophy," two papers by Prof. E. Durkheim and Mr Branford; "Sociology and the Social Sciences," by Prof. Durkheim and M. E. Fauconnet;—all published in "Sociological Papers," the first volume of the Sociological Society's Proceedings.

Sociology and History.—Something must be said in regard to Spencer's somewhat peculiar attitude to history. "I take," he said, "but little interest in what are called histories, but am interested only in Sociology, which stands related to these so-called histories much as a vast building stands related to the heaps of stones and brick around it." He went the length of saying: "Had Greece and Rome never existed, human life, and the right conduct of it, would have been in their essentials exactly what they now are: survival or death, health or disease, prosperity or adversity, happiness or misery, would have been just in the same ways determined by the adjustment or non- adjustment of actions to requirements." When we reflect on the complex ways in which the influence of Greece and Rome has saturated into our life, and has become bone of our bone and flesh of our flesh, in literature and art, in philosophy and science, so that the ideas and feelings among and in which we live and move are hardly intelligible apart from it, we can hardly believe our ears when we listen to Spencer's sentence. It seems to throw a weird light on his Sociology.

For lack of personal interest and in his preoccupation with general movements, Spencer failed to do justice to what is ordinarily called history. While we can sympathise with his recoil from historical studies which lose the wood in the trees, which are like palæontologies that never disclose the ascent of life, the same limitation befalls every kind of specialist study, and is almost a necessary evil, due as Spencer would phrase it to "the imbecilities of our understanding."

Spencer's point of view was this:—

> "To have before us, in manageable form, evidence proving the correlations which everywhere exist between great militant activity and the degradation of women, between a despotic form of government and elaborate ceremonial in social intercourse, between relatively peaceful social activities and the relaxation of coercive institutions, promises furtherance of human welfare in a much greater degree than does learning whether the story of Alfred and the cakes is a fact or a myth, whether Queen Elizabeth intrigued with Essex or not, where Prince Charles hid himself, and what were the details of this battle or that siege —pieces of historical gossip which cannot in the least affect men's conceptions of the ways in which social phenomena hang together, or aid them in shaping their public conduct."

Here, of course, Spencer was making game of what he termed "so-called histories," for, to do them justice, they are not wholly composed of gossip, else they would be more read, but he was scoring a definite point that history is incomplete without sociological generalisation. He did not seem to see that we need the most scrupulous historical scholarship if we are to make sure of our generalisations. Nor did he understand how essential it is to some minds to have in their vision of the past just those personal details and picturesque touches, which he despised as gossip.

The antithesis between the sociologist and the conventional historian is comparable to that between the biologist and the descriptive naturalist. The painstaking scrupulous describer, with an almost personal affection for his subjects, the gatherer of exact data to whom nothing is common or unclean, nothing trivial or without significance, often shrinks from the sweeping statements and far-reaching formulæ of the generaliser; his detailed knowledge makes him a purist in science, enables him to recall difficult exceptions, makes him distrustful of the summing-up phrases which cover a multitude of individualised occurrences. But just as the specialist is indispensable, so there can be no science without interpretation.

We presume, however, that the historians agree with Spencer that their chief aim is to give an account, as rational as is possible for them, of the movement of human history, as Gibbon, for instance, did in his "Decline and Fall of the Roman Empire," but that they have a scientific instinct of recoil from generalising formulæ, and probably doubt the validity of some of Spencer's. We presume that they admit that all events are not equally important, and that they are laws of perspective applicable to historical pictures, but that they doubt Spencer's competence—especially after that sentence of his regarding Greece and Rome—to act as judge of what is important or in proportion. Just as the descriptive naturalist justly resents any dictation from the biologist as to what is or is not worth observing, so the descriptive historian resents the sociologist's interference. And it is to be feared that men, both in history and in life, were too much mere "phenomena" to the Synthetic Philosopher, and that his Sociology was more biological than human.

Spencer's Sociological Data.—Spencer may be accused of a lack of personal interest in the details of human history, of a lack of appreciation of what modern societies owe to the past, and of taking too mechanical a view of social evolution, but to accuse him of *a priori* methods is gratuitously unjust. Darwin in his theorising was no less scrupulously careful than he was in his monographing of barnacles, and, however we may disagree with any of Spencer's sociological generalisations, we must remember the carefulness with which he prepared himself for his task. From 1867 to 1874, with the help of Mr David Duncan, Mr James Collier, and Dr Scheppig, he worked at the compilation of sociological data, showing "in fitly classified groups and tables, facts of all kinds, presented by numerous races, which illustrate social evolution under its various aspects." This detailed work was begun solely to facilitate his own generalisations; it was published "apart from hypotheses, so as to aid all students of Social Science in testing such conclusions as they have drawn and in drawing others."

Most admirable was the ideal which Spencer had before him in collecting his data of Sociology.

"Indications of the climate, contour, soil, and minerals, of the region inhabited by each society delineated, seemed to me needful. Some accounts of the Flora and Fauna, in so far as they affected human life, had to be given. And the characters of the surrounding tribes or nations were factors which could not be overlooked. The characters of the people, individually considered, had also to be described—their physical, moral, and intellectual traits. Then, besides the political, ecclesiastical, industrial and other institutions of the society—besides the knowledge, beliefs, and sentiments, the language, habits, customs, and tastes of its members— there had to be noticed their clothing, food, and arts of life."

Central Ideas of Spencer's Sociology.—The central ideas of Spencer's sociological work are thus summed up by Prof. F. H. Giddings:—

"Spencer's propositions could be arranged in the following order: (1) Society is an organism; (2) in the struggle of social organisms for existence and their consequent differentiation, fear of both the living and the dead arises, and for countless ages is a controlling emotion; (3) dominated by fear, men for ages are habitually engaged in military activities; (4) the transition from militarism to industrialism, made possible by the consolidation of small social groups into large ones, which war accomplishes, to its own ultimate decline, transforms human nature and social institutions; and this fact affords the true interpretation of all social progress."

Spencer sought to disclose the evolution of human ideas and customs, ceremonials and institutions. He emphasised the true idea that any society worthy of the name is an integrate like an individual organism, with the capacity of co-ordinated action or unified behaviour distinct from the life of the component units, and he used other biological concepts to render social evolution more intelligible.

He relied greatly on the influence of Fear in the early stages of social evolution: fear of living competitors gave rise to political control—to ceremonies and institutions; fear of the dead gave origin to religion whose primitive expressions are seen in ancestor-worship or worship of the dead. The conception of another life originated mainly in "such phenomena as shadows, reflections, and echoes," and gave origin to conceptions of gods.

Pressure of population and competitive struggle between societies have been potent factors in evolution, promoting differentiation and integration, and continually tending to disappear as their ends are achieved. Morality is developed as an adaptive expedient under the complex struggle for existence, and industrial organisation replaces military organisation as the social integrates grow and multiply and coalesce. As solidarity deepens with increased peaceful synergy, the severe centralised control, necessary when militarism is dominant, should be replaced by greater freedom of individual life, and by a restriction of governmental function to securing justice, to maintaining equitable relations, preventing one individual infringing on his neighbour's liberty. The formula of absolute justice is that "every man is free to do that which he wills, provided he infringes not the equal freedom of any other man." In militant times the individuals exist for the state; in industrial times the state is to be maintained solely for the benefit of the citizens, and a better than industrial freedom is to be looked for when it is more fully realised that life is not for work but work is for life. Spencer believed so much in the beneficence of peace and individual liberty, that he said "there needs but a continuance of absolute peace externally, and a vigorous insistence on non-aggression internally, to ensure the moulding of men into a form characterised by all the virtues"—a fine illustration of evolutionary optimism. To him the goal of human progress was a completed individualism, but "the ultimate individual will be one whose private requirements coincide with public ones.

He will be that manner of man who, in spontaneously fulfilling his own nature, incidentally performs the functions of a social unit, and yet is only enabled so to fulfil his own nature by all others doing the like."

The Idea of the Social Organism.—Spencer has been largely responsible for popularising the conception expressed in the phrase "The Social Organism"—that a society or societary form is in many ways comparable to an individual organism, *e.g.* in growing, in differentiating, in showing increased mutual dependence of its parts, and so on. It is true that the comparison of society to an organism is at least as old as the philosophy of Plato and Aristotle, but Spencer was one of the first to fill in the analogy with biological details. The idea was briefly expressed in *Social Statics*, and was elaborated in an essay which appeared in the "Westminster Review" in January 1860. There he likened government to the central nervous system, agriculture and industry to the alimentary tract, transport and exchange to the vascular system of an animal, and pointed out that like an individual organism a society grows, becomes more complex, shows increasing inter-relations, division of labour, and mutual dependence among its parts, and has a life immense in length when compared with the lives of the component units. At the same time, it should be carefully noted that it was Spencer who introduced the term *super- organic* as descriptive of social phenomena, indicating thereby that the biological categories may require considerable modification before they can be safely used in Sociology.

Parallelisms between a Society and an Individual Organism.—Spencer indicated four chief parallelisms between a society and an individual organism:—

(1) Starting as small aggregates both grow in size.

(2) As they grow their initial relative simplicity is replaced by increasing complexity of structure.

(3) With increasing differentiation there comes about an increasing mutual dependence of the component parts, until the life and normal functioning of each becomes dependent on the life of the whole.

(4) The life of the whole becomes independent of and far more prolonged than the life of the component units.

It is obvious that this pleasing analogy may be pursued far. Thus a society may be compared to an organism as regards the genetic kinship of the component units (the cells being compared to individuals); in the fact that continued existence depends on continued functioning; in the power of retaining integrity or viable equilibrium in spite of ceaseless changes both internal and external; in the internal struggle of parts which co-exists with some measure of mutual subordination; in owing its peculiar virtue to the subtle inter-relations between its unified elements; in its power of coalescing with another form or of giving birth to another form; in its power of varying as a whole; in its habit of competing with other forms, as the result of which adaptation or elimination may ensue; and so on. In fact the analogy is far-reaching and persuasive and it is helped over some of its difficulties by the consideration that just as there are many grades of social-group, from the nomad herd to the French Republic, so there are many grades of organism from sponge to eagle.

Schäffle, in his famous work on the *Structure and Life of the Social Body* (1875), carried the metaphor of the social organism to an extreme which has induced many to recoil from it altogether. The family is the cell, and the body consists of simple connective tissue (expressed in unity of speech, etc.), and of various differentiated tissues, such as sensory and motor apparatus. The comparison is as interesting as a game, but when we find writers speaking of the social ectoderm and endoderm, and so forth, we cannot but feel that the metaphor is being stretched to the breaking-point.

Spencer was himself quite conscious that the metaphor had its limitations, for he indicates four contrasts between a society and an individual organism.

(1) Societies have no specific external forms.

(2) The units of an organism are physically continuous, but the units of a society are dispersed persons.

(3) The elements of an organism are mostly fixed in their relative positions; while units of a society are capable of moving from place to place.

(4) In the body of an animal only a special tissue is endowed with feeling; in a society all the members are so endowed. The social nervous system is happily wider than the government.

There are other limitations, *e.g.*, that the social organism does not seem to pass *necessarily* through a curve of life ending in senility and death; that when a particular form disappears it is usually by being incorporated into another in whose life it shares.

As it appears to us the real analogy is between a human societary form and an animal societary form, such as an ant-hill or a bee-hive or a beaver-village, and not between a society and an individual organism. Moreover, since the biologist has not yet arrived at a clear conception of the innermost secret of the individual organism, notably the secret of its unity, the comparison implied in the metaphor of the social organism is an attempt to interpret *obscurum per obscurius*. The analogy, such as it is, is probably destined to be of more use to the biologist than to the sociologist.

In thinking of the unity of the individual organism—which remains in great measure an enigma to Biology—we have to distinguish (*a*) *the physical unity*, which rests on the fact that all the component units are closely akin, being lineal descendants of the fertilised ovum, and on the fact that they are subtly connected with each other in mutual dependence and co-operation, whether by intercellular bridges, or by the commonalty established by the vascular and nervous systems; and (*b*) the correlated *psychical unity*, the *esprit de corps*, which in a manner inconceivable to us makes the whole body one. That there are organisms, like sponges, in which the psychical unity is quite unverifiable is probably only a passing difficulty, greatly lessened by our increasing knowledge of the life of the simplest unicellular organisms whose behaviour is now seen to include trial by error and other traits which we cannot interpret without using psychical terms.

The same is true in regard to the social organism; we have here to distinguish (*a*) *the physical unity* which rests on hereditary kinship and on similar environmental conditions, and (*b*) *the psychical unity*, the "social mind," developed with relation to certain ends—"a unity which is the end of its parts." It seems probable that in early days, the physical unity was more prominent than later on, when, as in the case of mixed racial groups, the psychical bond is practically supreme. But genetic and environmental bonds do not as physical facts constitute a society. Until there is enough of correlated psychical unity for the group to act, however imperfectly, as a group with a mind of its own, controlling the egoism of the individual members, there is no human society.

In short, if we continue to speak of a society as a social organism, we must safeguard the analogy by remembering that the character of society as an organism exists in the thoughts, feelings, and activities of the component members, and that the social bonds are not those of sympathy and synergy only, but that the rational life is intrinsically social.

As Green said, "Social life is to personality what language is to thought."

The chief difficulty that Spencer had with his metaphor was that in the individual organism there is a centred consciousness in the nervous system, whereas the social group as a whole has no corporate consciousness. Thus "while in individual bodies the welfare of all other parts is rightly subservient to the welfare of the nervous system, whose pleasurable or painful activities make up the good or ill of life; in bodies politic the same thing does not hold, or holds only to a very slight extent. It was well that the lives of all parts of an animal should be merged in the life of the whole, because the whole has a corporate consciousness capable of happiness or misery. But it is not so with a society, since its living units do not and cannot lose individual consciousness, and since the community as a whole has no corporate consciousness. And this is an everlasting reason why the welfare of citizens cannot rightly be sacrificed to some supposed benefit of the State: but why, on the other hand, the State is to be maintained solely for the benefit of citizens. The corporate life must here be subservient to the lives of the parts, instead of the lives of the parts being subservient to the corporate life" ("The Social Organism," *Essays*, vol. i.). In other words, Spencer found the metaphor useful even when it broke down, for it enabled him to corroborate his doctrine of individualism. If he had pursued the analogy between the human social group and the animal social group, such as that of bees or beavers, the corroboration would not have been so easy, though Spencer would doubtless have arrived at the same result.

CHAPTER XVI

THE POPULATION QUESTION

We have not in this volume discussed any of Spencer's contributions to practical life, for the task of indicating his scientific position was more than enough. Furthermore, his *Education* is the best known of all his works, and many of its suggestions are now realised in everyday practice; his political recommendations are too debatable; and as to ethical advice he has himself said: "The doctrine of Evolution has not furnished guidance to the extent I had hoped. Most of the conclusions drawn empirically are such as right feelings, enlightened by cultivated intelligence, have already sufficed to establish." But there is one practical suggestion to which we must refer, namely Spencer's contribution to the population question.

"The Abundance of Life"—the title of a very suggestive essay by Prof. Joly— is one of the great facts of Nature. The river of life is always tending to overflow its banks. Hence, in part, the "Struggle for Existence."

There are great differences in the number of offspring produced by different kinds of organisms, and great differences in the mortality-rate among the crowds of those produced. The rate of reproduction depends primarily on the constitution of the organism, but it also varies in response to external conditions, notably in relation to the food-supply. Some organisms are intrinsically more reproductive than others, thus the unicellular organisms, such as Bacteria and Infusorians, which multiply by dividing into two or many units, head the list; and, on the whole, it may be said that relatively simple creatures multiply most rapidly, especially if their mode of reproduction, *e.g.*, the equipment of the germ-cells, is relatively simple and inexpensive, and if the period required for reaching reproductive maturity is short. But as we find very different reproductivity in animals and plants which occupy the same grade of organisation, we are led to the conclusion, which Weismann, for instance, has worked out, that the constitutional capacity of producing many or few offspring has been regulated by selection working throughout the ages, and is adapted to the particular conditions of life. As the continuance of the race is an ideal aim, which could not be present to the animal consciousness— not to speak of the slumbering analogue of this in plants—all that we can say is that in certain conditions variations towards greater fertility would be relatively more successful because there were more of them to survive, and that variations towards relative sterility would seal their own doom. The survivors survived because they were many and capable of producing many. Moreover it is possible in certain conditions that a variation towards greater fertility may have been correlated with some other variation, such as greater vigour on which the process of selection could immediately operate. In any case, however, we may work out the theory, the rate of reproductivity cannot be satisfactorily interpreted without regarding it as in great part an adaptive character.

But while the rate of reproduction depends upon the constitution of the individual organism, modifiable within variable limits by the direct influence of food, warmth, and the like, the rate of increase or decrease in an animal or plant population depends upon the wide and complex conditions of the entire animate and inanimate environment. In short, it is a function of the Struggle for Existence.

When there are no checks to prolific multiplication a single Infusorian may become, in the course of a week, the ancestor of several millions, and the same is true of a Bacterium within a day. Huxley has computed that the progeny of single mother Aphis or green-fly, if they all lived a charmed life, would in a few months literally outweigh the population of China, which probably amounts to between two and three hundred millions. If there were no checks to increase, a few pairs of cod-fish and conger-eels would soon put an end to fishing and much else, by making the North Sea solid. And apart from problematical cases, every now and then, with locusts or voles, with rabbits in Australia, or sparrows in America, we get a vivid glimpse of what a "spate" of life may mean.

In the main, however, the river of life overflows its banks only locally and temporarily. An adjustment of the abundance of life to the limitations of subsistence is speedily effected in nature, and the flood subsides. The "positive checks" of disease, starvation, lack of room, internecine competition, increase of enemies, and so on, re-establish a balance, though perhaps with a slightly changed centre of gravity. The struggle for existence punctuates the increase of population.

In the history of mankind various aspects of the population question are familiar. Whether we inquire into what is known of the history of uncivilised races, or into present-day conditions in more or less isolated communities and even in large countries, we read the story of population-crises—of increase in numbers out-running the means of livelihood. Among races in contact one often increases at a much more rapid rate than the other, and we hear of "perils" of various colours. Within a given race we find great differences in the fertility of different sections or stocks and dangerous results impending. One nation is troubled by its teeming millions, and another by its dwindling birth-rate. The whole question is one of great biological interest and human importance, and it is one to which Spencer had a very definite contribution to make.

But before we consider Spencer's theory, it may be profitable to notice what other suggestions have been made.

(a) *Malthusian.*—In 1798, in his *Theory of Population*, Malthus riveted the attention of all thoughtful men by seeking to establish the induction that population tends to outrun the means of subsistence. In its earliest form, his thesis was that population tends to increase in geometrical ratio, while the means of subsistence increase only in arithmetical ratio. So precise a statement cannot be justified, but Malthus was right in insisting on the general fact that in certain conditions and in certain stocks multiplication tends to exceed the means of subsistence. His discussion of this thesis, and the conception of "the struggle for existence" which he developed—for the phrase was his—had a profound influence on many minds, including Spencer, Darwin, and Wallace.

Malthus pointed out, with abundant concrete illustration, that the increase of population is met by "positive checks," such as disease, starvation, war, and infanticide, and that it may also be met by "prudential checks," such as late marriage and moral control. His practical corollary was that to avoid the "positive checks" which are almost always appalling and pity-moving, we must develop the "prudential checks," which tend to prevent further swelling of the population-tide. "To a rational being the prudential check to population ought to be considered as equally natural with the check from poverty and premature mortality" (Malthus, 1806). The obvious objections are, that extended celibacy or postponed marriage tends to increase of sexual vice; that very late marriages are biologically and psychologically inadvisable, tending for instance *on an average* to increased mortality in childbirth, to less fit children, and to a diminution of the happiness of married life; and that moral control is apt to be most exercised where it is least needed, namely among the more highly developed stocks, and that it is a very uncertain check since great conjugal temperance seems often to render conception the more certain.

(b) *Darwinian.*—The Darwinian theory, that is the theory of Natural Selection, supplied an important supplement to the Malthusian position. For it pointed to the course of nature wherein the struggle for existence has opened up the pathway of progress. Increase of population brings about or accentuates the struggle for existence wherein the relatively less fit are eliminated. Although this Natural Selection works slowly it works surely, hence the Darwinian corollary is practically nil, that is to say, a *laissez-faire* policy. The obvious objections are, that man as a rational and social being has a higher standard than mere survival, and that a confidence in uncontrolled natural selection is altogether optimistic. He cannot abrogate his task of endeavouring, by rational selection, to accelerate what he believes to be progressive evolution and to hinder degenerative change. Moreover, it is not in him to stand by contemplating the mills of Nature grinding slowly, ignoring the well-being of the individual in considering the merely possible advancement of the species. And as a matter of fact he is continually interfering with natural selection by introducing various modes of what he believes to be rational selection.

(c) *Neo-Malthusian.*—The general position of modern Malthusians may be summed up in a few propositions. Population has a constant tendency to outrun the means of subsistence; over-population is a fruitful source of pauperism, ignorance, crime and disease; the positive or life-destroying checks are cruel, and their reduction is in the line of social progress; abstention from marriage is for normal organisms unnatural and anti-social, postponement of marriage is also unnatural and tends to vice and unfitness; the check that remains to be advocated is "prudence *after* marriage," and by this the Neo-Malthusians most distinctly mean attention to methods which secure small families. So far as these scientific checks imply control and conjugal temperance and obviate or lessen misery, they commend themselves, but the obvious objections are, that their use is often not without its physiological risks, and that by annulling the responsibility of consequences, while allowing the gratification of sexual appetites to continue, they may have the result of increasing an already sufficiently intense sexuality, of facilitating unchastity, and of exaggerating the tendency of marriage to sink into "monogamic prostitution." On the other hand, it seems probable that the transition from impulsive animalism to deliberate regulation—somewhat mechanical though it be—would tend in some to decrease not increase sexual intemperance. While the ideal surely is that there should be a retention, throughout married life, of a large measure of that self-control which must always form the organic basis of the enthusiasm and idealism of lovers, it remains a fact that even exemplary temperance does not obviate an unduly large family, and that some form of Neo-Malthusian practice is in many cases the only practicable suggestion—*pis aller* though it be.

(d) *Spencer's Contribution.*—In his keen analysis of the conditions of multiplication,[20] Spencer showed that a species cannot be maintained unless self-preservative and reproductive powers vary inversely, and gave a physiological reason why these two powers cannot do other than vary inversely. If we group under the term individuation all those race-preservative processes by which individual life is completed and maintained, and extend the term genesis to include all those processes aiding the formation and perfecting of new individuals, the result of the whole argument may be tersely expressed in the formula—*Individuation and Genesis vary inversely*. And from this conception important corollaries follow; thus, other things equal, advancing evolution must be accompanied by declining fertility; again, if the difficulties of self-preservation permanently diminish, there will be a permanent increase in the rate of multiplication, and conversely.

[20] A summary of his argument is given in "The Evolution of Sex," by P. Geddes and J. Arthur Thomson. Walter Scott, London. Revised edition, 1901.

The next step was an inductive verification of these *a priori* inferences, and here Spencer utilised a wealth of evidence drawn from a wide survey of the animal and vegetable world. He measured individuation by amount of growth, degree of development, and fullness of activity, and his result always was that genesis and individuation vary inversely. To the question: How is the ratio established in each special case? Spencer answered: By Natural Selection. According to the particular conditions of the species, natural selection determines whether the quantity of matter spared from individuation for genesis be divided into many small ova or a few large ones; whether there shall be small broods at short intervals or larger broods at longer intervals; or whether there shall be many unprotected offspring, or a few carefully protected by the parent. In other words, natural selection determines the particular form which the antithesis between individuation and genesis will take. Finally, Spencer introduced the following qualification. If time be left out of account, or if species be considered as permanent, then the inverse ratio between individuation and genesis holds absolutely, but each advance in individual development implies an economy: the advantage must exceed the cost, else it would not be perpetuated. The organism has an augmentation of total wealth to share between its individuation and its genesis, and though the increment of individuation tends to produce a corresponding decrement of genesis, this latter will be somewhat less than accurately proportionate. In short, genesis decreases as individuation increases, yet not quite so fast. If the species be evolving, the advance in individuation implies a certain economy, of which a share may go to diminish the decrement to genesis.

Spencer then extended his hard-won generalisation to the case of man, in which, as everyone knows, very high individuation is associated with all but the lowest rate of multiplication. The same antithesis is seen on comparing different races or nations, or even different social castes or occupations. Where there is relatively low individuation, or where nutrition is in obvious excess of expenditure required to get it, there high multiplication prevails. Reviewing the various possibilities of progressive human evolution, he concluded that this must take place mainly on the psychical side. Hence the corollary that the culture of man's psychical nature constantly tends to diminish the rate of fertility, and pressure of population, which Spencer regarded as the main incentive to progress, tends to disappear as it achieves its full effect. The acute pressure of population, with its attendant evils, thus tends to cease as a more and more highly individuated race busies itself with its increasingly complex yet normal and pleasurable activities, its rate of reproduction meanwhile descending towards that minimum required to make good its inevitable losses.

This was Spencer's contribution to the population question, and it is one which suggests hope and action, and is in harmony with the growing ideal of racial eugenics. "For it is obvious that the progress of the species and of the individual alike is secured and accelerated whenever action is transferred from the negative side of merely seeking directly to repress genesis, to the positive yet indirect side of proportionally increasing individuation. This holds true of all species, yet most fully of man, since that modification of psychical activities in which his evolution essentially lies, is *par excellence* and increasingly the respect in which artificial or rational comes in to replace natural selection. Without therefore ignoring the latter, or hoping ever wholly to escape from the iron grasp of nature, we yet have within our power more and more to mitigate the pressure of population, and that without any sacrifice of progress, but actually by hastening it. Since then the remedy of pressure and the hope of progress alike lie in advancing individuation, the course for practical action is clear—it is in the organisation of these alternate reactions between bettered environment (material, mental, social, moral) and better organism in which the whole evolution of life is defined, in the conscious and rational adjustment of the struggle into the culture of existence."[21]

[21] *Evolution of Sex.* Chapter xx.

CHAPTER XVII

BEYOND SCIENCE

Metaphysics—Early Attitude to Religion—Increased Sympathy with Religion

Spencer was always clear that "life is not for work and learning, but work and learning are for life." Thus he valued science because it is "*fructiferous*," to use Bacon's word, making for the amelioration of life; but he valued it still more because it is "*luciferous*," "for the light it throws on our own nature and the nature of the Universe." He spoke with regret of "the ordinary scientific specialist, who, deeply interested in his speciality, and often displaying comparatively little interest in other departments of science, is rarely much interested in the relations between Science at large and the great questions which lie beyond Science." He ranked himself with those who, "while seeking scientific knowledge for its proximate value, have an ever-increasing consciousness of its ultimate value as a transfiguration of things, which, marvellous enough within the limits of the knowable, suggests a profounder marvel than can be known." Thus it is not surprising to find that he had a metaphysical system of his own, and if he had not a religion he had at least "a humility in presence of the inscrutable," and a reverence for Nature deeper than many religious minds exhibit.

Metaphysics.—"Metaphysician" was with Spencer a term of reproach, "employed (as Prof. Sidgwick says) exclusively to designate a class of thinkers who have followed an erroneous method to untenable conclusions," yet he himself had a metaphysical system—which Sidgwick defines as "a systematic view of the nature and relations of finite minds to the material world, and to the Primal Being or ultimate ground of Being." A critical discussion of Spencer's metaphysical and epistemological doctrines will be found in Sidgwick's "Philosophy of Kant and other Lectures," 1905.

In his doctrine of "the Unknowable," in which experts discover the influence of Kant through Hamilton and Mansel, Spencer reached the conclusion that "no tenable hypothesis can be formed as to the origin or nature of the Universe regarded as a whole." He offered for the reconciliation of Religion and Science the "Supreme Verity," that "the reality underlying appearances is totally and for ever inconceivable to us... but we are obliged to regard every phenomenon as the manifestation of an incomprehensible power, called Omnipresent from inability to assign its limits, though Omnipresence is unthinkable." Similarly when we try to understand Time, Space, Matter, Force, Consciousness, we have to confess that the "reality underlying appearances is and must be totally and for ever inconceivable by us." At the same time Spencer was able to attain to some knowledge of his Unknowable, concluding, for instance, in spite of the antithesis between subject and object, never to be transcended while consciousness lasts, that "it is one and the same Ultimate Reality that is manifested to us subjectively and objectively"; that while "the manifestations, as occurring either in ourselves or outside of us, do not persist: that which persists is the Unknown Cause of these manifestations"—"an unconditioned Reality without beginning or end."

Early attitude to Religion.—Spencer came of a religious stock, but the traditional beliefs took no grip of him. Even as a boy he had what may be called a cosmic outlook, but he tells us of no religious tendrils, and if there were any they found no support in the faith of his fathers. Though surrounded in early life by a religious atmosphere, he never seems to have moved or even drawn breath in it. He passed by theological beliefs as if he were immune; he developed into an agnostic without passing through any crisis or perplexity; he had not even what Prof. James has called "the religion of healthy-mindedness."

The explanation of this may be looked for partly in the self-sufficiency of his strong intellect, partly in the limitations of the emotional side of his nature, and partly in his fine heritage of natural goodness. When the religious mood does not arise naturally as an almost spontaneous expression of inherited disposition and nurture-influences, it is usually reached by one of three paths, or by more than one of these at once. These paths to religion, which apply to the racial as well as to the individual history, may be called the practical, the emotional, and the intellectual approaches to faith. When men reach the limits of their practical endeavours and find themselves baffled, when they feel the impotence of their utmost strength, when they are filled with fear of the past, the present, and the future, then they sometimes become religious. When men reach the limits of their emotional strength, and the tension of joy or of sorrow, of delight in nature or love of kin becomes almost an oppression, then they sometimes become religious. When men reach the limit of their intellectual endeavours after clearness and unity and are baffled, they sometimes become religious.

As Spencer was never at his wit's end practically, and was born too good to be troubled by a sense of sin, and as he had a somewhat lukewarm emotional nature, and was singularly devoid of any poetical or mystical sense, he was not likely to approach religion by either the practical or the emotional path. The third path, reached by baffled intelligence, was more or less closed by

Spencer's postulate of the Unknowable, though there was even in this some tinge of religious feeling.

He had been brought up among those who held almost as an axiom to the belief that "In the beginning God created the heaven and the earth," but this never seems to have meant anything practically or emotionally to him, while as a cosmological statement it seemed quite unverifiable. Most thinkers have tried by searching to find out God, to find some way of thinking of the ultimate origin, nature, and purpose of things, but at an early age Herbert Spencer foreclosed this quest, and was quite comfortable in so doing, chiefly, it must be suspected, because it never appealed to him save as a purely intellectual puzzle. *"Nur was du fühlst, das ist dein Eigenthum."*

> Thus when he was twenty-six (1848) he wrote to his father, "As regards 'the ultimate nature of things or origin of them,' my position is simply that I know nothing about it, and never can know anything about it, and must be content in my ignorance. I deny nothing, and I affirm nothing, and to any one who says that the current theory *is not* true, I say just as I say to those who assert its truth—you have no evidence. Either alternative leaves us in inextricable difficulties. An *uncaused* Deity is just as inconceivable as an uncaused Universe. If the existence of matter from all eternity is incomprehensible, the creation of matter out of nothing is equally incomprehensible. Thus finding that either attempt to conceive the origin of things is futile, I am content to leave the question unsettled as *the insoluble mystery*"... (*Autobiography*, i. p. 346).

This was written in 1848, twelve years before *First Principles*, in which he afterwards sought more fully to justify the position which Huxley called "agnostic."

Just because his emotions were so little engaged, the agnostic position seemed to him a very simple and satisfactory one, and we find no evidence that he ever tried to get below the surface of theistic or Christian doctrine. He was so much repelled by particular anthropomorphic and superstitious expressions or formulæ of religious belief that he never appreciated their true inwardness or value. Otherwise, he would never have spoken of "the radical incongruity between the Bible and the order of Nature." Otherwise he would never have written the following passage, "The creed of Christendom is evidently alien to my nature, both emotional and intellectual. To many, and apparently to most, religious worship yields a species of pleasure. To me it never did so; unless, indeed, I count as such the emotion produced by sacred music.... But the expressions of adoration of a personal being, the utterance of laudations, and the humble professions of obedience, never found in me any echoes."

Later Attitude to Religion.—But while it seems to us preposterous to speak of "the religion of Herbert Spencer," beyond a reverence for the mysteries beyond science, it is important to note that in his later years he became more appreciative of the important rôle that religion has filled, and continues to fill in human life. The 'Reflections' at the close of the *Autobiography* illustrate this change of outlook.

In his earlier days Spencer was an uncompromising critic of many of the established governmental forms, such as the monarchy; in later years, while he did not change his views, he became more acquiescent, feeling that institutions must be judged by their relative fitness to the average characters and conditions of the citizens at any given time. He saw, moreover, that mere morphological changes matter little since the temper of a people alters so slowly. There is a rhythm of change in external forms, but the actual constitution of the social organism varies very little.

> "We have been living in the midst of a social exuviation, and the old coercive shell having been cast off, a new coercive shell is in course of development; for in our day, as in past days, there co-exist the readiness to coerce and the readiness to submit to coercion. Here, then, I see a change in my political views which has become increasingly marked with increasing years. Whereas, in the days of early enthusiasm, I thought that all would go well if governmental arrangements were transformed, I now think that transformations in governmental arrangements can be of use only in so far as they express the transformed natures of citizens" (1893).

A similar change marks his ideas about religious institutions. In early days he was an uncompromising critic of particular theological doctrines and religious customs, but a wider knowledge convinced him almost against his will that some sort of religious cult has been an indispensable factor in social progress. Quite aware of the great changes in theological thought which had taken place during his life-time, he looked forward to a stage in which, "recognising the mystery of things as insoluble, religious organisations will be devoted to ethical culture." As Prof. Henry Sidgwick puts it, "Spencer contemplates complacently the reduction of religious thought and sentiment to a perfectly indefinite consciousness of the Unknowable and the emotion that accompanies this peculiar intellectual exercise."

> "Thus I have come more and more to look calmly on forms of religious belief to which I had, in earlier days, a pronounced aversion. Holding that they are in the main naturally adapted to their respective peoples and times, it now seems to me well that they should severally live and work

as long as the conditions permit, and, further, that sudden changes of religious institutions, as of political institutions, are certain to be followed by reactions.

"If it be asked why, thinking thus, I have persevered in setting forth views at variance with current creeds, my reply is the one elsewhere made: It is for each to utter that which he sincerely believes to be true, and, adding his unit of influence to all other units, leave the results to work themselves out."

Largely, however, Spencer's change of mood in regard to religious creeds and institutions resulted from "a deepening conviction that the sphere occupied by them can never become an unfilled sphere, but that there must continue to arise afresh the great questions concerning ourselves and surrounding things; and that, if not positive answers, then modes of consciousness standing in place of positive answers must ever remain."

"An unreflective mood, he said, is general among both cultured and uncultured, characterised by indifference to everything beyond material interests and the superficial aspects of things."… "But in both cultured and uncultured there occur lucid intervals. Some, at least, either fill the vacuum by stereotyped answers, or become conscious of unanswered questions of transcendent moment. By those who know much, more than by those who know little, is there felt the need for explanation. Whence this process, inconceivable however symbolised, by which alike the monad and the man build themselves up into their respective structures? What must we say of the life, minute, multitudinous, degraded, which, covering the ocean-floor, occupies by far the larger part of the Earth's area; and which yet, growing and decaying in utter darkness, presents hundreds of species of a single type? Or, when we think of the myriads of years of the Earth's past, during which have arisen and passed away low forms of creatures, small and great, which, murdering and being murdered, have gradually evolved, how shall we answer the question— To what end? Ascending to wider problems, in which way are we to interpret the lifelessness of the greater celestial masses—the giant planets and the Sun; in proportion to which the habitable planets are mere nothings? If we pass from these relatively near bodies to the thirty millions of remote suns and solar systems, where shall we find a reason for all this apparently unconscious existence, infinite in amount compared with the existence which is conscious—a waste Universe as it seems? Then behind these mysteries lies the all-embracing mystery— whence this universal transformation which has gone on unceasingly throughout a past eternity and will go on unceasingly throughout a future eternity? And along with this rises the paralysing thought—what if, of all that is thus incomprehensible to us, there exists no comprehension anywhere? No wonder that men take refuge in authoritative dogma!"

"So is it, too, with our own natures. No less inscrutable is this complex consciousness which has slowly evolved out of infantine vacuity— consciousness which, during the development of every creature, makes its appearance out of what seems unconscious matter; suggesting the thought that consciousness in some rudimentary form is omnipresent. Lastly come the insoluble questions concerning our own fate: the evidence seeming so strong that the relations of mind and nervous structure are such that cessation of the one accompanies dissolution of the other, while, simultaneously, comes the thought, so strange and so difficult to realise, that with death there lapses both the consciousness of existence and the consciousness of having existed."

"Thus religious creeds, which in one way or other occupy the sphere that rational interpretation seeks to occupy and fails, and fails the more the more it seeks, I have come to regard with a sympathy based on community of need: feeling that dissent from them results from inability to accept the solutions offered, joined with the wish that solutions could be found" (1893).

CONCLUSION

Even those who have criticised Spencer's system most severely have been generous in recognising the grandeur of his aim. Thus Principal James Iverach, while never sparing in his disclosure of what he regards as the weaknesses and inconsistencies of the Synthetic Philosophy, writes as follows: "It is a great thing to be constrained to recognise that a system is possible which may bring all human thought into unity, that there may be a formula which may express the law of change in all spheres where change happens, and that the universe as a whole and in all its parts forms one system. Suppose that the particular formula of Mr Spencer is inadequate, is a failure, yet is it not something worthy of recognition, that a man has lived who gave his life to the elaboration of this thought, and has so far succeeded as to make men think that such a consummation is possible and desirable? He has widened the thoughts of men, has enabled them to think in larger terms, and has done something to enable men to overcome a mere provincialism of thought. In an age of specialism he endeavoured to be universal. And such an endeavour is worthy of the highest admiration."

Perhaps the greatest of Spencer's services was his insistence on the Unity of Science, on the ideal of a unified outlook and inlook. It may be that his "Synthetic Philosophy" left most of the problems of philosophy out, but no one will deny the grandeur of his aim in seeking to present a unified system of scientific knowledge. As Prof. A. S. Pringle-Pattison has said: "It was much to hold aloft in an age of specialism the banner of completely unified knowledge; and this is, perhaps, after all, Spencer's chief claim to gratitude and remembrance. He brought home the idea of philosophic synthesis to a greater number of the Anglo-Saxon race than had ever conceived the idea before. His own synthesis, in the particular form he gave it, will necessarily crumble away. He speaks of it himself, indeed, at the close of *First Principles* (ed. i.), modestly enough as a more or less rude attempt to accomplish a task which can be achieved only in the remote future and by the combined efforts of many, which cannot be completely achieved even then. But the idea of knowledge as a coherent whole, worked out on purely natural (though not, therefore, naturalistic) principles—a whole in which all the facts of human experience should be included—was a great idea with which to familiarise the minds of his contemporaries. It is the living germ of philosophy itself."

HERBERT SPENCER'S WORKS

(PUBLISHED BY MESSRS WILLIAMS & NORGATE)

A System of Synthetic Philosophy.

First Principles. 1862 and 1900.

Principles of Biology. 2 vols. 1864 and 1898-9.

Principles of Psychology. 2 vols. 1855 and 1876.

Principles of Sociology, Vol. I. 1877.
Do. Vol. II. 1886.
Do. Vol. III. 1896.

Principles of Ethics, Vol. I. 1879.
Do. Vol. II. 1892.

Justice.

An Autobiography. 2 vols. 1904.

Other Works.

The Study of Sociology. 1873.

Education. 1861.

Essays. 3 vols.

Social Statics. 1850.

The Man *v.* The State.

Facts and Comments. 1902.

Various Fragments. 1897.

Reasons for dissenting from the Philosophy of M. Comte. 1864.

A Rejoinder to Prof. Weismann. 1893.

Weismannism once more.

Factors of Organic Evolution. 1886.

Descriptive Sociology.

Compiled and abstracted by Dr Duncan, Dr Scheppig, and Mr Collier. Folio. Boards.

English.

Ancient American Races.

Lowest Races, Negritos, Polynesians.

African Races.

Asiatic Races.

American Races.

Hebrews and Phœnicians.

French.

SOME REFERENCES TO LITERATURE

1876. Bowne, E. P. The Philosophy of Herbert Spencer: being an examination of the "First Principles" of his System. Nelson and Philipps, New York.

1897. Clodd, Edward. Pioneers of Evolution. Grant Richards, London. Pp. 250.

1889. Collins, F. Howard. An Epitome of the Synthetic Philosophy.

1904. Crozier, J. B. Mr Herbert Spencer and the Dangers of Specialism. *Fortnightly Review*, lxxv. Pp. 105-120.

1875. Fischer. Ueber das Gesetz der Entwickelung mit Rücksicht auf Herbert Spencer.

1874. Fiske, John. Outlines of Cosmic Philosophy, based on the Doctrine of Evolution. MacMillan & Co., London.

1904. Gribble, Francis. Herbert Spencer: His Autobiography and His Philosophy. *Fortnightly Review*, lxxv. Pp. 984-995.

1879. Guthrie, Malcolm. On Mr Spencer's Formula of Evolution as an exhaustive statement of the changes of the universe. Trübner & Co., London. Pp. 267.

1882. Guthrie, Malcolm. On Mr Spencer's Unification of Knowledge. Trübner, London. Pp. 476.

1884. Guthrie, Malcolm. On Mr Spencer's Data of Ethics, London. Pp. 122.

Green. Mr Herbert Spencer and Mr G. H. Lewes: their application of the Doctrine of Evolution to Thought. *Contemporary Review*. December 1877, March and July, 1878.

1894. Hudson, W. H. An introduction to the philosophy of Herbert Spencer. Popular Edition. Watts & Co., 1904. Pp. 124.

1904. Hudson, W. H. Herbert Spencer's Autobiography. *Independent Review*, July.

1904. Hudson, W. H. Herbert Spencer. A Character Study. *Fortnightly Review*, January.

1904. Iverach, James. Herbert Spencer. *The Critical Review*, xiv. Pp. 99-112, 195-209.

1899. Mackintosh, Robert. From Comte to Benjamin Kidd. The appeal to biology or evolution for human guidance. Macmillan & Co., London. Pp. 287.

1900. Macpherson, Hector. Herbert Spencer. The man and his work. Chapman & Hall, London. Pp. 227.

1872. Martineau, James. The Place of Mind in Nature. Williams & Norgate, London.

1879. Martineau, James. Essays. 2 vols. Trübner & Co., London.

1882. Michelet. Spencer's System der Philosophie. Spencer's Lehre von dem Unerkennbaren. Leipzig, 1891.

1898. Morgan, C. Lloyd. Mr Herbert Spencer's Biology. Natural Science, xiii. pp. 377-383.

1900. Pearson, K. The Grammar of Science, 2nd. Edition. A. & C. Black, London. Pp. 548.

1904. Pringle-Pattison, A. S. The Life and Philosophy of Herbert Spencer. *The Quarterly Review*, vol. 200, pp. 240-267.

1902. Sidgwick, Henry. Lectures on the Ethics of T. H. Green, Mr Herbert Spencer and J. Martineau. Macmillan & Co., London, Pp. 374.

1905. Sidgwick, Henry. The Philosophy of Mr Herbert Spencer. In "The Philosophy of Kant and other lectures." Macmillan & Co., London. Pp. 475.

1904. Sorley, W. R. The Ethics of Naturalism: a criticism, 2nd Edition, Blackwood, Edinburgh. Pp. 338.

1892. Sorley, W. R. Herbert Spencer. Article in Chambers's Encyclopædia.

1879. Sully, James. Article, "Evolution." Encyclopædia Britannica, ninth edition.

1899. Ward, James. Naturalism and agnosticism. 2 vols. A. & C. Black, London. Pp. 302 and 291.

British Quarterly Review. October 1873, and January 1877.